Astride a Grave

Astride a Grave

Bill James

A Foul Play Press Book

The Countryman Press
Woodstock, Vermont

This edition published by arrangement with Macmillan
Publishing Company in 1996 by Foul Play Press, an imprint of
The Countryman Press, Woodstock, Vermont 05091

ISBN 0-88150-361-4

Printed in the United States of America
10 9 8 7 6 5 4 3 2 1

Chapter 1

Harpur said: 'Oh, "Make my day, punk." Without doubt.'

'Really?'

'Wonderful,' Harpur said.

He was taking part in one of his wife Megan's literature discussion evenings at home, and the group had been asked by the creative writing expert running things tonight to quote their favourite single slice of speech in fiction. Whenever he could, Harpur attended these little soirées, often with fair pleasure. He knew he needed improvement. A moment ago the speaker had said: 'And now I'm going to ask Colin Harpur, because he has to slip away shortly on urgent police business. I hope the rest of you won't think I'm currying favour with the fuzz!'

It was a session on the making of dialogue. A gymnasium owner in the group had gone first and cited something about all of us being born in a gleam by a woman standing astride a grave, which he stated had a multiplicity of overtones and came from the very well-known play, *Waiting for Godot*, by Samuel Beckett. Harpur had heard of both and was ready to agree with the gym owner that the line might be 'seminal'. Now and then Harpur had to deal with graves – mostly shallow, hastily made, ineffective – though he had never encountered a woman standing astride one.

'So, now we take, "Make my day, punk",' the creative writing speaker exclaimed, a tall, fleshy lad with a First World War moustache, and wearing red cords and a green cord, open-necked shirt. 'We do get around! From *Dirty Harry*, yes, Colin? Clint Eastwood as Detective Harry Callahan.'

'He's being provocative, Greg, that's all,' Megan remarked a bit wearily. 'As bloody ever; low-browing for effect.'

'No, no, I'm sure he means it, don't you, Colin?'

7

'Oh, he means it, all right,' Megan replied. 'But he's still trying to stir.'

'So tell us why, Colin.'

Harpur said with enthusiasm: 'You remember the scene? Callahan has just stopped a bank robbery, blasting off his magnum. He has one of the crooks lying in front of him on the ground, wounded. The crook thinks about reaching for the weapon he's dropped.'

Greg whooped: 'And Clint says, "Go on. Make my day, punk." '

'It's got the lot,' Harpur replied.

'What lot?' Megan asked. 'Magnum force. Outright fascist-pig savagery.'

'Oh, no,' Harpur said, 'not outright at all. That's the whole thing. To finish off this robber might give Harry total pleasure but— '

'No might. Would,' Megan commented.

'It could be just a witty, deterrent threat,' Harpur said. 'But the real point is, Harry cannot pull the trigger. Why? He's a cop and inhibited by rules. He's wild and he's dirty, but he must not shoot unless the other guy makes a move first. The man's a degenerate, well, a "punk", and deserves all that might come his way, but still has rights which Harry recognises – to a trial and so on. Harry must forgo his little treat. In four words it's a line about constitutional treatment of the vile, about the absolute centrality of law. It celebrates civilisation. No shoot-to-kill policy here.'

'Oh, God. The film should have been called *The Venerable Harry Callahan*?' Megan asked. 'What about the social conditions that forced the robber into crime? He's black, isn't he? Ever heard the term "Underclass" – the way some in the States are driven to law-breaking?'

'I don't think Harry has time to consider that.'

'Fascinating,' Greg said, as if genuinely pleased. 'A contribution from well outside the so-called canon, though by no means the worse for that, I'm sure. Ephemera certainly has its own validity.'

Harpur left them soon afterwards and drove out to Caring Oliver's place, Low Pastures. There were walls and high gates. He pressed a button and when a woman replied he spoke into the grille. 'Detective Chief Superintendent Colin Harpur.'

'Who did you want?'

'Whom,' he said. 'I've just come from a literary evening, for heaven's sake. That Mrs Leach?'

'I'll see if she's in.'

'Don't fart about, Patsy. Open up.'

In a minute the gates swung back. Caring's wife was waiting for him in the porch of the big old country house when he reached the end of the drive, wearing jeans and scarlet angora, like an ad in one of the rougher colour supplements. 'I'm afraid Oliver isn't here, Mr Harpur,' she said. 'He'll be sorry to have missed you. He's abroad.'

'Yes, I know. Spain way, the last we heard. Not a trite, villainous Costa. Somewhere select and churchy, in the North?'

'I'm not at all sure. Business. Flitting about, rather.'

She took him into a big sitting room, which had bare stone walls heavy with heritage and some genuine-looking beams, plus a view out over fields and woods and eventually to the sea. A lot of the soil and trees belonged to Caring. He had found good funds these last few years.

'Here's Lynette, my daughter. This is Mr Harpur of the police.'

'I thought you were away at school in Cheltenham,' Harpur said.

'In dad's dossier, is it?' the girl replied. She was about fourteen.

'Lynette's home for a few days.'

'Suspended,' Lynette said. 'Fighting. Gouging, they called it.'

'I hope you did the damage,' Harpur replied.

'Why I'm sent home, isn't it? History's written by the defeated.'

'Can the medics get the teeth out of your elbow?' Harpur replied. Lynette took after Patsy, large in the face, heavy cheeked, with dark eyes lying low in all the sombre flesh. Harpur knew Caring thought something of both of them, but not enough to stay close when there might be a crisis. There would have been one now, if Harpur had been able to find him.

'So you're missing Oliver?' Harpur asked.

'We make the best of it,' Patsy Leach said bravely.

'Poor mummy has to shop alone. Guyless in Asda.'

9

'I wonder if we could talk, Patsy,' Harpur said.

Lynette stood up from the settee. 'I was just going out to practise a few wrinkles from *The Terrorist's Handbook*.'

When she had left and he and Patsy were sitting opposite each other, Harpur said: 'You'll know that a great friend of Oliver was killed taking part in a bank raid in Exeter. Peter Chitty. Several other men got clear with the haul.'

'Peter, yes. Such a foolish fellow. Indeed, he *was* a friend of Oliver, or perhaps more accurately an acquaintance, but that would be a long, long time ago, Mr Harpur. We were shocked to read about him. Of course, his marriage had broken up, and the children are with her. Anna is it? That kind of disruption can do terrible things to a man, even drive him to violent crime. I always say men are a lot more sensitive than some of us give them credit for.'

'Yes, well Chitty was being sensitive with a .357 K-frame pistol in his hand when someone blew the side of his head off. There were two gangs there, identical tip-offs, presumably, and competing for the same big load.'

'Appalling. Such a waste.'

'Yes. Around £1.8 million went.'

She came to terms with grief and shock for a while. 'I know it's your job to worry about that – about the accounting, as it were – but when there's loss of life, well, the money, no matter how much, seems almost immaterial.' Her voice and weighty face grew grave.

'Obviously, we're very keen on finding the other people who took part.'

'Obviously.'

'That's to say, the men who did the actual raid on the bank and another who held the manager's family hostage in their house. The manager was also killed at the bank, of course. You'll have read about it. Two children left behind, one of them a daughter, though much younger than yours. Her name's Gloria – five years old, still at nursery school the last I heard. I wondered if you could help us, Patsy. When did Ollie go abroad?'

'Oh, it's a little while now. I'm poor on dates. But, if it's important, I would have thought Heathrow might be able to help.'

10

'Except we don't think he took a conventional route.'

'No?'

'Some exceptional luggage? Sensitive luggage, you might say.'

'I don't follow these things, Mr Harpur.'

'He's in touch?'

'Indeed yes. By telephone. Unpredictable times. You know Oliver.'

'I'd like to know him better. What kind of business is he into these days?'

'Very various. I'm something of a dumbo about such matters, I'm afraid.'

'Oh dear.'

'He'll be extremely concerned about Lynette and the school.'

'Cheltenham Ladies' College?'

'Not exactly that. But very good, and certainly in Cheltenham.'

Harpur said: 'Well it might not be such a bad idea to have her at home with you for a while.'

She blinked a little. 'I don't understand.'

'Where you can keep an eye on her, and on people who might show an interest in her.'

She smiled in bafflement. 'Mr Harpur, I'm sorry, you're still losing me.'

'There's a lot of spare money in circulation, Patsy. Some folk could start looking for access to it. Lynette might fit the bill. She's a way of getting at Caring, isn't she?'

Patsy shook her head to signify continuing failure to understand. 'Kidnap? But how would Oliver be linked with "spare money", as you call it? He'll want her to return to school. Education is so exceptionally major with him.'

Chapter 2

She was a pretty kid, nice and full of energy, but they almost all were at four or five years of age, weren't they? Something in them reached out. You had to respond. Well, Ralph Ember did. That was his weakness. Why he was here now. Gloria. He remembered the name very well. Of course he did. Gloria Kale. If you had held a couple of children and their mother hostage you remembered everything about them.

He knew it would be madness to loiter around the nursery school watching for her when she came out with the other children into the playground, or when she went home. In any case, her mother picked her up with the car, so there would be no chance of anything, no time. Even if he just stood at the fence and gazed at her at break time, someone might notice and remember him: the teacher who supervised them, or people window-gaping from one of the houses near. An unknown man idling near a nursery, with an eye on one of the little girls, a really special eye: it would be sending signals.

All the same, he must see her. He felt he knew this child. He had spoken to her and she to him and he had even touched her. Eventually, it had not been possible to protect her from pain, though he had really tried. No, no, he could not be blamed for the pain. These things were utterly beyond him. He had taken no direct part in her father's death. Ember had been in the house with Gloria, Robert and their mother at the time. It made him sad and sick when he thought of Kale's murder, but those events were beyond him, and he definitely had no responsibility. He had never even been able to find out whether it was necessary, nor who did it.

What he decided was to walk past the playground when they

were having their break. That would be all right. He could be any adult watching children enjoy themselves, no other motive. He would take it slowly, but not stop, like being out on a stroll which happened to go near the school at break time. Nothing could be more harmless. So, he parked far off and watched until he saw the first of them skip out into the yard and then left the car and started his saunter.

Was she all right now? Of course she was not all right. What had happened to her father had happened. The child's life had been changed and stayed changed, maybe ruined. It was a question of whether she would recover. They said children could be wonderfully strong at coming back from even the worst of distress and violation. Surprisingly strong. Everyone knew this. In a way, the race depended on it.

When he was still twenty yards away he could pick her out among the rest of the kids. Easy. She was wearing the lilac track suit like that other time in the house, and her hair was in a pony tail like then. Perhaps her mother should get her something new. As he reached the yard fence, she disappeared behind a knot of children and he slowed his pace, waiting for her to emerge, certain he must not risk either pausing or walking back. God, you would think a colour like lilac would show, no matter where she was, but for a couple of seconds he lost her completely, just a swarm of those other fucking kids in sight, and he felt the sweat start across his shoulders and down his back. How could she drop out of sight?

And then the group splintered suddenly, the children running all ways in some game, and Gloria came capering towards the fence with a couple of girls and a boy, all of them shouting and laughing. Laughing, that was the thing. She laughed as much as any of them. She looked as happy as any of them, didn't she? Didn't she? And she was as pretty as ever, her eyes alight, her little teeth shining as she shouted and laughed, her skin bright and hopeful in the strong sun. He saw no damage. He could not help smiling. The relief.

She and her friends ran right up to the fence. The children with her turned and stared back towards where the group had been, as if expecting one of the other children to chase them in the game. But she did not turn. She stopped a yard or two back from the

13

fence and stared through it at him, gazing up at his face, her eyes puzzled now and a frown starting. He cut the smile and walked a little quicker. Her hand seemed to start to come up as if she was going to point and maybe speak. Speak or even scream. But why? She could not recognise him. That was impossible. All his clothes were different today and his face had been fully masked the whole time before. A near-babe of this age would not be able to spot someone from his physique. He looked away. When he came to the end of the fence he glanced back and, thank God, she had moved from that spot and was running hand in hand with another little girl again. She seemed to have forgotten about seeing him. Well, of course. He kept walking, circled the block and returned to the car. In a little while, he saw the children go back into the building, the lilac track suit up towards the front of the crowd. Yes, she had forgotten him.

He drove into the country and idled for a while. Half an hour before it was time for the children to go home, he returned to the town, but this time made for her house. He watched there from the car again and when he saw Mrs Kale leave in the Lada to pick her up, he took three large brown envelopes from the glove compartment, left his car and walked quickly to the front door. The envelopes were already addressed with capital letters. He posted them, then returned to the car and set off at once for home. It was a risk, walking in that street after being around the school, and he did not stop trembling until he had driven thirty miles on the motorway. Yes, a risk, but how else did you get £25,000 in fifties to someone without any chance of slip-up? Send it through the post? What a laugh. Register it? If you registered you shouted value. By hand was the only safe way. After fifty miles he felt pretty good. He had put things right with Gloria and Mrs Kale and Robert, as right as they could be.

Chapter 3

Anna Chitty hung about outside the club for a while, watching people come and go, trying to pick the right moment for entering the place herself. There probably wasn't one. She had never been inside the Monty, but had heard way back that unaccompanied women were not admitted. This might still be the rule. The customers entering or leaving were in pairs, or larger groups. The women looked rough, but they did have escorts, most of them rougher.

'So here goes,' Anna muttered and pushed the door open. She found it surprisingly elegant: dark wood-panelled walls, a lot of brass work and a handsome mahogany bar. True, there were pool tables, too, and a couple of fruit machines, and a few of the faces and suits were frightening. But her first feeling was that she need not have worried. A man behind the bar glanced up as she approached and then resumed pouring a round of brandies from the bottle, not an optic. He had a scar of some sort along the line of his jaw, faded but still noticeable. He was good looking in a bony, big-featured way, rather like Charlton Heston.

'This is a members and guests club only, I'm afraid, madam,' he said, taking a ten pound note from the man buying the brandies. He held it in his hand, looking her over, showing a decent quantity of lust, but no friendliness.

'Yes. It's just that I'm here about Pete Chitty,' Anna replied.

The brandy customer turned to look at her, too, his eyes swimming, but sharp. 'Chitty? You're quite a bit late there, love.'

She ignored him. 'Are you Ralph Ember?' she asked the man behind the bar.

He gave a tiny nod, his face still unwelcoming. He turned and put the money in the till and counted out some change to the customer. Over his shoulder he said: 'I don't think I can help you in this respect, madam.'

'I know Pete's dead,' she replied.

'You can say that again,' the customer muttered, gathering his drinks very capably, drunk or not. 'Well, with all respect.'

'He was still a member here?' she asked.

'This is quite untoward, you know, coming here, quizzing,' Ralph Ember replied, facing her again. 'I can't really allow you to remain on the premises, regrettably. It's the law. I have to think of the club's reputation, you see.'

'Ralphy's a stickler in that matter.' The customer lifted up his four brandies between the fingers of two hands and moved away. Then he came back nodding and smiling. 'Except you're the law yourself, of course? Police inquiries re Peter Chitty? But with legs and an arse like that? No chance police. Look, you can join me and some friends. I'll sign you in. That's permitted.'

'Thank you, no.'

'Oh, my. Really?' He made a ladylike face. He was squat and dark in a sad purple and gold cardigan, with a heavy mop of black hair and a smile that was meant to be provocative but which came out only Goebbels. 'Looking for Pete Chitty, are we? Well, whatever he was giving you he won't be giving it any longer.'

'Piss off, Cheapy, would you?' she said.

He took a second to register this and then, drinks out in front of him, lunged towards her, grunting, 'Now, look, whore princess, you can't come in here and— '

She swung her handbag violently across him so that it caught all four glasses and knocked them from his hands. In untidy squadron they flew at the genuine mahogany bar and shattered, the fragments gleaming brilliantly in the air for a moment under the club lights, like a firework cascade. Grief-stricken and astonished, the customer gazed down at the wreckage and the expensive little pools.

Ember came quickly around from behind the bar and took her by the arm. 'I said out.' He began to march her towards the door.

'I'm Pete Chitty's wife,' she said. 'I wanted to talk to you about money. A split that somehow went astray? Pete always said you were a fount of information, Ralphy.'

They were at the door. 'I can't help you.'

'This was £1.8 million. Where did it disappear to? I have children, you know. Pete couldn't collect, obviously, but we're entitled. We were separated, but I'm still entitled.'

'I can't help.'

'A club like yours. There must be talk. Where's the cash?'

'Don't come back, right?'

'Oh, I'll come back. I know you know plenty. I can smell it in your sweat.'

Chapter 4

In a couple of days, Ember forgot about her, almost. 'Oh, I'll come back.' Mouth. They shouted their heads off, discarded women like that, and especially if they caught a whiff of cash. Well, as far as she was concerned, there bloody wasn't any, and perhaps she had picked up the message. All right, he might take something to Mrs Kale and her children, because he felt he owed. He was not going to start spreading money and information all ways, though. There had to be parameters.

Then, lying awake alongside Margaret on a Sunday morning, joyously re-re-counting big funds in his head, he thought he heard a couple of sounds from somewhere downstairs in the club. It was just after 3 a.m. and he had not been in bed long, after a reasonable night's business. Maggie said they should fit alarms. That always angered him. She was not dim, but refused to understand, though God knew he had explained enough: alarms were noise and noise meant police swarming and police swarming meant probing and disclosures and all sorts.

He slipped out of bed, put on his dressing gown and picked up the heavy flashlight which would do as a weapon if it came to that. The joy had gone and terror held him in the racking style it often did, and which was neoned in his nickname, Panicking Ralph: shakiness in the legs, the sweat the woman had spoken of the other night, and a fierce, spreading ache across his shoulders and neck and back of the head. If it was a couple of locals after the till he could handle that, and takings did not matter a fuck, anyway, now, not even a heavy night's. He feared intruders with something else on their mind. No question, the call by Chitty's one-time lady had upset him. For a long while he had been waiting for visitors along those lines, only worse – people not happy with their share from the bank, maybe with no share at all. There'd been a lad named Harry Lighterman and another who was never called anything more than Fritzy. So, tonight, one of them, or both, might be here.

He did not switch the flashlight on but made his way slowly in the dark towards the stairs down to the club and bar, leaning against the wall now and then to give his legs a spell. Halfway he paused and listened but heard nothing. Quietly he took the last few stairs and gently pulled back the bolts on the door. Then he opened it in one sudden movement. A couple of low-powered security bulbs burned all night down here. Someone spoke.

'Ralphy, I was going to wait quietly till morning, but I should have known you'd hear. A pro.'

'Caring? You're back?' He stared towards where the voice had come from, a table in shadow over beyond the pool tables.

'We sat here once before, way back, remember that, Ralphy?' Caring Oliver said. Ember did not like it when people grew reminiscent. Often that meant shit would fly.

'How come you're in this country, Caring?' Ember replied, 'though glorious to see you. Obviously.'

'We were sitting here, talking business et cetera, and your daughter came down, a pretty kid, remember that, Ralphy? This was God knows what time, four-thirty, five a.m., you late back from shagging half the populace, and this lovely-looking kid comes down to see what's going on. Valmai?'

'Venetia.'

'Exactly. Full of it. We were discussing your safety among other matters that night, as I recall. Daughters. One reason I'm back. My Lynette, she's giving problems. Been sent home. I want you to take me up to the house to see her.'

'Tonight?'

'Well, now you're here. I haven't got a lot of time, Ralph.'

'Can I get you something, first?'

'Winston was here that other night when Venetia arrived, yes? Where did he end up after the Exeter thing, Ralphy? I must have missed it in the Press. Winston, the only one taken.'

'I lost track. Twelve years, even though he coughed some to police. Otherwise fifteen the judge said.'

'Well, I saw bits of it in the continental *Daily Telegraph*. That

19

paper costs, but it's a warm link with everything that really matters back home.'

Ember poured a couple of brandies and took them over. Although Caring was young, his hair had gone silver and he kept it long and pushed back behind his ears. In the faint light it had a flat, yellowy gleam, like an industrialised river. His face seemed thin and longer. 'You're looking grand, Caring. Bronzed. It suits you. Not like me. I go lesser-breed if I tan.'

'I didn't know if you'd still be here in the Monty. Not now you've got a bit acquired.'

Ember sat down: 'I thought, act as usual for six months, maybe a year, before making big changes. These people, Harpur, Iles, they watch. They read spending.'

'Wise.' He put the glass to his lips but Ember had the idea he did not take any of it. 'Can you get up to my place soon and check whether there's a police reception waiting?'

'Right.'

'Thanks, Ralphy.' He gazed into the darkness for a couple of moments. 'Recall someone called Fritzy? He was with us at Exeter.'

'The name, yes. I didn't meet him. I was at the other end of the job, if you remember.'

'Right. And looked after it a treat, the hostage side.'

'Well, it did go passably.'

'Class, that's you, Ralphy.' Caring Oliver leaned over and squeezed Ember's arm through the dressing gown. 'That fucking Fritzy traced me.'

'No! Where? Not abroad?'

'It's my own fault. I picked him for that bank outing for cleverness, and he turns out to have too much of it. This is Spain. And I don't mean sodding Malaga and all that criminality where anyone would search. This is in the North, nearly Portugal, almost a nowhere place, but enough to keep me occupied – casino, races and no end of young fanny. Anyway, Fritzy turns up in that town, Santiago de Compostela, a deeply religious spot in many respects, with floral displays. Making inquiries, using my name. I mean, my real name. Is this thoughtless? But I had some friends there, and I get an early warning. One reason I'm back. This was a handsome Iberian town with nice little dark streets. You'd think a man could get fully lost there.'

'He's— '

'Concerned about his take-home pay from Exeter, that's obvious, Ralph. I didn't wait to ask him, but this is what it would be. He ran when we all ran that day at the bank, but Fritzy had to run with nothing in his sack. That was just the way it turned out. And then he didn't arrive for the split, as you know. Lying low. In a way, he's got only himself to blame, you see. Well, what Fritzy ought to remember is he could have been killed at Exeter, like poor Pete Chitty or the bank manager. Fritzy had the breaks, really. He's not seeing it like that now, though.'

'I had someone here calling herself Pete's wife. The same motivation, Caring. They want to collect. They all sniff it a mile off, don't they, though? Still quite a body on her, legs and so on, so it might be his genuine woman.'

'I think there was a wife, way back. Anna. Yes, legs. And kids. So she knows you're holding some of the packages, Ralph?'

'Bold? Tempestuous?'

Again Caring lifted the glass and again he did not appear to drink. 'Well, I had to up roots from Spain because of this Fritzy.'

'It's a tr— ' He had been going to say it was a trial, but you did not want technical terms like that around. 'It's a real trouble, Caring.'

'And needing to see about my daughter. Some complication at school. So, I thought, kill two birds. What I'd like is you to drive up to my place now and have a good look around first, Ralph, then take me there, if it's clear.'

'Patsy doesn't know you're back?'

'Can't be done, Ralph, can it? Phone? Who's listening in? Write? You heard of steam kettles?'

Ember went upstairs and picked up some clothes, without waking Maggie. When he rejoined Caring in the bar, he said: 'This is a bit problematical, if they've got surveillance around your house. I could encounter it. How do I explain?'

'Oh, they'll think you're giving night comfort to Patsy while I'm away. They know your flair, Ralphy. Forno's not illegal.'

Indignantly, Ember said: 'Never, Caring. Would I? Your Patsy?' She had skin like cake mix.

21

'You and I know that, Ralph. But I'm talking about police dirty minds. They judge others by their own lust. That Harpur, for instance. Iles as well.'

Caring had a sort of manor house place outside the town, called Low Pastures although it was halfway up a hill. Maybe you didn't reach High Pastures until heaven. Alone, Ember drove to about half a mile from it and then had a good inspection on foot. It looked all right. No parked vehicles with big lads in. Funny, but he had never thought of doing anything with Patsy, even though Caring had to stay abroad. Patsy's looks were not much, but plenty of life in her. His failure at trying her alarmed Ember. He was in terror of ageing. When he returned to the Monty, Caring lay sleeping with his head on a table. Outside, it had begun to get light.

'So have you eaten, Ollie? Pickled eggs?'

Caring held up a hand. 'The guts are not too brilliant.'

'That Spanish rubbish?'

'I love it. No, it's nerves. Separation from the family.'

'This can affect the digestion. It's well known,' Ember remarked. They left the Monty and drove.

'Another thing in the continental *Telegraph*, Ralph, is the widow of that bank manager killed in the raid – Kale? – gets a mystery £25,000 in cash through the front door. She hands it over to police.'

'I didn't hear that.' His voice was fine. 'Strange.'

'So, what the hell goes on?'

'Mysteries.' He got off this. 'Caring, if Fritzy traced you to Spain, you don't think he could— ?'

'Dog me to your place? I approached very roundabout. But, if it came to the worst – which it won't, don't get jumpy – what I'm saying is, you've got his quantity somewhere? And Winston's? You're still the team's banker? You could pay them?'

As they approached Caring's place this time, Ember could see it from a distance in the dawn light, with big chimneys and looking like genuine old money. Caring had done sweetly. Ember said: 'This is one hell of a situation, Ollie. You remember when I went up to London to pick up the armament for Exeter and to meet Winston?'

'Well, of course. You did a nice job there, too.'

'I've been worried that chum of Winston would come looking for Winston's share, since they're not going to let Winston out of jail to make inquiries himself. This is the lad called Leopold. Small, but there's calibre venom in him, I'd say.'

'Leopold from Kew? Our armourer. Yes, it's possible.'

'This makes a number of dangerous people, Caring.'

'The point is, I run into problems and who do I think of first as a rock, a real source of help – Ralph Ember, obviously? Even from Santiago de Compostela.'

'Thanks, Caring.'

'Only the truth.'

There was nothing on the roads. That was part good, part bad: you could be unobserved, and you could be conspicuous. 'To be frank, Caring, I've got to say this, I never worked out the arithmetic of that Exeter job.'

Let's hear the sod get out of this one then.

Caring laughed. 'Oh, you're talking about £1.8 million,' he replied, full of top-grade heartiness.

'That's what the bank said.'

'I saw that in the *Telegraph*, too.'

'Six of us working the job. That should be £300,000 each. But my split, when I opened up the parcel – £120,000. And the same for the two spare packages I was holding for Winston and Fritzy. I did a count, just for security, you understand. This is on the light side, Caring. Notably, really. This is more than a million gone missing, much more.'

Caring had another big giggle. 'Those bastards, the bank. Makes it look as if I took a bigger slice? Or me and Harry Lighterman. I see your point, Ralph. It's the oldest gambit. Of course they say more went. Insurance. You'll have run across that before. They're all crooks. Believe me, £721,000 total, and lucky to get it, the mess-up there and carnage. Bank manager dead, Pete Chitty dead, some other guy, too, from the opposition outfit. And then Winston captured. It came to a perfect six-way split. Me, you, Pete, Winston, Fritzy, Harry Lighterman. Harry's all right. In Liverpool? We didn't realise Pete was dead when we were parcelling, or Winston caught, did we? You know me, Ralph, I have to have things right, exact, like Bradman couldn't play a bad stroke.'

'That's what you were always famed for, Caring.'

'Well, it's part of that, isn't it – of caring?'

'But you're holding a spare parcel, yes? When we split, you took one extra, and I took two extra. Couldn't you have given that to Fritzy, no problem? He'd have left you in peace then, maybe, in Spain.' This sod could suggest Ember paid out, but he would never do it himself.

'You've got a point, I suppose. But my extra one was marked down for Pete, originally. We were long-time partners, as you know, really close. This will do, Ralph.'

Ember pulled in not far from Caring's big, curving drive.

'Sentimental of me?' Caring went on. 'You're right, though: I could have said OK, Pete won't be needing it, give it to Fritzy. But someone like him, coming all that way, Santiago de Compostela, you can't tell how he'll behave. You didn't know him. He's no joke, Ralphy. Would £120,000 be enough? A sacred town's not going to make his sort ease up and turn pious. Has he heard £1.8 million? Of course he has. I tell you, he's sharp. So, how much is the bastard looking for? He'd want the super-maximum, that's how he's made. He's still got that K-frame Smith and Wesson from the job? I'm not volunteering to get knocked off in some run-down, bell-chiming bit of Spanish history, am I, Ralph? Do you know what it costs to bring a body home from there?'

'Christ, Caring, I don't want any of them nosing at the Monty. That's my home, as well as work, you know.'

'These are genuine problems. Pick me up here about this time tomorrow, four a.m., Ralph? I'll have sorted things out. I've got a hire car parked down in the town. If you could take me to that. Then I'll do France for a disappearance, I think. Some contacts there. Bordeaux way? Atlantic side, not that slurpy Med. They're calling it passé.' He left the car and walked towards the gates to his grounds, carrying a holdall.

When Ember returned to bed, Maggie stirred: 'What's up?'

'Caring's back from Europe.'

'Jesus. What for?'

'Some eye-wash about his daughter. How he had the news about her he doesn't say, though. Probably big funds in the house and Patsy can't get them to him. If there's any left, and she ever tried. So he comes harvesting. Like the rest of the greedy sods.'

'What about the £1.8 mill?'

'He gave me a lot of supreme balls about the bank lying. I'm seeing him again.'

She yawned and folded down into sleep. 'Living free-range over there? I hope he's condommed for Patsy then.'

Chapter 5

Looking ahead in his own, very personal, very fretful way, Ralph Ember saw there might be a confrontation when he went to pick up Caring, and during the afternoon climbed into the loft at the Monty, took his old Baby Browning pistol from behind a cupboard, and put it in his jacket pocket, ready for 4 a.m. He was shaking in his own very personal, very fretful way, too, and sat up there in the half-dark for a while on a clothes trunk hoping to recover. After ten minutes he felt worse and thought about putting the little gun back and accepting that he would simply be Caring's taxi man. 'Well, stuff that,' he muttered. From hidden corners of himself he could sometimes dig out small, unreliable quantities of fight, the same way he had dug out the mini-pistol from a hidden corner of the loft.

The weapon, with a box of bullets alongside, had remained untouched for years, and brought back prime, troublesome memories from days long before Caring Oliver. Ember would have preferred something heftier now, but that Smith and Wesson K-frame issued by Caring for Exeter lay under brown water in a pretty Devon stream, ditched there an hour after the job. Unfired. Anyway, the Baby could do classic chest or head damage up to about twelve metres, and if there was crisis with Caring he expected to be closer than that, much. It upset him to think badly of Caring like this. The man had to be regarded as a grand friend, with some decent ways, not just a colleague. But, when you came down to it, a full million had gone absent.

No question, and very regrettably, Caring was playing fast and loose. He could pump out geniality, yes, flash his silver hair about and do the daddy chat: such harmonious stuff about daughters, and a happy recollection of Venetia coming downstairs the other time.

But that did not take any noughts off the million he had slipped into his waistcoat pocket. Although Ember would occasionally disintegrate through fear, there was this other side: the smell of missed cash could act on him like stiff drinks and do limited marvels for his backbone and aggression. He sometimes thought of himself as two people, neither of them top flight or loveable but one slightly less lousy than the other. Perhaps everyone was like that. Human complexity. Think of church ministers.

Altogether it had not been much of a day. Around noon, when he was repairing the window where Caring came through during the night, the legs woman, Mrs Pete Chitty, had rolled up again, in the yard. 'Break-in, Ralph?' she remarked.

He had ignored her, name or not. It was wisest, even kindest in the long run.

'You're vulnerable here,' she said. 'You should have alarms. People must think you've got a stack of cash on the premises. They would, wouldn't they?'

There was quite a bit along those lines. He kept quiet, though, trying to work out what she knew, or thought she knew which could be just as unhelpful – what was often referred to as 'perceived'. Had she picked up whispers, somehow, about this Harry Lighterman or Fritzy or the Botanical Gardens elf, Leopold?

She had said: 'Of course, I'll be going up to Caring Oliver's place, stalking information there, too. But you can't get past the voice box on the gate, I gather. Patsy doesn't want to know. Who'd blame her?'

'Excuse me,' he had replied. 'I have to go. Preparations for a Mother's Day function in the club this evening,' and closed the window. There was no harm in basic politeness, even to someone of this mould, but he had been glad to get clear of her. Grab in a woman he loathed.

Crouched under the roof slope in the loft now, he grieved that the Monty seemed to be turning into an assembly point for all sorts of scroungers, and there could be more. What big money always produced was a focus. People came from all over. Ember had begun to feel like one of those sticky flypapers. So, make a move away sooner than he had planned? If the Monty was pinpointed, he had to think about his daughters' safety, not to mention Margaret's. The money, even in its present state, would probably stretch to buying something nice a long distance from here, possibly even London. Luckily, he had those two extra shares, bringing the gain up to £360,000 total: after the way Caring had behaved, Ember considered these were very, very definitely his. No question, Fritzy was entirely correct to go hunting his slice from Caring, even though Ember officially held Fritzy's part of the split. Lighterman was probably all right, in on the original share-out with Caring. This woman, Mrs Chitty, should concentrate on Caring, too, and so should Kew's Leopold the Stunted, if he came looking for Winston's quota. Perhaps it would be an idea to use some of the money to send his daughters away to school, like Caring's, out of reach. But would they be? Lifting a kid from a school would be pretty simple, what with games fields and walks in the countryside looking for the lesser ragwort.

Ember brought the Baby Browning out from his pocket and loaded it, then descended the loft ladder, taking it nice and slowly because worry was knocking his co-ordination. Here he was, a father and club proprietor, kitting up like a bandit. He had another short recuperation in the bedroom before going down to help Margaret get the club ready. Lying on the duvet, thinking some more, he could feel the Baby Browning poking pleasantly into his side. What a soft, guilt-jinxed sod, to shed that £25,000: how he had always been, though – a sucker to tenderness and conscience, especially where children were involved. That money could have come in handy now. Widows he was getting highly pissed off with. That Exeter woman's name could not have been clearer on the envelopes, and the little fortune delivered personally to the front door, but she still hands it over to police, complete. Ember had missed this in the Press and felt really ill when Caring mentioned it. Pathetic cow, no stature and no gratitude. All right, living around banks, she might have been trained up to honesty re cash, he would admit that. Just the same, couldn't she have kept part? Honesty had to go whole fucking hog?

The thing was, Caring and whatever he might have in that holdall on the return trip to Europe could come into these calculations about moving from the Monty. Very much so. It might make the difference between a nice place somewhere else, and a really very nice place somewhere else, which Ember felt he deserved this far on in life. Deserved, that was the point: worked for. Greed? No, never. Greed he despised, entirely. All he was looking for was what he was undoubtedly entitled to. He certainly did not seek violence with Caring Oliver: that idea had made him shake and undid his knees, and it still gave lung pain. Ember put his hand in his jacket pocket and ran a finger over the Baby's small, hard muscles.

There was always a good turn-out on Mother's Day. Ember liked members to bring their parents in for the occasion. It gave the club a warm feel and a homely touch of old world quaintness, the shoes and suits. Each year he had plenty of daffodils in big pots around the bar and made sure the music was period, such as *Shrimp Boats*. Of course, some years there had been grim, Mother's Day fights, trampled flowers everywhere, pool table baize furrowed by pissing competitions, and D-Day Landings language: families were very complicated matters, all with hidden hate webs, and he knew nothing worse than the elderly yelling knife threats or with a broken nose. Ember always stayed alert and moved around all evening talking to groups, trying to keep the tone up and make them feel like a tidy community, not just toe-rags' mums and dads.

He could tell Margaret knew there was something wrong with him, though the gun was too small for her to spot the outline through his coat. Once the bingo had started she said: 'You'll really do a head-on with Caring?'

'He'll take it reasonably. An account book matter.'

They were standing close to each other at the rear of the bingo and she gripped his wrist and squeezed it gently. 'Ralph, Caring's a— '

'I'll be all right.'

'Worth the risk, when we're not doing at all badly, Ralph? I wonder if— '

'You want to be running bingo and Mother's Day with this lot for the rest of your life, Maggie?'

'So, how?'

'How what?'

'How will you deal with him, if he turns awkward?'

'Well, sensibly. We respect each other fully. Friendship, not just business.'

'I mean, if it comes to the point.' She always hammered away. She could bring her mind to bear hard on detail, visualising situations, which he was not too good at himself.

'I know Caring so well. He'll try and talk his way clear – the whole distance to the car he's got waiting for the flit. I'll hear about his bloody daughter, the history of education in the Western world, decline in twentieth-century house architecture, probably.'

'And yet I quite like him.'

'He's marvellous, a very lovely man. It's full agony, Margaret, to think that on money he can act low, and that I might have to sacrifice loyalty.'

She squeezed his wrist again. 'I know, Ralph.'

'Yes, agony. I thought this sort of life was far in the past.'

'This could be the last of it. Couldn't it, Ralph?'

'I hope.' He went down to congratulate some old thing who had landed the jackpot and make sure there was no brutality over the win. But it looked as if this year Mother's Day might go very sweetly. The Monty was developing what was known as an ambience.

He was at the pick-up point at 3.45 a.m. but Caring had not arrived so he drove on. It would be stupid to hang about in the car at this hour: although he saw no surveillance, there were patrols and his vehicle would be on the lists. He did a tour and came back at just after 4 o'clock. Caring had still not appeared. Again Ember drove on. He began to feel less sure of himself. That often happened and he recognised the gathering symptoms now. Even when he had been at his best a long time ago, running as an equal with really heavy, hard people, he was always liable to lose his guts if the waiting stretched out or if difficulties suddenly piled up. Now, the uncertainties began giving him a truly bad time. Would Caring have big money with him? Might he be carrying armament himself? Would the Baby function after nearly a decade of neglect? The mess in the car? Getting rid of Caring afterwards? He had not given it real planning, because the situation had come fast, out of nowhere. He was not used to handling planning, anyway. He worked for people who had fully schemed things for him, the way Caring organised Exeter, even if it did all fall apart and get blood-soaked.

Ember took another twenty-minute drive and decided that, if

30

Caring was not there this time, finale. Christ, he was not in the export business. The bugger could find his own way to France. Ember would go back to the Monty, count again what he already had, and forget him. That would be a lot less good than getting the additional entitlement, especially as he was already twenty-five grand uselessly down, but at least it would mess Caring up and let him know there were definite limits. The gun could go back into the loft. Bye-bye Baby.

It was almost 4.30 when Ember returned to the spot and this time Caring stood waiting. As well as the interesting holdall he had two suitcases alongside him on the ground, like someone for a coach tour. Jesus, this had to mean something glorious and unrationed. It was always a boost to know the old instincts still worked, no problem. He felt grand again. Ember drew up and muttered out of the window, with a real light touch, 'Your carriage, my lord.' Then he saw that Caring had someone with him, hanging back in the shadows. He recognised Lynette, the daughter, from photographs Caring had produced once: a kid with a doughy, oblong face, worse now from no sleep, up-and-coming breasts, and some-colour hair in the usual frizzed sofa-stuffing style. 'Well, this is a nice surprise,' Ember remarked. The sod must have realised there could be trouble. He had a brain, Caring.

The girl climbed into the back with the two cases. Caring took the passenger seat, keeping the holdall on his lap, gripping the handles. 'I'm going to see you very right, Ralphy. There's a couple of hundred in it for your trouble.'

'What trouble, Caring?'

'Cheltenham. We're taking Lynette back to school. Nice early start? She'll be there for first lessons today, if you put your foot down. I don't want her missing stuff. This is a crucial year, the run-up to GCSEs. Double chemistry later this morning. There's a big future for chemistry, what with all these tablets.'

'I thought she'd been sent home.'

'Not that I could care less,' Lynette remarked. 'It's Maggotsland, believe me, Ralphy. The BO off the Geography mistress – really Third World. Even the rest of the staff complain. Where that saying comes from, Hell is other teachers.'

'Patsy rang the head at her house yesterday,' Caring replied. 'Things can be smoothed out, but she said she must see a member

31

of the family. I can understand, but it's not on for me, really, at present. So at once I thought, "Ralphy". Well, an especially close friend, an honorary member of the family. Patsy agreed.'

'See the head?'

'You handle that sort of thing very well, Ralph. Your own daughters' school. You could be doing this as a friend for a club member, which is right enough, too.'

'Oh, look, Caring, I— '

'Shall we get moving then? You're someone with class and weight, to prove Lynette's got background, Ralph. Yes, a couple of hundred minimum. On to the motorway and more or less straight through. I'll come and wait outside. I need to know it's all fixed, for peace of mind while I'm heavily engaged abroad.'

Ember turned the car. 'Couldn't Patsy take her?'

Lynette had a big, helpless laugh. 'My mother flogging all the way to a school in Cheltenham? I like it. You've heard of intensive care, Ralphy? That's what she gives herself.' She folded down to sleep.

'Patsy was convinced you'd make a much better job of it. She mentioned gravitas? That the word?'

'And he doesn't want mummy down there, anyway, because he's sniffing around one of the teachers,' Lynette said, 'gravitas, grab its arse.'

Caring put his seat back to doze, too. He must have decided the girl would be safer in school. Ember wondered still. It would not be hard to find which school and where if someone really tried, and someone looking for a route to a million really would try.

And it was quite a school, Ember had to admit. He loved grey stone, especially with plenty of good, old trees and no empty 7-Up cans. This school looked like a term bill to make your teeth ache, unless, of course, you were sitting on a stack ripped from your best bloody friends. There should be a chance to deal with this aspect on the way back, when they had left the child. The distance from home could be a plus, if you thought about it. They put Caring down in the town to wait and Ember went on alone with the girl.

The headmistress was small, but with a voice that left no doubts. 'Bullying – of a particularly distressing kind.'

'She was bigger than me,' Lynette said. 'She had it coming.'

'We shall require very firm undertakings before readmitting Lynette.'

'These she will give,' Ember declared. 'Lynette?'

The girl shrugged.

'That's just her way,' Ember said. 'Children these days – you have to be able to read the signs, don't you, Mrs Partridge? I've been proud to watch Lynette grow from babyhood into a fine young girl. So much community spirit, like her father, indeed. Help the lifeboat to mention but one. Any problems, I know she will wish to put right. I speak for her and her mother and father. He is in very close touch by telephone from major commitments overseas.'

'Well, he's lucky to have someone like you to do his dirty work, Mr Ember.'

'I don't see it like that. Friendship is friendship. One doesn't swerve.'

The head let them have a minute on their own in a side room. 'Ralphy, thanks,' Lynette said. 'Give dad a goodbye from me, the two-timing toad. Have this for your help. It's all I've got.'

She put into his hand what he thought for a moment was a fifty pence piece and decided she had picked up his value from her father. When he looked, though, he saw it was a silver badge with the word MONITOR printed on it in red.

'They'll take it away from me, because of what's happened, Ralphy. So sod them. You have it. My name's on the back.'

He turned it over and saw, handwritten, 'Lynette Helen Leach'.

'Oh, look, I can't take this, Lynette.'

'Please, Ralphy. Just to remember me. You're so busy.'

'Of course I'll remember you.'

'Did you see that head-cow?'

'What?'

'Fancying you, juicing her gusset.'

'No, that's silly.'

'You know you look like Charlton Heston, Ralphy?'

'Who? The actor? That's something I never heard before.'

'Anyway, you're here with me, not her. So help me stop them getting this badge, yes? I really want you to have it.'

'Well, all right. Thank you, Lynette.' He looked at it with a bit of reverence for a while and then put it in his pocket.

33

She stretched up and kissed his cheek. 'Cheers, Ralphy. You're all right, and more, whatever they say. I've got to go and do *Jane Eyre* now.'

'Who?'

'You know – "Reader, I married him." All that crap.' She turned away and walked from the room.

In the car, Caring said: 'Where the fuck d'you think you're going, Ralph?' He had put the holdall on the floor in front of him this time.

'See a bit of the country.'

'Balls to the country. Get back to the motorway.'

Driving with one hand, Ember brought the Baby from his pocket, pointed it across his body at Caring and after a mile stopped in a lay-by on a quiet stretch. He leaned across and checked Caring for armament. He was clean. 'But what about the holdall, Ollie?'

'You can't cope with something like this, Panicking. That water-pistol.' Caring had a big, protective smile on, stuffed with non-worry.

'I'm coping.' Seated, he might be all right. He would not trust his legs, though.

'The split? You're still uneasy about the split?'

'You've hit it. Un-sodding-easy. I'll open the holdall. You sit back.'

'There was an entitlement to extra for me, Ralphy. I ran that show, start to finish. I'm management.'

'That entitlement's not seven figures.'

'Seven? Oh, come on. Don't forget Harry Lighterman. He picked up extra, too, just by being in the right spot on the day.'

'So, you and Harry half a million each clear, not a full one. It's still worthwhile.'

Ember held the gun against Caring's body, pressed into his chest. He saw Caring glance down at it now and again, trying to sort out whether it could do anything, whether age and dirt had finished its little sting. He still had the nice smile on. But, of course, one thing Ember knew: the point about Caring was he had heavy respect for Ember's past. Caring might call him Panicking on the quiet, but he also knew Ember had seen real activity with good people, people who went through with it. Caring would spot risks.

'You're sweating, Ralphy.'

'Yes. I'm sweating on more cash.'

Caring did not pause. 'And this is certainly possible. Yes, I can see your point.'

'Fine. You mean two hundred for bringing you?'

Caring turned the smile into a laugh. 'You saw that as an insult? I don't blame you, Ralph, now I come to reconsider. You're no car hire. No, I was thinking bigger, of course. I can see you might be entitled. You did really well at your end, with the hostage family. You've earned a bonus.'

'That's it. That's just what I've earned. I'll open the holdall. You stay back in the seat.'

'No, look, I agree with you, that's a fact. I'll open it,' Caring said, and swung his hand hard towards the Baby, reaching with the other one at the same time for the holdall. And Caring's fist hit the little pistol, and hitting it knocked it an inch or two sideways so that Ember's finger on the trigger tightened without him knowing it had and the gun went off. The barrel was still half sunk into Caring's clothes and there was only a small noise. For a moment, Ember thought it was a blowback of some sort and no bullet had left the muzzle. Then he saw Caring's face. It was very close to his own in the car and he could easily read the last agony in the eyes and a serious lapse in concentration, and he heard the tiny, laboured whisper: 'School trips were always a pain.'

Ember pushed him up so he was supported by the door and his seat belt. Blood had begun to form a jagged triangle on Caring's shirt above the heart. 'Are you going, Ollie?' Ember asked. 'Suicide, despite all your successes?'

He leaned down and unzipped the holdall. A big automatic pistol, perhaps a Walther, lay on top of a folded pair of beige slacks, lightweight for the Bordeaux area. He pulled them aside and saw underneath a beautifully heavy collection of fifty pound and twenty pound notes in wrappers. How the hell would Caring have got that lot and the Walther through Customs? Well, he didn't have the problem now.

Ember drove on until he came to wooded country. He stopped and pulled the body from the car and hid him in bushes. Caring's eyes were still open and Ember left them like that. Manhandling the corpse from the car had almost set one of his full, top-to-toe panics going, and he did not fancy any further contact. He made sure none of the blood had soiled his own clothes, then went back into Cheltenham and bought a mattock and spade. Returning to the wood, he took a couple of hours to dig a reasonably deep grave. Before putting Caring into it and covering him he did close the eyes and took the suit off. He could nerve himself for that now the thing was nearly over, although rigor had begun and made matters tricky. The suit and everything in the pockets could go into the Monty incinerator.

He gathered leaves and foliage to conceal the newly turned earth. Caring must not be found, or the child could say how he came to be in that area and who with. As long as he remained hidden, nobody would know where he had disappeared. When he did not contact Patsy from France she would eventually deduce something was wrong, but probably say nothing. Caring's family were not ones to go to the police. If Patsy asked him about Caring all he had to say was he had set him on his way to France, as planned. She might suppose Caring had chosen to drop out of sight for keeps. And anything could have happened to him abroad if he had been carrying a load of funds like that. There were some supreme savages even today in Europe. This was well known. It did not stop with Hitler.

Thinking of Lynette pained Ember. This was Caring, a two-timer, but still her father. Reader, I buried him.

Chapter 6

Anna Chitty took a taxi to Caring Oliver's place and asked the driver to wait while she tried the security intercom. She'd rather not be stuck here among mud and hedges if she failed to get in. Anyway, she liked to feel she had an exit. It was taking it out of her, sapping her courage, these visits to places like Ember's and this house, badgering people who might easily turn out resentful and dangerous. Anna had never been strong or pushy or hard, and had to force herself now: but she believed she and the children were owed, and that Pete would want them to have something. They needed it, badly. This grand place in its grand grounds, with the newly painted, spiked gates, made her angry, which was a help.

When Patsy replied, Anna introduced herself on the machine: 'We met, years ago.'

'Anna, yes of course, but, yes, so long ago. I'm terribly sorry about Peter, but I can't really— '

'I've some information that might interest you.' She had to stoop to talk into the thing and put her head close when listening. She felt abject.

'Information? I can't see how, really. Oliver did know Peter through business, true. But, as we said, in another time.' Even through the crackle of the voice box it sounded unfriendly. Of course it did: she would know why Anna had rolled up out of the blue.

'Patsy, this is information about a man called Ember.'

'Ember? Would I know him?'

'This is important.'

There was a pause and then she heard the gates click open. Anna paid off the taxi and began to walk up the tarmac drive through an avenue of trees. Yes, Oliver Leach knew how to take care of himself. From the road, the house was part hidden, but now she came around a bend in the drive and saw it before her, sleepy, beautiful, weathered, full of noble history and Caring's gear. In the days when she was with Pete and used to hear about Caring Oliver he and Patsy lived in a couple of rooms by Marl View School. Hadn't there been a daughter with the same looks as Patsy, even when a baby, poor little mite?

'Mostly mid-eighteenth century – not my favourite period,' Patsy said when Anna exclaimed in the porch about the house's loveliness. 'You're looking wonderful, despite. Unchanged. So much grief over Peter. But at least it's quite a while since you split up. Distance helps? Still a terrible shock for you, the death, and knowing he was into that kind of— Was it necessary? The Spanish consul lived here at one time last century, and then a lord lieutenant. We like it. Large enough, yet not pretentious or unmanageable. One of Oliver's things – he was sure he had to have the house as soon as he saw it. You know how it can be?'

No, she did not know how it could be to have things she wanted, especially not eighteenth-century bits of bijou. They went into a room that Patsy called the library. Why not? It had some books and shelves and a nice old leather-topped table, in case Caring wanted to sit down and pen his rather selective memoirs one day. They sat in big hide armchairs. There was an outlook over fields to the sea. 'Oliver's not here?' Anna asked.

'A long business trip abroad.'

Patsy had never been beautiful, or even near, and people used to wonder why Caring had picked her and sort of kept faith, but she had something now – a nice comfortable-looking cheerfulness, plus, somewhere far back, a trace of fear that made you feel for her. Anna could feel for her, had always quite liked Patsy, but was here for something else today and had to go through with it. 'I don't begrudge you and Caring any of this,' Anna said.

She gave a nice, kindly nod. 'Some luck. What information? Ember?' She had not offered tea or a drink.

'I went to see him,' Anna replied.

'Now I think about it, I believe I know who you mean. The club? A man with a scar on his jaw? What information?'

'An impression.'

38

'An impression – not information?' Her voice became harsher.

'An impression that he knows a hell of a lot and that he's full of greed, and that I wouldn't trust him, not with anything that mattered.'

'No? Not trust him? All right, if you say. But how is this going to affect me, Anna?'

'Perhaps it won't.'

'No, perhaps it won't.'

Anna had begun to feel clumsy and weak. She blurted: 'What I'm really here for is— '

'To beg?' She turned that plump, dull, serene face to stare at her. 'It's not on, you know. I know nothing about the details of the business. And I've no cash box.'

'Listen, I think— '

Patsy waved a hand to dismiss the subject. 'Not trust Ralphy Ember in what way?' she asked.

'That's right – Ralph. You do know him, then.'

'I said.'

'And you're worried about him, after all?' She had mentioned Ember only as a means of getting in, but perhaps she had been cleverer than she knew.

'He does one or two things for us now and then, I believe.'

'What sort?'

'Does it matter?' Patsy replied. 'Driving. Ferrying.'

'Yes, it might matter. Ferrying? What? Where, Patsy?'

'I don't really follow you – not trust him. He's harmless, surely. Impressions? What impressions?' She was speaking with some urgency now.

'I've upset you? I wouldn't want that.' Patsy's sudden anxiety was getting in the way. She had begun to look less serene.

'But you have seen Ember? And you— '

'Fear. Greed. They'd push him to anything. That was the impression. But then, this goes for all of us, wouldn't you say? What do you mean, ferrying?'

'It doesn't matter.'

'Not carrying money? Not ferrying anyone you care about?'

'Why do you say that?'

'As I said, an impression.'

'Yes.' Patsy stood up. 'It was pleasant to see you after all this time. I'm so sorry I can't help, Anna. I have to go now. I've promised to take some things to Oxfam. Forgive that word – that word, beg. It was wrong of me. I have to be a little wary since Oliver grew successful. Perhaps you do feel entitled, in some way I don't understand. It's something to do with the old, past friendship between Oliver and Peter, is it? I can't possibly become involved in that. I know nothing of it. And Oliver being abroad.'

'You bet the bugger's abroad.'

'I don't understand.'

'No?'

'You were always so intense, Anna. Myself, I like that in a person. Oliver found it disturbing.'

'I need to talk to him, Patsy. I'd try not to be intense. I've a right to talk to him.'

'That's certainly possible. It would be best if you left me an address. I'm sure he'll make contact.'

'Yes?'

Chapter 7

'Here's Mrs Chitty, sir,' Harpur declared.

'This must be so painful – something troublesome from deep in the past reaching out suddenly to disturb you,' Iles said, getting up from behind his desk. 'A husband shot on a bank job. Well, it's a while ago now, so I hope the pain has abated.' To Harpur the Assistant Chief seemed at his most benign and silky, which could mean anything at all, or worse. His white shirt collar gleamed like a signal from a gorgeously organised life.

'Mrs Chitty believes that, given the passage of time, she's now entitled to entry to her late husband's flat.'

'Of course she does.'

'She feels she and the children have a right.'

'The lawyer says so,' she added.

'Lawyers sometimes mean well. Please, do sit down, Mrs Chitty,' Iles replied. Harpur noticed that, when she did, Iles kept his eyes off her legs. Now and then the ACC would show baffling traces of politeness. He sat down again himself. 'A right? To be sure. The flat's been sealed since the death, naturally, but I can see no objection at all. Unquestioned as next of kin, even though there had been a separation. You and the children can't be having an easy time. Again, as I understand things, there's some nice stuff there which should come to you. Oh, yes, Pete Chitty had taste. Decent green leather furniture and Jackson Pollock prints. All right, Pollock was a piss artist, literally, but he certainly had a great way with coloured dots.' He turned to Harpur. 'An American painter, Colin. Harpur's appreciation of art doesn't go much beyond underpass graffiti, Mrs Chitty – Anna, isn't it? Well, take a squint at him. He's not employed to look like Anthony Blunt, is he?'

Anna Chitty said: 'I thought that if—'

'Your husband was an out-and-outer, you know,' Iles continued genially. 'Sophisticated villainy from arsehole to breakfast time, but I hope that does not mean we can't show a little humanity to you and the children.' Iles made a sympathetic groan. 'Basically, you're in search of bank loot, I take it. Peter's split? Well, you won't be the only one sniffing for a share, Anna. I'm afraid you're unlikely to find anything. We've no information. Caring Oliver is abroad. Europe we understand, but that's as close to pinpointing as we've got. And there'll be no significant parcel waiting for you up at his place.'

'Caring Oliver?' she replied.

'Oliver Leach,' Harpur said.

'Ah, I believe I do recall that name from way, way back,' she replied. Harpur thought she did it pretty well.

Iles nodded fondly: 'That's it. He and your husband worked together very productively, like Beaumont and Fletcher or Burke and Hare.'

'Low Pastures? That still their place?'

'Caring's of international dimensions now, silver quiff, hand-made brogues,' Iles replied. 'Why, here's the Chief himself come to see you.' The ACC stood behind his desk. Mark Lane, in uniform today, entered and sat down. Iles resumed his chair once more. 'We were just commiserating with Mrs Chitty, sir,' the ACC said. 'Widowhood is a state demanding sympathy, even when the husband was foul.'

'We would very much like to trace Peter's associates, Mrs Chitty,' the Chief remarked. 'This was a crime of great seriousness, and several people remain unpunished for it.'

'Exactly,' Iles said, striking his desk to endorse the sharpness of this comment. He smiled and shook his head: 'Anna is allegedly here for permission to look over that rubbish in Pete Chitty's place. We're supposed to believe that of a woman with a body and legs like hers? I ask you, sir. She's called to find what we know about the disbursement of the take, obviously.' He beamed at her. 'Well, not much, Anna.'

'There's a lot of money loose,' Lane said.

'Had you realised that, Anna? That there's a lot of money loose?' Iles inquired.

The Chief added: 'In fact, what we have here is the classic case of thieves falling out over an illicit carve-up.'

'Classic case,' Iles told her.

The Chief said: 'We have the feeling that you and the children had drifted from Peter Chitty on account of his criminal activities and have no desire to be associated with that part of his life. We know that you would wish to help us in any way you can.'

'I would,' she replied. 'I don't see how.'

Iles smiled and shook his head again. 'Of course you don't.'

'Shall I take Mrs Chitty to the flat, then?' Harpur asked.

'I don't see why not,' Iles replied. 'You won't need a chaperone, I'd say. What's your feeling, sir? Harpur safe?'

Chapter 8

'Oliver said to get in touch should there be any further trouble, Ralph – that you wouldn't mind. But I don't know. Perhaps you're— '

'Trouble, Mrs Leach?' Ember replied, noosed by an instant sweaty tremor. He shook so that the receiver gave him a small bang on the ear.

'It's Lynette again. Further aggro at that damn school. Children sense something marginal about her background? Persecution? Lynette hits back, that's all.'

Jesus. 'Look, I'll come out there, Mrs Leach.'

'I know the telephone is— '

'I'll come out there. Now.'

In the big drawing room of Caring's place, with all the lumps of stone and beams showing through the walls like one of the very best new–old pubs, Patsy Leach shook his hand with both of hers in a gesture of high gratitude. Well, gratitude was all right. He did not want her moving on to anything heavier than that, what with her feeling neglected up here: there were a lot of alcohol bottles on a sideboard, though he smelt no drink on her, even when she came very close, which seemed often. 'Look, Ralph, I did go out to a booth to telephone,' she said. 'I know Oliver is paranoid about being tapped, probably especially now.'

'Very wise.' Well, wise: going to a pay-phone might dodge a phone tap at her end, but not at his. On his way up here now, he had taken another good look around Caring's house to make sure there was still no surveillance.

'Yes, the school rang last night, Ralphy. Some further unpleasant incident. Incidents. Fighting. Involving staff as well, apparently. They're not used to these brutalities in fee places.

44

You and I – our teachers were getting thumped all the time, weren't they, even knifed, but they don't really know how to cope down there. They're calling for what they term "parental presence" again. It's a terrible bore for you, I know, but Oliver did assure me you would be willing, in an emergency. He said he would be seeing you all right. Such a patronising phrase.' She took his wrist, again in that double grip and gave a warm, sad smile, then ran her knuckles up and down the lapel of his jacket twice. That was some sort of code, was it: Please fancy me, Ralph?

But Ember thought, Whatever happens, I'm not fucking this, and definitely not on a regular basis. Christ, what kind of man would he be to do that? To shoot someone's husband and then move in? Despicable. It reminded him of a Shakespeare play to do with a king which his daughters were talking about not long ago – killing someone, then having a run at the widow. In those historical days, kings were rampant. Patsy had no real looks, anyway, nothing demure, and hips very run-of-the-mill. The other strong point against any flesh intimacy: Caring was home lately from months of loaded, celebratory, all-round Euro-shagging and, despite what Margaret had said, he would not have been one to sheath up, there or here, making hygiene moot.

'Kiddies,' he said. 'Do we know what we're letting ourselves in for, Patsy, when we have them? And yet we would not be without them, either, would we? They bring such lasting joy.'

'Oh, you'll do it? You'll go and put things right again? Thank you, thank you, Ralph.' Her body twitched and her voice rose into an excited cry of partnership. 'Look, I'm going to come with you. Yes.'

He did not like that. 'Both of us?'

'I feel I should. My daughter, after all. Perhaps I've been remiss, even neglectful. Yet I'll be more comfortable if I know you'll handle the talking.'

He could still have refused. That was not the way he functioned, though. In him was some strange, powerful element that recognised obligations to people he had deprived or hurt – why he had flogged down to deliver the twenty-five grand to the wife of the dead bank manager, and why he had wanted to check her little girl, Gloria, looked all right. Of course, a total sodding waste, as it turned out. Who could have guessed, though? You did what your nature ordered.

As for Patsy and Lynette, they did not even realise they had been deprived of Caring, of course. All the same, Ember felt for them. He rang Margaret to say something unexpected had come up which would keep him away from the club for the rest of the day, and asked her to get their relief barman. Then he and Patsy set off for Cheltenham.

'If Oliver hears of this latest episode he'll withdraw Lynette and we'll all go to live abroad permanently,' she remarked in the car. 'He dearly wants her to complete her time at the school, and yet he worries. I mean about her safety, Ralph. There are odd people about, vile, avaricious people.'

'You don't have to tell me.' He was tied up in his thoughts: sympathy for victims was not the only way the past could give Ember a rough time, and these last few days, he had found himself fretting badly about Caring's very improvised resting place. He would like to confirm that it was as well hidden as he felt when he drove away, and perhaps he could do that on this outing. Although he had originally meant to burn all Caring's stuff and Lynette's badge, he had decided against: they might come in handy. If necessary, those things could be dumped somewhere to send false signals. He had them well hidden, and the digging tools were in a reservoir. He had managed to clean up the staining in the car pretty well by acting quickly. There would be a swift identification, though, if the body came to light, especially if it came to light soon: to date, Caring would still own usable finger prints.

Patsy talked on: 'I've had a woman at the house. I ask you, at the house! Threatening, in a roundabout way. I see this as an intrusion. And, I have to tell you, Ralph – she did not speak well of you. Absolutely absurd. She said not to let you drive anyone dear to me. I ask you!' After the anger, she laughed. 'Well, it's only too clear Lynette was delivered safely, isn't it? More bother!'

'These slanders come from Pete Chitty's wife, so called?'

'Right.'

'Mad because I kicked her out of the Monty. Scrounging, unhinged bitch.'

'Obviously, I suspected something of the sort.'

'Yes, avaricious, as you say.'

'I'd prefer to take Oliver's judgement of people. He prizes you so, Ralph. Trusts you totally. Track record, integrity.'

'Thanks, Patsy.'

'But then there are others: Oliver himself spoke of men who might cause bad difficulties, might well locate our daughter, as a means of pressuring him, you see. Of getting to his little nest egg.'

His sodding what? The little nest egg had upwards of half a million in it, at least. 'Fritzy Something and a Kew Gardens runt called Leopold? Even, possibly, someone named Harry Lighterman? They're swarming.'

'Exactly. Men who frighten Oliver. Not many can.'

'Just more people in sickening pursuit of gain, Patsy. Yes, they are dangerous, no question.'

'There are times when I feel so exposed, Ralph.' Sitting alongside him in the car she put her head for a moment against his shoulder. He still smelled no booze. Perhaps she could get things throbbing in herself without its help, even a.m. Always his damn problem was looking like Charlton Heston. Women craved it with El Cid, anticipating a mythological experience. 'Exposed as to myself, and my child,' she added.

Patsy with him would be a complication when he went to look for the grave of her husband, this was very plain. But could he reasonably refuse her request to make the trip? A mother concerned for her daughter. Such relationships had to be treated with the fullest consideration, even if Lynette said Patsy never gave a shit about her.

'Perhaps we could buy some food and wine and pull off the motorway for a picnic lunch,' she suggested. 'It's such a day, and I need strengthening before meeting these schoolies.'

'That's an idea.'

They picked up supplies and not long afterwards he took the exit for the little road leading to the Caring rest-patch. 'This is so therapeutic,' she said.

'We should be able to find some woodland.'

'Really? In Nature I love woods more than anything.'

It was hard to recall the layout and for a few minutes one of

47

those gilt-edged panics hit him, so that his vision became misted and he could not move his feet easily between the pedals. Then, when he started to get the feel of the place again, more fear came his way: suppose Caring had been found and there was a reception.

'Woods have a sort of primeval serenity,' this nutty tit added. 'Red wine sipped among trees seems so in harmony, don't you think? An aptness.'

'How about here?' He had spotted the track where he drove off last time.

'Anywhere. You choose, Ralph.'

The area looked all right, undisturbed, and he began to feel better. When he dragged the body from the car it had flattened some foliage, which made a trail. But it was the beginning of spring now and everything had recovered: there was plenty of new growth, here on the edge of the wood, where enough sunlight got through. He had chosen pretty well for the interment. He must have an instinct.

In the car, he kept an old coat and they spread this now and brought out the wine, plastic cups and cutlery, bread, potted mussels, sausage rolls, tongue, ham and fruit. He went off a little way for a pee and had a really good examination of the grave. It seemed perfect: no sign of recently turned soil, and grass, weeds and creepers matting over it so well at a grand pace. Nature, which she had mentioned, knew how to take care of itself. Standing there, his cock in his hand, with a small breeze blowing the stream out in an almost pretty arc over three fat clumps of primroses, he congratulated himself for eventually shutting Caring's eyes before shovelling down on to him. This was certainly a lovely place if you were living, but dead was dead, and Ember felt conscious for a moment of the column of mud that would be bearing down: the way it would squash in around Caring's face and eyes and make a thick, rubbish pie of the grey hair that used to be such a show, brushed back behind his ears. Yet there was no need for Ollie to be there at all. If he hadn't tried to be smart and as full of mastery as ever, banging his fist on the Baby Browning, he probably would never have been shot – as long as he had handed over a fair slab of takings, obviously. Ember would have sent him off to the Bordeaux wine regions, or wherever, with an 'Au revoir, Caring', and no hard feelings. Anyone who knew Ember would vouch it was the way he preferred to work, no unnecessary violence. Oliver's had, indeed, been a kind of self-destruction.

'It's ready, Ralphy,' Patsy called. 'You haven't been borne off by a nymph, have you?'

Was it worth snarling at her over 'Ralphy', which sounded like somebody's retarded cousin kept upstairs out of sight? It was Ralph, or for formal things, Ember or R.W. He would not be seeing much of her, though, so perhaps he could ignore it. Zipping up, Ember thought Caring had deserved something better than dust to mud so early in his career. Although Patsy might be right and woods could be unbelievably great, Caring Oliver had had a hell of a lot of mileage left, and who wanted to spend eternity on the edge of fucking Cheltenham?

Patsy had laid everything out very neatly on the coat. 'Some won't eat cold sausage rolls,' he remarked, 'but for myself I think you get the full flavour much better then.' As an afterthought, he had picked some of the primroses and, having given them a shake, presented the bunch to Patsy with a great sweep of his arm, while making a bow. Laughingly, she placed them in the top of her dress. They sat down.

She speared a mussel from the jar with a cocktail stick and said: 'Oliver thought it was probably you who went back to give that money to the bank manager's widow, Ralphy.'

The bugger had no right at all to talk business with her. 'That would be a stupid thing to do, wouldn't it? And, look, I like to be called Ralph.'

'No, not stupid in the least. A delightful insight into character, as a matter of fact. Indicating someone really worthwhile, Ralph.'

The sausage roll was like eating one of his mother's shoes. 'Well, yes, as a matter of fact, I might have offered that cash to her. Kids to clothe. They'd be up against it.'

'Lovely. I do realise Oliver might not see it like that, but please don't worry, Ralph: I'll never talk to him about it. This is a personal thing.'

No, she never would talk to Caring about it, but she meant a close, secret link. It was an intimacy. She had a strategy, this one. 'Thanks, Patsy. These feelings run away with me sometimes.'

'It's called humanity. This is an incident that opens you up.' The dress and the way she was sitting on the ground let her show a fair length of leg and so on. It could have been worse. 'I often wonder about that scar on the line of your jaw, Ralph.'

'Some stupid youngster. But, then, I suppose we were all stupid youngsters in those days. Life was a fight for dominance.'

'I don't mean it's unsightly or anything. Fascinating, indeed.'

For politeness and warmth, he wanted to say something kindly about her, too, but knew it could lead on, and that still seemed wrong to him: worse now, right alongside Caring, who hadn't been too bad a lad, other than wolfing the bloody split bare-faced. Was it seemly to have someone astride a grave – her husband's grave? 'There are some of us who don't need a knife scar to look interesting, Patsy.' Hell. But you did what you could.

'Thank goodness.' She smiled and ran a hand over her own biggish jaw.

Yes, it would be wrong, a sort of treachery and insult to the departed, yet it seemed to him, the more he thought about things now, that she deserved a lot of wholehearted comforting. Even if Caring had stayed alive, he would be away nearly all the time, leaving her in that big place to cope, and, as far as he had heard, nobody else looking after her requirements. Genuine wood beams and raw stones in the walls were fine, but it could not be much of a scene for someone in her thirties, with lots of ideas and verve, plus obvious feelings about Nature and probably other matters. All right, she was short on looks, but this did not mean she lacked desires. And if that woman, Anna Chitty, had been spreading slander, it made another reason for trying to make Patsy think in yet more friendly fashion of him. He leaned across the coat and with a finger retraced the line of his knife scar on her face. 'That's where it would be,' he said. His wrist brushed the primroses in her bodice, making things even more rural.

'Yes.' She reached up and held his arm again, this time keeping his hand against her cheek. 'Wouldn't it be wonderful if a trip that really started out as a bit of a pain turned into – well, into a plus, Ralphy? Ralph.'

'I'm surprised you even noticed I had a scar.'

'Oh, yes. I've noticed. Of course. A lot of people notice you, Ralph. A lot of women. You must know.'

'Because I kick them out of the Monty, you mean?'

50

She laughed, but not stupidly: a good atmosphere was getting constructed here. 'Hardly.' She was still holding his hand to her face. With the other, he shifted the mussel jars and ham and tongue wrappings to the edge of the coat and moved over to sit close. She had a cup of Rioja in her free hand but put it down away from her. She turned her face to him and when he kissed her it was as he had expected, a sense of someone aching for contact and affection: not fierce or mad or gnawing at him, but gentle, as if she was taking something from his lips and wanted to make the most of it.

'You'll do the whole thing slowly, too, won't you, Ralph?'

'Well, to start with.'

'Yes, to start with.' She lay back. 'I like to be naked, even in the open air. And you to be naked, too. No coarse garments intervening. That's in harmony with the locale, as well.' He began to undress her, stacking her stuff on the side away from Caring. It was only a little matter, but seemed protocol. She started to take his clothes off, too, and had her hand around him before he had really touched her properly at all. 'I love it,' she muttered. She swung around on the coat to get her mouth low. 'It's talking to me,' she muttered. 'Do you want to know what it's saying? It's saying, "I'm going to fuck your cunt, Patsy, till you squeak." '

Some of them went in big for crude language. As to words, he himself preferred restraint. After all, what else was there to fuck? But he said: 'Cheeky of it.'

'Yes, but I don't really mind. It's primitive here.' Then she could not speak any more for a short while.

Ember put his head between her legs. She smelled and tasted beautifully sweet, as if she had done some preparation for this outing. Women believed in going for what they wanted these days. This was the whole point, and he approved. They had had a bad time over the ages. The situation here might still seem what could be called treacherous, but she did need something and how could he honourably ignore that?

He progressed with his mouth up her body and then got into her, keeping it slow and deliberate like an answer to a plea. So, Caring had been along this route. The cleanliness problem did not seem to matter. Not much ever seemed to matter at this stage. She knotted her legs behind him, pulling him closer and deeper and

51

spread her arms wide, her fingers gripping the grass and weeds, as if wanting communication with the soil. That was all right. She murmured: 'The leaves make such fascinating patterns against the sky. I could lie here for ever and ever and ever.'

He did not like that thought, and for a second felt unable to go on. Then he recovered. Life had to continue, for some. This was Nature's law. 'So, squeak,' he said.

'Later.'

Later she did.

When they reached the school, the headmistress and a young, pretty woman teacher were waiting in the head's room. They looked sombre, but at least Lynette had not burned the whole lot down yet. Caring had told him once about a teacher here that he was hoping to have it away with eventually, and Ember wondered whether this might be the one. All he knew from Caring was that she liked the music of Loudon Wainwright the Third, taught physical fitness and computers and had a great arse. This one's arse seemed along those lines.

'Something quite appalling has happened,' the head said.

'Is it really that bad?' Ember replied. He had decided to get some control from the start. In business it was known as setting the agenda.

'I'm afraid Lynette has disappeared,' the head went on. 'We believe taken against her will. The police are here now, including a Mr Iles and Mr Harpur from your part of the world. Of course, you were on the road, and we had no way of reaching you.'

'Here's a good turn then on your part, Ralphy, coming down to see about the child. And we hear you've been to the school before,' Iles declared. 'A sort of honorary daddy.' Ember had learned a long time ago that most of what the Assistant Chief said was meant to do damage. He had on a suit like a banker's and a dark tie covered with silver shields, with a motto in French, like heraldry. It was all supposed to show the bugger came from social background and had seen twenty better schools than this. He had grey hair early, like Caring, but still well above ground, regrettably.

'Ralph very kindly offered to help, since Oliver is abroad,' Patsy replied.

'Friendship through the club.' Ember said. 'I felt a duty.' These two, Harpur and Iles: you had to try to keep your voice casual with them. Iles was the nasty one, Harpur the one who stuck at it. So Iles had higher rank.

'Well, it's grand,' Iles replied. 'In character.'

The headmistress had given them a small room to talk privately. They sat around a table.

'Everything is being done to find Lynette, Mrs Leach,' Iles went on. 'It's a different police force here, of course, and Harpur and I are, in a sense, guests only. Myself especially. I came along solely to ensure liaison at the highest level in the search for the child. I can assure you our colleagues have everything very much in hand.'

Harpur said: 'I tried to contact you, Patsy, as soon as we had the news. But you must have already left.'

'We didn't rush down,' Ember replied. 'There seemed absolutely no need. It looked a minor crisis then.'

'Quite,' Iles remarked. 'We must have passed you on the motorway. Didn't spot you. Obviously we're very worried about the motive for taking the girl. Or, of course, what I should say is, we're worried about the motive, though our prime anxiety is for the child's well-being.'

'Motive?' Patsy replied.

'Is it a way of putting the screws on Oliver?' Harpur said. He wore a suit, too, but brownish and more like a police suit.

'But who would want to do that?' Ember asked.

'That's the question,' Iles replied.

'Perhaps she's simply done a runner,' Ember said. 'She's headstrong. And this trouble with the school.'

'Certainly possible,' Iles replied. 'Our colleagues here are giving that idea proper weight, and one hopes it may be so – though even this is enough to cause you great anxiety, Mrs Leach, we realise that. But I gather the evidence so far suggests she was forcibly abducted. I'm sorry.'

Harpur said: 'Clearly, we need to know where Caring is, Patsy. We see two possibilities now. Either those who have taken the child know how to locate Caring and may make ransom demands direct. Or, if they don't know where he is, they will apply that pressure via you. This second seems to us the more likely.'

'Ransom? Pressure?' Patsy replied. 'I don't understand.'

'Do you mean someone thinks Ollie has a lot of funds?' Ember asked.

'We wondered,' Iles said. 'Big gains? Recent coup of some sort?'

'This is ridiculous,' Patsy told them. 'I know of nothing like that.'

'These stories get about, I'm afraid,' Iles said, 'and the amounts involved tend to expand with the telling.'

'Kidnap my daughter because of mere rumour?' Patsy said.

'Somehow Caring's turned into a target. Have you had any callers – people looking for him, for money, threatening in any way?' Harpur asked.

'Nothing,' she said.

'Patsy would certainly have mentioned that,' Ember said. He wished she could have looked more agonised over Lynette.

'To be blunt, we're thinking about a connection with Exeter, Mrs Leach,' Iles told her, sitting back in his chair and smiling, like he had just announced she had won the school prize.

'Exeter? What's Exeter?' She frowned for a while. 'Oh, this is to do with what Mr Harpur saw me about? Peter Chitty? The bank and supposed connection? Didn't I explain that Oliver had no link with Peter Chitty these days?'

'Someone cornered a lot down there,' Harpur said.

'These sorts of situations set up reverberations afterwards,' Iles remarked, still grinning. 'People get very edgy about their bit of the split. That's so, isn't it, Ralphy?'

Ember shrugged. The movement caused a slight noise as the shirt came free of his shoulder flesh, where it had been stuck by sweat. 'I think Patsy deserves rather more considerate treatment in view of what has happened,' he said. It came out pretty firm.

'So where's Caring?' the Assistant Chief asked, as if he had not heard.

'That I don't know,' Patsy said. 'A lot of rather frantic travelling. Business. He keeps in touch, from time to time, of course. I never know where he is, though.'

'Any particular part of the globe? Fiji? Greenland?' Iles asked.

'Europe. I think,' she replied.

'This is a help,' Iles said.

'When did you last see him?' Harpur asked.

'Oh, quite some weeks,' she said.

'How many?' Iles asked.

'I'll need time to consider. I'm not thinking well.'

'Look, Patsy's obviously deeply upset because of Lynette's disappearance,' Ember said.

'Of course she is,' Iles replied.

'We could be talking about the child's life, Patsy,' Harpur said.

'You mean that if there was a ransom demand you'd recommend Oliver to pay?' she replied.

'Can he pay?' Iles asked, leaning over the table. 'So there *are* big bucks about?'

'He has to be told the situation,' Harpur said. 'It might be necessary to seek delays by pretending to put a demand to him. People seem to believe he's had a windfall. Spinning things out is crucial when dealing with a kidnap. Why I said Lynette's life could hang on finding him.'

'And the suggestion that Ralphy should handle matters with the school?' Iles asked. 'Where did that come from? How?'

'It's just something I knew Oliver would want, if I needed help. Oliver's always trusted Ralph and thought highly of him.'

'Quite right, too,' Iles remarked. 'Ralphy's a jewel.'

In the car on the way back, Patsy said: 'My view, Ralph? That Oliver has taken her. It's damn obvious.'

'But, look, Ollie is— '

'This has always been on the cards. He thinks of her, her, her, only her.' Patsy's voice grew high and wild, then sank suddenly and, when he looked, Ember saw her harmless, bread-pudding face show real electricity for a second. 'Myself, I can rot up there in that big crumbling house for all he cares. He's planned this, with his usual fucking aplomb.'

'But he was overseas when she disappeared, Patsy.'

'How do we know?'

'I don't understand.' What ideas had that bloody woman Chitty put into Patsy's brain?

'The other night, he went down with you to the school and, afterwards, you took him somewhere, yes?'

'Yes.'

'Where?'

'What?'

'Where did you go?'

All right, he had this worked out, ready, but to be asked straight still shocked him. 'Oh, to a hire car he had waiting. Then he was going somewhere to cross to France. Air, boat? I don't know.'

'Exactly. So what proof he ever actually went abroad? Went abroad at that time? He's gone now, all right – with Lynette. That's what he always wanted. The two of them over there with all the cash. Not me. Just bloody daddykins and baby. Oh, Ralph, it's nauseating. It's so damn cruel. Thank heaven you're with me, darling. I don't know what I should do otherwise.'

'My God. Patsy, this is so – so cruel. Yes, damn cruel. But it would be terribly difficult to get abroad – two people – without being spotted. On his own, yes. A man and a girl is different.'

'He could manage it. Oliver has ways. More to the point, Oliver has money. Did you see that holdall he was carrying?'

'Holdall?'

'Full of more cash. That's on top of the load he's already taken. All of it from the Exeter thing.'

'What, that ordinary holdall?'

'A couple of hundred grand in there.'

'That's one hell of a risk.'

'He's used to risk.'

They were passing the exit lane to Caring and the primroses and she touched his hand on the wheel. 'No, not there this time. I want you in my own bed, Ralph. His bed. That's important to me now. When we get back. Make some speed, darling.' She gazed from the car for a few minutes. 'I think the police realise what's happened. That Iles. What does he miss? Don't tell me they're unaware he's been back in England.'

Jesus, he hoped they were. 'They'll want to move in at your place, in case of messages from— '

'The kidnappers? They're perfectly sure there aren't any. Did you ever see two people more unworried? But, yes, they will set up shop with me, I know. Phones and recorders and what all. Why I want you predatory in my bed before they arrive, consuming, being consumed, Ralphy. Ralph.'

'It's dangerous, Patsy.'

'Yes, but I think it's the kind of man you are.' She touched the scar on his jaw, then did that thing with her knuckles on his lapel again.

He looked in the mirror to make sure those two cop tyrants weren't behind, watching. 'Well, yes, I've seen some danger in my time,' he remarked. 'One gets fairly used to it.'

Chapter 9

'Mummy, contact daddy and say half a big one. Tell him he owes. When you've done it, put a notice in the Personal of the *Independent*, "Thanks for caring." There'll be another call then. No media. Please, mummy. You will?'

Patsy Leach said: 'Lynette, love, oh I— '

But Harpur, sitting opposite in her drawing room, listening on an extension, heard the receiver put down at the other end. He leaned across and gently took the telephone from Patsy and replaced it. 'In case they try to get back at once,' he said. 'It's possible.'

Francis Garland, in shirt sleeves, sat at another extension across the room, with the recorder. 'Too brief for us to trace,' he said. 'These people know what they're doing.'

'Yes, probably,' Harpur replied. No question of that, but it was better unsaid.

'You've no doubt it was your daughter, Mrs Leach?' Garland asked. Francis always handled the details of a situation right, but could occasionally hit the wrong tone: whizz kids had to think about whizzing, not sensitivity.

She was white but dry-eyed. 'Of course it was Lynette.'

'Terrible for you,' Harpur said. 'Shall I get one of the lads to make some tea, Patsy? Or a drink?'

In the far corner, Garland played the tape back. 'Sounds as if she's reading, except the last words. "Please, mummy. You will?" That came over as herself, didn't you think, sir?'

'Did it?'

'Oh, as if she feared – excuse me, but as if she feared you might fail her, Mrs Leach,' Garland said. He replayed the tape.

'Fail her? What does that mean?' she asked.

58

Garland seemed to realise he had been treading heavily. 'I thought we were suddenly getting a kind of special appeal, mother to daughter, Mrs Leach.'

'Special appeal?' she replied, and for a moment then Harpur thought Patsy would weep: that heavy, plain face seemed to lengthen.

'Direct words to you, not a script,' Garland explained. He was managing to keep his voice tender, but went on: 'Afraid you won't contact her dad.'

Patsy Leach gazed down at the table where she and Harpur were sitting. When she raised her head she had recovered: 'What else can I do but fail her? I don't know how to reach Oliver.'

'Mrs Leach, no idea at all?' Garland replied.

She did not bother to answer that. 'And, if I did? Half a big one? Half a million?'

'That's it,' Garland told her.

'Absurd,' she said.

'Is Caring carrying that sort of money?' Garland asked.

'Carrying?'

'Does he have it on tap?' Garland said. 'Wherever he is.'

'Wherever he is is right,' she replied.

'Is he in touch with half a million?' Garland asked.

'How would he be, for God's sake?' she said.

'Some windfall,' Garland replied. 'Caring's doing well? This place and so on.'

'Christ, is that one of your words, "windfall" – a police word?' She pointed at Harpur. 'He said that, "a windfall".'

'Was there one?' Garland persisted.

'Where does half a million drop off a tree? Look, are you here to find my daughter, or what?' she said.

'Of course we are,' Harpur replied. 'This is a step forward, Patsy. It's horrible, I know, the worried voice out of nowhere, speaking what she's told to speak. But it's better than silence. We're into something of a pattern now. I've had this sort of case before. We'll do what they say for as long as possible and keep it from the papers and broadcast people.'

'Probably not a public phone box,' Garland said. 'No traffic, no boom.' He was listening again to the tape.

'Oh God, must I hear it over and over?' Patsy Leach asked.

'No, no, of course not,' Harpur told her. 'Take it elsewhere, Francis, will you?'

Garland stopped the tape immediately and softened his voice once more. 'At least she seemed all right, Mrs Leach. She spoke well.'

'They do elocution at school. Can you tell if it was from abroad?'

'Why? Do you think she's abroad?' Garland asked. 'Where abroad?'

'God, doesn't he pounce, though?' she said. 'Next life he's a ginger tomcat.'

'Would you rather talk to one of the girls?' Harpur asked. 'Look, here's Jane Bish. Sergeant Bish, one of our best officers. Has children of her own. If she didn't have to give them so much time, she'd be outranking all of us. Francis can go and make the tea.'

'What?' Garland grunted.

Harpur saw the anger was reasonable: he had let him ask all the cruel, totally necessary questions and kept the sob stuff for himself. 'Tea, yes. Thanks, Francis.' Jane Bish came and sat alongside Harpur.

'All we want is every bit of information that might help us find Lynette, Mrs Leach – Patsy,' Jane said. 'The sole object of all this.' She waved a hand to take in the special phones and equipment and the other people.

'Is it?'

'Of course. I know how you feel.'

Patsy stared at her: 'No you don't. You're a cop doing a job. So, a woman cop doing a job. So, a woman cop with a family doing a job. You still can't know what I feel. I don't know what I feel myself.'

'Confusion – inevitable,' Harpur commented.

'Yes, it's a job,' Jane said quietly. 'Yes, I'm a cop. I can still want to get your child back.'

'That's part of the job, maybe,' Patsy replied. 'But the main part's to nail Oliver, isn't it, find what money he's got and where he got it? That's more important? It is for *him*, anyway.' She nodded at where Garland had been seated with the recorder. He was in the kitchen now. 'Lynette's a way into some other investigation. This bank thing I keep hearing about.'

Jane was silenced for a second, but Harpur knew it would be wrong to try to help. In any case, he had no idea what to say. Patsy had it mostly right: she might not have the looks but there was a tough brain operating. Perhaps Caring went for that, at least in a wife.

Jane said: 'We have to look at everything. Oliver must be relevant. I know you see that. I hope you see that.'

This was one of Jane's strengths: she could go slowly, sound uncertain and hesitant – not gallop into the middle of someone's troubles and expect them to scatter. Dark, slight, not very tall, about twenty-six, she could look child-like herself, a face generally solemn, attentive, bright. Probably none of it would work the magic on Patsy Leach. If you lived with Caring Oliver, you knew police were police and, as she said, they did a job. Good ones were good because they did the job better, not because they held your hand. Harpur saw a flimsy chance Jane might build some contact with Patsy, that was all.

'Why do you think abroad?' Jane asked.

'It has to be a possibility, hasn't it?'

'Very difficult to take a child out of the country against her will,' Harpur said.

'Is it? I suppose so.'

Garland came back with the tea.

'Abroad was just a guess?' Jane asked.

'And we're interested in how Ember comes to be involved,' Garland said.

'Friendship, through the Monty. I expect you all have good friends, too, don't you?' She looked at the three of them in turn.

Harpur wondered whether there was something he did not know about between Garland and Jane Bish, something Patsy had picked up. Women were gifted at that. Or, had she heard gossip about himself? 'I've always been very fond of Ralphy,' he said.

'You treat him like shit,' Patsy replied.

Chapter 10

My darling Ralph,

Forgive me, but this is the only way I can communicate at present. The phone's been taken over and a sow sergeant is always with me, but always – supposed to be in case I need help, but really hoping I'll crack and can tell them things about Oliver, and especially money matters and where he is. So, I can't even get to a public phone alone, love. But, fear not, I will try if I get a chance. I so need to talk to you, Ralph. Writing things is risky, but believe me it was the only way.

Ralph, perhaps it really is a kidnap. Lynette called. Or maybe Oliver made her do it, to confuse police, I don't know. He is capable. They don't show what they're thinking, not that Harpur, nor his girl angel of alleged mercy. Harpur terms you 'Ralphy', but I didn't say anything to correct that, it would be such a give-away. Don't worry, I will never mention Oliver came back and was at your place, and the school trip with Lynette. That might be dodgy for you, Ralph, making them think you and Oliver were partners. They asked how come you were at the school with me and so on, but I did NOT give any indication so DON'T WORRY. Ralph, I am thinking about you and our glorious times in the woods etc. When I can I definitely will telephone so DON'T WORRY.

Your Patsy.

The letter was bad, but the envelope a fucking coronary: *Mr Ralph Ember, Monty, Strictly Private and Confidential, By Messenger*, in very black ink. And sending it down with the milk boy. Thank God he had been on his own in the club when it turned up. By the time he read it, the boy had disappeared, or

62

he would have slipped him at least a twenty to try to make sure of eternal silence. How much had she given him? Did she realise about security and what it cost to keep shut mouths shut? 'Terms you "Ralphy".' What the hell was that 'terms', like a specimen?

Plus DON'T WORRY. DON'T bloody WORRY, linked to a crazy woman? Jesus, where the cock could lead you, even with a dud piece like Patsy. He thought about taking the phone off or unplugging it, but if they had a tap they could tell and would wonder. And, when Patsy could not get through, what would she try next? At this moment, she was up there in a house full of cops using every bit of her brain to find ways of sneaking out to drop him in it. This meant two women now who could be full perils for him, giving pointers to anybody listening or watching. There was Patsy, of course, and there was also Pete Chitty's so-called wife, Anna, probably still around, sniffing non-stop and shameless and always liable to turn up at the club, though, God knew, that one he had never given even a smile to encourage, legs or not.

With old newspapers he made a blaze in the yard incinerator and said a swift goodbye to the letter and envelope. He watched until they curled up in the flames and the last word he saw was 'etc.' – that is, 'glorious times in the woods etc.' Etc. was Caring's bed. Could they do that genetic tracing and find specks of his character on the sheets? Panic approached fast. Although it was still early morning, back inside the club he drew himself a slab of armagnac and sat under the framed photograph of an almost trouble-free Monty outing to Paris last year, gazing occasionally at the half-full glass on the table in front of him. But he did not drink. Somewhere he had read that Churchill would often have a glass of spirits near him but not touch it, content simply to know it was there if needed. How he beat Jerry. If you were like Churchill as well as Charlton Heston you had to be doing all right, though, naturally, before they grew old. When he viewed things from that angle, he felt forced to admit it was inevitable that women such as Patsy would struggle to come back for more.

In a short while he began to feel much better and had a small grin. Who, coming in to the Monty now, and seeing him in his worn black and scarlet track suit, huddled against the wall under this photo of half-pissed nobodies and small-score villains and their slags, would think he had £511,000 spread around in various safe, very accessible nests? That was three times the £120,000 in the split, because he was holding for two who could not collect, plus what was in Caring's holdall. Of course, it would have been £536,000 if he had not felt sorry for that bank manager's widow and her family, but no man could suppress his nature.

He would not deny that to any outside observer the Monty was a shit heap: full ash trays, a broken pool cue and part of a denture after some untowardness last night, plus a range of dirty glasses. It did not look like the imperial palace or probably even the Garrick. Beams of morning sunshine reached in through the drawn curtains and put light where shadow would have been helpful. Just the same, this interestingly scarred, seated, unpushy guy, who owned the place, deeply irresistible to women and smelling of burned paper, was somehow worth a fortune, cash. Well, no somehow. It happened because at the right times he saw what had to be done and did it. This was instinct on top of quality training from way back. In a word, calibre.

He heard a car draw into the yard and tensed for a moment: some of the people liable to walk in at the Monty's door would not be here to admire his pedigree or loveliness. But in a second he realised it must be Margaret, back after taking the girls to school. He put the armagnac out of sight. When she appeared, he had begun emptying the ash trays into a cardboard box. He smiled again: Mr Big still had his chores, like Prince Philip straightening the anti-macassars.

'Venetia and Fay are so excited today,' she said. 'Auditions for a school play.'

'Which play?'

'*A Midsummer Night's Dream*. William Shakespeare.'

'Well, I know. One of those laughable comedies? I'm in favour of all that.'

But an awkward thought had hit him, the way awkward thoughts did sometimes. So, his kids were happy and bubbling over, but what about Caring's Lynette? Where was that girl and, above all, *how* was she? He worried about her as he had worried about the bank manager's widow and her children. All right, Lynette was no picture and a smart-arse, yet he had nothing against her, really. And the point was, his £511,000, or some of it, might be the only means of keeping her alive. Of course, nobody knew this.

Obviously, whoever had Lynette expected Caring to cough up: Caring was the daddy, so care, Caring, and pay. And Caring might have cared and paid, but Caring was dead.

In some ways, this secret made things easier for Ember, but in others much worse: he had a real problem here, which was, what should he do about the life of this menaced child? It was right on his plate, even if he was the only one to know. Shagging the mother was a thoughtful means of bringing some comfort to the family, but it might not be the whole answer. What he had before him was what definitely had to be referred to as a moral dilemma.

Total. There was another difficult aspect, wasn't there? Did he really want the child found? Did he really want the child found alive? If that happened, police would naturally be talking to her a lot and asking questions. All right, she might know she was not supposed to say her father had been home lately, but this was only a kid and could she keep quiet? Could she cope with someone like Harpur or that ace interrogator the bastards used, the one they called Erogenous Jones? How would it be if she told them Caring and Ember took her back down to school together that night? This was the kind of information he had to keep buried, in a way of speaking. It could lead on.

He had another very troublesome thought, too, which produced more of his spate sweat. Suppose the child was already talking – not to police, but to whoever was holding her. Suppose this kidnapper heard that Ralph W. Ember was the last known person in touch with Caring and, therefore, most likely, the last in touch with Caring's acquired funds. This was going to set up another very unpleasant pointer, especially when the kidnap did not produce, which it wouldn't and couldn't. Someone might come looking. Ember went and recovered the glass of armagnac and downed it, then tipped in another – into the glass first, then himself. Sod Churchill.

Chapter 11

'Please, mummy. Please. This is Lynette Helen Leach speaking. Free me. You will do it, won't you? Tell daddy. Put a notice in the *Independent*.'

After the opening call, they had two like that, the identical words each time, an hour and ten minutes apart. Harpur found it touching that the girl should formally identify herself. Who else would it be? But, of course, she was reading from a script, as before. All the same, who else would it be? Again the brevity and speed of the calls gave Patsy no chance to speak or keep the conversation going for a trace.

'There's a lovely directness in the girl's tone, Mrs Leach,' the Chief said. 'Like a friend to a friend, rather than daughter to mother, but the blood connection, too. An inspiration. Yes, I know she's reading words prepared by someone else, yet the voice reaches out to you, and only you, with such affection, such unaffected trust. One does feel like an intruder.' A small flush of pleasure appeared on Lane's sallow cheeks. He was wearing one of his older C&A greyish suits today, maybe not wanting to overawe.

'Lynette and I are very close,' Patsy replied.

'Not something easily attained with a teenager,' Lane said. 'Many parents would envy you.'

'So what's the soft soap in aid of?' Patsy said.

'Not at all,' the Chief assured her.

'We really love it,' Iles remarked. 'We think we should do what Lynette asks and put the notice in the *Independent*, even though you say you don't know where Caring is.'

'Not just say. I don't know. How would I?'

'Or, to take the flip side, how wouldn't you?' Iles replied. 'He's your man.'

'To place the notice is Colin Harpur's opinion as well, Patsy,' the Chief told her. 'He's our expert. He's dealt with a previous kidnapping.'

'We have to prolong contact,' Harpur said. 'It's the only way.'

'And when I can't come up with the money?' she asked. 'Won't that make for frustrated rage?'

'A valid point, certainly,' the Chief said. 'We have somehow to stall, hope for a breakthrough: possibly tracing, possibly something else.'

'Such as?'

The Chief did not answer. He and Iles had come out to Low Pastures in time for the second call, and listened on extensions. Now and then, Mark Lane insisted on personal involvement in exceptionally sensitive cases, and this would rate: a life at risk, another police force concerned. Iles accompanied him here as Head of Operations. In anything to do with a child, Lane could be brilliantly considerate. The ACC sometimes referred to the Chief's 'velvet mitten on a soft-as-shit fist'. Iles loved alliteration and vowel music, which came from his admiration of the poet, Tennyson.

Harpur said: 'Patsy, we're trying to draw up a list of all those with motives for taking Lynette. We wondered whether Peter Chitty's lady, Anna, had been in touch with you at all.'

'Why should she?'

'Oh, you know, darling: Peter and Caring were great confeds and Anna might be in distress now – is it three children to support?' Iles replied. 'That sort of nice comradely thing. Suppose she decided to apply some leverage. So, just fucking answer, would you? Did she get in touch?'

'Why should she?'

'Looking for money, of course, you prevaricating fool,' Iles replied. 'Do you care about your kid or not?'

Lane said gently: 'It would help us to know if she contacted you, Mrs Leach.'

'What money?'

'Hefty bank money,' Iles answered. 'She might think you or Caring had some, some that might by rights have gone to Peter, if he hadn't accepted those street bullets.'

67

'How would that be?'

'It might be very relevant to Lynette's disappearance,' the Chief said.

'If she was sent away unsatisfied,' Harpur explained.

'Was she in touch – visiting, or by phone?' Iles asked. 'She came to see us, ostensibly about the laughable tat in Pete Chitty's flat but obviously feeling out the land. And, naturally, we've had our people really talk to her since the kidnapping. No joy, though. Not yet.'

'I don't know her.'

'Patsy,' Lane said, with supreme gentleness, 'you wish to prevent any appearance of association between your husband and the bank robber, Peter Chitty? I do understand, but— '

The telephone rang and they waited while Patsy crossed the room and picked up the receiver before lifting their extension phones. It was the same message.

At the end, Garland, with the recording apparatus again, said: 'A tape? Tape talking to tape, *inter alia*.'

'No, surely. So personal, so warm,' the Chief replied. 'I'll swear that's a blood relationship crying out.'

'Did Anna come here?' Iles asked her again.

'No.'

In the car on the way to headquarters, Iles said: 'Lying – on auto-pilot. People like that refuse the truth by habit: if it's police, give them fuck all. Nothing to do with loyalty to her husband. In fact, I believe the malign bitch thinks Caring nipped back and took the child abroad.'

'My impression, too,' Harpur said.

'Which?' Iles asked. 'Anna did visit her, or she's sure Caring's got the kid?'

'Both,' Harpur replied.

'Patsy obviously hates the girl, and probably hates Caring as well,' Iles said. 'Jealousy? I'm not necessarily suggesting anything unseemly between father and daughter, sir, just an alliance against mother. Routine happy families stuff, really.'

Obviously appalled, the Chief muttered, 'My God, no. That child's deeply loving voice.'

'You've a wonderful nature, sir, if I may say,' Iles replied.

'Now, listen, Desmond, Colin: I want this woman and Lynette

treated with full decency. There's a potential tragedy here and genuine feelings, even if they are part of a rotten dynasty.'

'We'd better talk to Anna again,' Harpur said. 'I might do it myself this time, though if Erogenous Jones can't get anything out of her, my chances— '

'Someone else shagging Patsy Leach?' Iles asked. 'Caring's been absent a long while.'

'Don't think so,' Harpur replied.

'And yet she's not an utter dog,' Iles went on. 'Near thing, though. The end-of-terrace face and those hips. Not up your street, I suppose, Harpur?'

Chapter 12

Ember had a joyous call on the bar phone of the Monty. 'Ralph, it's Patsy. I've managed to give them the slip, darling. I'm talking from a booth. Can we meet? Oh, please.'

It was a quiet evening at the club, and he had help in to serve, but he muttered: 'Regrettably, very awkward.'

'There's so much to say, Ralph,' she replied.

She could sound pretty definite. But, God, how could she be sure she had really given those buggers the slip? They knew their trade. How did she know, or he know, that the club phone was secure? 'It will have to be brief.' She might roll up here loud if he did not go.

'The foreshore?' she said. 'There's an old army defence post near the— '

'I know it. In half an hour.'

He went upstairs and told Margaret he had been tipped off about cut-price crates of spirits going at a docks warehouse. On the way, he watched his mirror and left his car at the end of the little foreshore road and walked. He saw nothing to worry him. When he arrived, she was already there, and he joined her in her dark car, close to that last war pill-box, meant to throw Jerry back into the water. 'They think I'm asleep, sedated in my room. Oh, Ralph,' she said, clutching him, 'such a long time.' Again her mouth seemed to be gently sucking comfort from his, unwilling to break away or to endanger the flow of sweetness by growing too passionate and fierce. Her two hands held his head, covering his ears, her fingers tenderly playing up and down the back of his neck. This was a woman in such need. He felt really sad about her, plain or not. Even choosing to marry someone like Caring Oliver did not mean she was unentitled to a life, for God's sake.

70

After a time, Patsy slowly pulled back her face from his, eyes wide open and alert, wanting to gaze at him in what light there was. Women often did this. It was the El Cid factor. They liked to stock up rich on fantasy before making love. Fantasy was recommended to many women by experts, owing to orgasm handicaps. He did not mind too much. It still felt the same for him, whatever they dreamt about.

This was a red Volvo estate and she already had the back seat folded down. 'How the hell did you get out in the car without being seen?' he asked, full of terror.

'I didn't. Couldn't. I came out on foot through the gardens. Mucky. This is borrowed from the All Nite Garage, which we own half of.'

They lay on his jacket. He had never made love in a Volvo before, but Volvos were Swedish and it was well known they went in for brilliant sex over there with tall blondes, so the leg room turned out a treat. She did like oral, giving and receiving, which you could not object to. He always felt it showed a real willingness to share, plus first-class trust, even when things might be dicey healthwise. She moved herself with a nice, steady rhythm on the tip of his tongue, growing gradually faster as suited her own sensation needs, and she held the back of his head again, keeping him hard to her for as long as it took. Then, her mouth on him was sweetly tight, but not too tight, not liable to bring on a rush between the wrong lips. He liked to finish where, in his view, it was right to finish, meaning mouth on mouth, the woman's legs locked around him, her body pushing up and up, tireless and real in response. What was in her mind did not matter to him, but her body had to be saying this something real and keep on saying it.

Near the end, Patsy was chortling noisy rudenesses in her special way, which he could have done without, but never mind. If it worked it worked, and why not? The lights of another car worried him for a moment, but it had parked a good distance away and her yells probably would not carry. He remained alert for a while, in case she had been tailed, but eventually relaxed. This was a known haunt for lovers and couples stayed private.

'It's so wonderful to see you, Ralph. I've had a lot to think about, worry about. Ransom? How much? Half a million? A

71

million? What a laugh. The police think Chitty's woman has Lynette. Where? Idiots. I know as fact that ugly little schemer's with Oliver. Don't ask me what goes on between them, please. Probably France.'

'But how do you know, Patsy?'

'I just do. And he's left a tape of her for someone to play and confuse everyone. Clever? Sure: Oliver's trade-mark all over. Well, there'll be no ransom paid, I mean, even if I had the money. I'm not second mortgaging Low Pastures, either. The demand's for a reply in the papers, but I'll refuse. The police can't do it regardless, can they? It would only bring more nuisance calls.'

'But, Patsy, if the police say it's Anna— '

'Kidnapped by a woman? How the hell could she bring it off? How could she hold that little demon against her will and force her to speak on the phone? Police get an idea and then can't let it go. You know what they're like at the top. And, listen, one of them's supposed to be banging the other's wife. Harpur, Mrs Iles? You heard that? Can anyone rely on such people?

She had brought a bag of prawns and olives, plus Ovaltine in a vacuum flask, with plastic cups, and they enjoyed a picnic back in the front seats. He hated this spot on the coast – the sound of the filthy, mysterious sea, just over the earthwork wall, trying to sneak in on mankind's built-up areas all the time, and the festering concrete bunker that never did a day's work in fifty years. Ember found he was growing unbearably anxious about this child whose life could depend on him without a soul knowing. The kid had a right to decades yet. She had given him her little badge and kissed him. Police would not worry too much about her or split a gut to bring her back: she was a villain's daughter whose disappearance could be used to squeeze him, or so they'd think. And did her mother worry? Here she was – clothes chucked on again almost anyhow after full gratification, loudly spitting out olive stones, breaking open prawns at a hell of a rate and washing them down with the famous old, hot, sweet drink. She spoke evil of the girl, could not care less about her and seemed glad to see her gone, except for the money that she thought went, too. He had a duty to Lynette.

It meant he had to get urgently to Chitty's Anna. He could not wait for her to appear at the Monty again. That would be a mad hope, anyway: if she had Lynette, she would stay hidden. He had no idea where she lived, and she would probably not be listed in the telephone book. Did Anna even go as Chitty any longer? He felt desperate, and enraged with himself for coldly turning her away twice from the club.

Patsy cleared up the food wrappings and put the Ovaltine flask and cups to one side on the floor: in Ember, that milk drink had started strong recollections of his childhood, especially times with his mother. Patsy reached down to his knee and held it for a few moments before beginning to move her hand slowly up. This poor creature really did hunger. His trousers were going to smell of prawns on most of one leg, probably, but it was only a working suit and you could not quibble when a woman was in such a bad state for human warmth.

'I'll always find a way to get out, or at least be in touch, Ralph,' she promised him, 'no matter how many of them are around the house.'

'Great,' he replied.

'Do you know what I want, above all?'

'What, Patsy?'

'Can't you guess?'

'Well, I— '

'One day to go back to that spot in the woods where we first made love. Cheltenham? That place has such a special significance for me now. Symbolic?'

'It's— '

'It's a long way, I know. But you do understand?'

'It's a lovely thought.'

'It's lovely and sensitive of you to agree, Ralph. Something like that, Caring would never be able to appreciate. Some things are beyond him.' She re-undid his zip and went in with two hands: Patsy was boisterous and very self-centred, yes, but she had diplomacy. 'Well, here's a surprise,' she said.

He would have liked to be quick, so he could do something immediately about looking for Anna and maybe fixing a deal for the child. But Patsy wanted all their clothes off again, saying sex otherwise was furtive, which she supremely hated, apparently. They had climbed into the rear of the Volvo once more, and he was glad of distance from the food and drink smells, most

73

especially now the Ovaltine: it had come to seem wrong to have his hand on pussy while recalling moments as a boy with his mother just before bed, sipping from steaming Winnie the Pooh mugs.

Patsy turned languorously on to her side, her back to him, folding up her legs. 'Sometimes I think extra things can be said the Italian way,' she told him. 'As they call it.'

'Yes?'

'Caring's so routine and British, despite travel. Waistcoats etc. But, look, why else did God make us like this? In a way, I think I'm seducing you, the great Ralphy. Ralph.'

'In a way.'

She grunted a lot and put a palm up on the car window, her fingers massaging and digging at it, as she had on his neck at the start. From outside it could look like someone sealed in, pawing hopelessly at the glass for escape. This might all be part of her individual requirements. These days women were constantly told to create their sexual menu, that was the phrase. You had to go along with it, for the sake of progress, honouring what suffragettes had fought for. He would wipe the finger marks off the window eventually. It was not right for a Volvo.

When they parted she told him once more that she would be doing all she could to break out and see him again soon. He kissed her on the forehead and said how wonderful that would be. 'Please, let them put the reply in the newspaper, Patsy,' he said urgently. 'You never know, she might not be with Oliver after all, and it's crucial to keep contact.'

'That's what the big cop said, the one giving it to Mrs Iles.'

'It could be right, just the same.'

She turned her head sharply towards him. 'Christ, don't tell me you fancy that creepy kid, too,' she yelled.

'Patsy, this is a child's life, that's all.' God, women jealous of their own daughters?

It was late when he returned to the Monty, but there were still a few customers around and Margaret had not gone to bed. 'They want ready cash for this warehouse booze,' he said. 'That kind of deal. I've got a bit in the loft.' He would have to tell her in the morning that the bargains had all gone by the time he returned.

Although most of his new special savings were spread in vault deposit boxes, Ember had kept about £120,000 up there for fear he

74

had to buy himself very fast out of trouble. He had been thinking of Fritzy or Leopold the Little arriving at the Monty in a froth, possibly even Harry Lighterman, but now he knew Anna could be trouble, too, and probably was – more than any of them. He packed £100,000 in fifties and twenties into a case, then looked out one or two do-it-yourself items that might help with a break-in, and included them. He went out to the car again.

The only possible place of contact with her he had been able to think of was Pete Chitty's flat, which had stood empty since his death. She had not lived there at the end, or for a while before, yet Pete had kept in touch with the children, so there might be something around with an address for them and Anna on it. Once, Ember had been to the flat himself, on the first floor in a good, private block, and knew the layout. It was a very long shot. He could think of no others tonight, and with a child's life involved he must hurry. An exciting, fresh idea had come to him: was it even possible that Anna had a key to Chitty's place from their better times and would use it now to house Lynette? Surely that would be crazy. Police knew the flat, probably even before Pete's death, and certainly now. If Anna was up against it, though? If she had nowhere else?

It was just after 2 a.m. and he stood a fair chance of being stopped on the road. At least they would get only Ovaltine and prawns on his breath, but how did you explain a hundred grand in a bag? He made his approach to the flat as cautious as when he met Patsy, driving past the block at first and getting around into a street at the rear for a view from there. Everything was dark, which you would expect so late. The flat block stood in quite a decent area, near Grant Hill, and would certainly have a security system. Things could be very difficult. He was sweating a bit and shaking in his personalised fashion, two more reasons he did not want to be waved down by police.

He stayed at the back and parked. Then, taking a flashlight from the glove compartment and carrying the loaded case, he walked to a service lane behind the block, put the case on its end against the wall and used it to help him climb over. He unbolted the door and brought the case into the yard with him. There was a fire escape and he thought he could identify Chitty's place alongside the first floor landing. Burglary had never been one of Ember's skills, but he knew how to break a window without making too much noise. On the landing he opened the case, brought out his small hammer and wrapped the head in a handkerchief. He worked on a pane in the french windows and after a moment was able to undo the catch and let himself into the sitting room. The curtains had been over, but when he pushed them apart to get in he saw at once it was the right flat: even in the near dark he recognised the crap art around the walls and Chitty's horrible green leather chesterfield sofa and chairs. Briefly, he stood still, listening for the sound of anyone disturbed by his entry, and for the noise of alarms, though one of those might be going off secretly somewhere: he would have to take the chance.

After a minute or two, he made sure the curtains were tight again and switched on his flashlight, keeping the beam directed close down, restricting the spread. Again he listened. It seemed obvious now that nobody had been aroused by the noise of glass breaking, and, instead, he tried to pick up the sound of breathing in a bedroom. No. He began to move slowly towards the door, which would take him into a small hallway. Then he could do the rest of the search.

He had not reached the door when he found his legs starting to fail him. They grew stiff and very weary, hard to keep going. These were symptoms he had suffered from before, even when younger and into regular rough work. The sweats, the freezing of the legs, plus a misting of his eyes – these were attacks he would fight to resist, but they could almost always beat him, always take away his strength. Now and then, the result had been real disasters – one reason he had tried to leave all that stress and make a go of the Monty.

But, Jesus, what was he doing here, standing so exposed, a flashlight advertising his position, the heavy suitcase in his other hand, giving him no hope of protecting himself? A bit of nausea began to get at him, too. He thought he had better rest for a spell, and managed to make his way to the chesterfield. For a moment he switched off the flashlight and sat hunched forward with the case between his feet, trying to listen again, but finding it hard now, because of the noise of his own frightened breathing. Basically, he knew he was not El Cid.

The whole thing had come to seem mad to him. There would

be nobody here, nor anything to find worth finding. Often when a woman was all over him, giving him a throb, like Patsy, he began to believe in himself and might decide then to try things he would run like hell from usually. That had happened tonight. It was stupid even to consider continuing the search. The police would have turned this place over and over after Chitty's death and taken all material that could lead on. He should get out while he could. Police might be on their way, alerted by an alarm. He found the darkness very frightening and switched on the flashlight again. Would his legs get him to the french windows and down the escape?

Two small, sharp sounds from very near brought added sudden alarm, until he realised it was sweat from his face dripping on to the case. Momentarily, in his panic, then, he considered leaving the money in the flat. He would be able to move more easily. And, if Anna really was here with the child, perhaps she would get the message and accept this as enough. What more could she ask for – hand delivered, no trouble?

Standing, he found he did not feel too bad, as long as he knew he would be out of here soon. He took a couple of steps, then went back and picked up the case. After all, this was a hundred fucking grand. Despite everything, you could not just leave it around. It had taken a lot of collecting and holding, one way and another. He would be able to cope with this situation all right. On some things, such as money, he was still strong, still in control. This was Ralph Ember, with a career going right back.

From outside, he pulled the curtains close to and fixed the latch. Yes, he was cool again now, calculating: with any luck the break might not be noticed for a time. He had no trouble descending the escape and from the yard threw the case over the wall into the service lane. Then he scrambled over the wall himself, without any help this time. He could have let himself out of the back door, but wanted it to stay re-bolted, so there would be no obvious sign of a break-in. The case had not burst open, thank God, and he recovered it, took a rest, leaning against the wall for a few minutes, then made his way quickly to the car. On the whole, he thought he had not done badly, after all. That had been a well-organised, planned exit from what had turned out to be a crazy peril. He had nothing to be ashamed of, had he?

77

Back at the Monty, he put the case in the loft, showered, and climbed into bed. Margaret, warm and smelling nicely of Campari, turned his way and reached down for him in a leisurely, happy style. 'Successful night?'

'Not altogether, as a matter of fact.'

'Never mind. I was dreaming about you, Ralph,' she murmured. 'You were being *very* successful. Very, well, manly.'

'What was I doing?'

'Something so nice.'

'This?'

'Why should I need to dream?'

'Exactly,' he said. He began to feel altogether fine again. He had made a gesture tonight on behalf of that child, and it had been a sound and honest one, one based on humanity.

Chapter 13

Harpur had a call at home from Jack Lamb, asking for a meeting at one of the rendezvous spots they sometimes used, an old defence post down on the foreshore. As so often seemed to happen when Jack rang, Megan picked up the phone first and her voice fell at once into that hostile chattiness she kept on ice especially for Lamb. Megan loathed Jack, or at least loathed the *quid pro quo* arrangement Harpur had with him. She still thought all police work should be spruce and open, and hated the use of what she called 'epically tarnished' informants such as Jack. Harpur's daughters were worse and spoke of him as 'father's foul fink' or 'whispering grass'. Lamb read their dislike, even though they all stayed more or less polite to his face. Only a fool would fail to feel the edge, and nobody was less a fool than Jack, otherwise he would be dead. He never allowed their antipathy to affect him, though, thank God, or Harpur knew his career was on stop. Harpur did not let it affect him, either. He tried to be tolerant: Megan's parents, doctors in Highgate, were a fine, brilliantly radical couple, and she had not yet grown out of their haze.

Lamb seemed fond of this bleak slab of coast, with its wide, glinting mud flats at low water. Often there were frothy patches of gorgeously coloured effluent, and a scatter of tree trunks, lavatory paper, rail sleepers and seaweed dumped high in strange, festooned shapes by the tide. At night, it was a spot for motorised lovers and, now and then, when she could get away for a couple of hours, supposedly for bridge, Harpur would bring Sarah Iles. They were here briefly last night, when he should really have been waiting for calls at Patsy Leach's house. You had to grab the time. The chances with Sarah were scarce. She had had some messy entanglements and Iles watched her carefully these days.

79

Soon, Lamb appeared wearing shorts and a purple sweatshirt, with the head of a toothy wild animal snarling on the back. For someone who rightly insisted on secrecy in their dealings, Jack could choose oddly noticeable gear. 'Thought I'd make a jog of it along the sea wall, Col.' He looked huge and powerful, like someone who had fought heavyweight fifteen years ago and almost kept in shape since. 'I heard about Caring's kid.'

'Oh, how?' Harpur would ask such questions, knowing they would never be answered, or even acknowledged.

'Taking a child is beyond. Not decent. So I've tried to do some listening for you.'

'Nobody's supposed to know.'

Lamb by-passed that, too. 'But I haven't done too well.'

All the same, Harpur paid attention. What amounted to not too well for Jack would be bloody brilliant coming from anyone else. 'Caring was nicely settled in North Spain then moved on in a hurry, possibly disturbed by someone stalking his share of the Exeter loot, and more. Caring might have an even bigger slice of that than everyone thought.'

'Move on where?' Harpur was riveted.

'I told you, I haven't done well. Perhaps intending to make for France eventually. Bordeaux way? Arcachon? That's the tale. But in the meantime I don't know where.'

'Could he have come back home?'

'It's possible. I don't know.' Jack sounded genuinely ashamed of his failures.

'Who made him move from Spain?'

'Don't know that, either.'

'Christ, this is crucial. It could be everything, Jack. Caring's own whereabouts are secondary.'

He did an echo. 'Christ, don't I know it's crucial? Don't I know it could be everything?' Lamb was almost shouting in his rage at being asked what he could not answer. 'Obviously someone formidable, if he can frighten Caring. Maybe, also, someone who grew tired of trailing him across Europe, came back and grabbed the girl instead, as a short cut. Yes, I do see that, Col, and all the hazards to her. But I can't help you.' His massive face looked angry, but sad, too.

'Jack, if you know so much about where Caring was, you— '

80

'Yes?'

'If you— '

'Look, Col, the police themselves never discovered who else beside the dead and jailed were in the Exeter bank raid. You don't even know for sure it was Caring. If you can't do it, how should Jack Lamb?'

'Just because you're Jack Lamb, of fucking course.'

'So kind. And you've tried Winston Acre at Strangeways, the only one you picked up alive at the raid?'

'He doesn't talk, except to tell my lads Chitty was on the raid. Really? Why else would he be dead in a mask on the bank steps? Winston's only other disclosure is there's going to be a riot soon in his jail. Routine stuff.'

Lamb pondered and then his mind seemed to switch. 'Do I hear there's something between you and Sarah Iles?'

But Lamb was not the only one who could stonewall. 'Jack, look, Lynette Leach might finish dead. It's hard to make police worry and work at full pitch over the kid of a villain. Stretch a point – let me talk to your source direct.'

Lamb ignored that. It was one of those conversations where sequence had little chance. 'Yes, Caring was hoping to get to France. Could be Les Grand Lacs? Sauvignon vicinity? Know the area at all?' He began to bend and flex, loosening his great muscles.

'Ever hear anything to connect Panicking Ralph with Exeter, Jack? We wonder now and then. That £25,000 returned would be just like the soft bugger. And a few other points.'

'Ralph? A jerk, but a clever jerk. I'll probably do a really big run today. I'm in that sort of all-conquering mood.' He set out. Harpur leaned against the pill-box, thought about his times down here with Sarah, and gazed at the forlorn view. It seemed to say something just right about his relationship with her, maybe about all love. Then, he muttered to himself, 'Oh, weep no more, Harpur, you self-pitying jerk: consider yourself lucky.' The other couples who turned up here in the dark probably felt it was all delightfully remote, even romantic. For a moment last night he had glanced across at what seemed to be a Volvo estate and thought he saw a hand pressed against the glass, perhaps a woman's, convulsively loosening and tightening, like some sort

81

of urgent signal, though not one he was able to interpret or answer.

When Lamb was almost out of sight on his run, he turned suddenly and came pounding back. He reached Harpur and, running on the spot, said: 'Please, Col, I meant nothing disparaging about Mrs Iles. She's a very lovely woman, not in the least a routine stuff.' Then he was away again.

Harpur left. At the station, the ACC and Lane drifted into his room. 'Garland tells us he thinks Patsy Leach sneaked out of Low Pastures on the quiet last night,' the Chief said. 'He noticed mud on her shoes this morning.'

Iles stared at Harpur: 'I thought you were supposed to be up there, too, keeping an eye.'

'Yes. I had to slip out for a short while.'

'Oh, where?' Iles asked.

'Home. One of the children not well.'

'I'm very sorry to hear that, Colin,' Lane said.

'Which child?' Iles asked.

'Hazel.'

'I do hope she's all right now,' Lane said.

'Thank you, sir, yes.'

'What was wrong with her?' Iles asked.

'Some bug.'

'Which bug?' Iles said. 'Did it require your presence? You're a healer now?'

'We don't know where Patsy went?' Harpur asked.

'Obviously we bloody don't,' Iles said. 'Where the hell were you, Harpur?'

'Come now, Desmond,' Lane protested. He had on a country-style twill check shirt today, not quite big enough and opening up around the chest buttons. 'Colin has explained.'

'Colin has,' Iles said. He jerked his head to throw back a wedge of grey hair that had dropped over his eyes.

'Patsy went somewhere on foot?' Harpur asked.

'Or picked up by arrangement,' Iles said.

'Garland's view is that she could have got out to contact Caring Oliver, either phone or face to face,' the Chief said. 'It's an ingenious notion. He thinks Patsy and Caring are running this whole kidnap thing between them, to get the money-hunters

off Caring's back. Eventually, they'll let the child reappear –
great jubilation, and everyone is supposed to deduce that all the
Exeter take has been paid out in ransom. So, no point in putting
pressure on Caring any longer, switch it elsewhere. He'd be clever
enough.'

'All balls,' Iles announced. 'But tell me this, *à propos* your
absence: have you got something extra going again, Harpur?'

'Please, Desmond. Let's concentrate on this child's safety,
shall we?'

'Patsy doesn't know we think she broke out last night?' Harpur
said.

'Not at all,' Lane replied.

'We must really watch her next time, in secret,' Harpur said.

'Yes, we really must, next time. If there is one.'

'We're putting the announcement in the *Independent* for tomorrow,' Lane said. 'She doesn't want it, but is there any choice?'

Chapter 14

Standing in Pete Chitty's place again late at night, Ember grew suddenly sure he heard someone make a quick movement elsewhere in the flat. For a second, he felt only overwhelming joy: the child was here, alive with Anna. He had been right after all to think the flat would lead to her, and right to return. Those famous Ralph Ember instincts from the old days still did the job, then. Very briefly, his belief that he had triumphed made him keep the flashlight burning, even prompted him to swing the beam around towards the sound, ready to call a greeting and make clear he meant nobody any harm, meant only a blessing and a rich deal.

He had not brought the case of fifties and twenties with him this time, because he remembered what a drag it had been, and knew he could scale the wall without help. But that money was just as available to buy back the girl as before.

The light beam meant Lynette would see him and recognise him, what she called the Charlton Heston face, which was absolutely fair enough, and she would know he was a friend – not like that bank manager's kid at the school, staring at him, unsure and alarmed, sad little bugger. Lynette would realise it was a rescue, and share his own sense of victory.

He had woken up the other morning wondering how the hell he could have chickened out of the first search. And not just chickened out: hadn't he conned himself into feeling so all right and glorious about it, like Dunkirk? Christ, that really was Panicking Ralph: start something, then run for no reason, no reason except built-in Ember terror. And so he had forced himself to come back. He had a soul to be saved.

'Lynette,' he murmured. 'Lynette Helen. It's Ralphy. I've come to take you home.'

Although he hated that 'Ralphy', she had used the name, and he felt it might make him sound less dangerous, more like the good friend she knew. He thought only of Lynette's reactions, not Anna's. The child was top in his mind, those awful fears and confusions she must have. If you killed and rough buried someone's dad you had obligations to her, to her in person, and giving it all ways on request to the mother was not a full answer.

There was a second sound, again like quick movement. This time he thought the tread might be heavier than a child's. Some of his happy excitement began to drain off, the way it often did with him. But that made no sense. After all, he did not expect Lynette to be here alone, and Anna was just as likely as the child to be woken by somebody entering the flat. He switched off the flashlight and stood still, his face turned towards the sound. He felt puzzled. It seemed to come from the sitting room, yet he had certainly seen nobody when he passed through after entering by the french windows again. Now, he was in the tiny hall, on his way to the kitchen and bedrooms. He would have liked to speak Anna's name, too – to tell her she could do fine for herself trading with Ralph Ember and not to worry. But he found speaking suddenly difficult.

He still felt it was right to have come here. There had been a real choice. For an hour, he had sat in the Monty loft with Caring Oliver's clothes and possessions, and the green, cash holdall spread on the floor in front of him. Ember had wondered about putting everything into the holdall, including the monitor badge, crossing to France and leaving it somewhere, say at a rail station, or an airport. When it was eventually picked up and opened, would police deduce Lynette and Caring must be together over there and ease up on the inquiries? They might, if they believed the luggage had really been lost. It could just about work.

But Ember had found he could not do it. Although he dreaded what might come out if Lynette ever showed up alive, he dreaded more causing a scaled-down search that could mean her death. Ember knew he was jelly almost right the way through, but only almost. Somewhere far inside, he had a slab not quite of steel, but of genuine oak veneer, maybe. He would not write Lynette off.

In Chitty's hall he turned slowly so he could face the open door

to the sitting room square on. There was only silence now. He
began to feel very bad again and edged a little towards the flat's
front door, ready for another of his tactical withdrawals. If the
sounds had come from the sitting room, he would not try to get
back out that way, whoever it was, woman or not. Thank God
he had left the money load. He could really gallop if he had to.
'Anna,' he called, in a loud whisper, 'it's Ralph Ember. I'm on
your side, Anna. You're entitled, no question. I'm here to talk,
to talk business.'

There was no answer, and, for a while, no more sounds at
all. Ember was just about to call again, louder this time if his
voice would do it, when a man suddenly appeared in the sitting
room doorway and stood there, gazing at him, so bloody relaxed.
Because Ember had been looking for Anna or even the child, this
shock took all his thinking powers for a few seconds. In the dark,
he did not recognise the figure, only made out that the man was
young – early twenties, maybe – and thin and into those loose
double-breasteds that could tent all sorts of metal.

'So, who's Anna, Ralph?'

The voice, full of a sort of sleepiness, yet hard as hell at the
edges, almost reminded Ember who he was, and might have done
it completely if his mind had not taken such a thump.

'So, what business with Anna, Ralph? Can't your old pal Harry
be in on it?'

'Harry?' He tried everything to make his mouth do rapture.
'Harry! Harry Lighterman!'

'Right.'

'We worked together.'

'Right, again. You guarding the hostages in the manager's
house, me with Caring and the rest doing the bank. What a
balls-up, except for a happy few.'

'Harry, this is great.' Ember thought it would be decent to step
forward to shake his hand, then decided the movement could be
read wrong, so stayed still. This boy you did not want jumpy.

'Yes, isn't it great? You still look the same, Ralphy. Like that
guy on the screen whose name I always forget.'

'Oh, I know, people say— '

'Cardew the Cad on TV, that's it. That stuttering, half-baked bugger. I've been in this flat before, but through the front door last time.'

'We met here for the planning of the bank project, all except Fritzy. A while now.' He enjoyed talking about the past and comradeship. Did Harry Lighterman believe in comradeship, or much at all?

'Mad paintings everywhere, right? A blue horse?' Harry said.

Ember laughed: 'Right. Pete's. Taste. Known as Jackson Pollock, I recall. Only prints.'

'Well, yes, Pete Chitty. That was bad.'

'Bad, bad.'

'So what are you doing, coming in that way, Ralph? You do it a lot? The window already broken? Thieving? What is there?'

'We could sit down, Harry. It's quite a story.'

Harry went back into the sitting room and lounged in one of the green armchairs. Ember took a corner of the green chesterfield once more. 'The art's better in the dark,' Harry said. 'Obviously, I'm down here looking for that sodding magician, Caring.'

'Oliver? Abroad, I heard. That was the last.'

'I heard so, too. It's why I wanted to find you first, Ralphy, a point of contact. You came batting out of your club and lead me here.'

'Good tailing. I didn't spot.'

'But you heard me in this room? The flashlight came reaching. You're not as dim as they say. And the ears still OK.' Harry leaned forward, and Ember could just make out that youthful face which looked so worried about the troubles of the world, and so ever-ready to be open and giving. Ember remembered the bastard as a total me-first clam. He was talking now, though. 'Ralph, I picked up next to nothing at Exeter, you know.'

'You? I thought— '

'You thought Caring and I had a lovely consignment each, a nice split down the middle.'

'This was— '

'This was what Caring told around. Naturally.'

'Harry, I'm— '

'You got a slice?'

'Just my entitlement, Harry. Not a whisker more.'

87

'He turned up to make the share-out with you? That's like Caring, yes? Bits he'll do so strictly by the rules. The little bits. Your entitlement being?'

'Well, just over the hundred grand.'

Harry leaned back in the leather, his face invisible. 'Yes, the little bits. And now I hear his daughter's gone.'

'How did you find out?'

'It's around.'

'Not in the media.'

'Around.'

'Even so far? You were in Liverpool, yes?'

'I said it's around, Ralph.'

In a while, Ember asked: 'So, do you hear who's got her?'

'Ah, you worry about the rest of the cash, too? Good. Shows you only got what you said.'

'And about the kid. I'm worried about the kid.'

'Yes?'

'This is a schoolgirl, that's all, Harry.'

'You doing something affectionate there?'

'No. I mean just the life of a kid.'

Harry seemed to dream for a while. 'Who's got her? Oh, someone who knows how much Caring collected.'

'How much did he collect, Harry?'

'Well as for me, I had sixty-two grand.'

Could Ember believe that? 'But, my God— '

'The get-away, a shambles. Another gang on the scene, trying to muscle in, armed, too. Well, I don't have to tell you. Caring was somehow into the right car at the end, though. Yes, very somehow. Have you thought what that much money looks like in bulk, even big bills? This must be £1.7 or £1.8 million if the bank says true. He drives off like a loaded refuse van, suspension worse than Orson Welles's shoes. I'm left and have to grab a vehicle – steal it there and bloody then – and one bag of cash. He didn't wave. So, Caring's very desirable now.'

'This is a grief, what he did to you, Harry.'

'What he did to all of us, Ralph,' he said. It sounded like a fucking question, though.

'Well, yes, too true.' Ember held up a hand, as if listening. 'We ought to get out of here. This place is sealed by the police.'

He had had enough of Lighterman. The snotty insults: Cardew the Cad, for God's sake!

Lighterman did not move. 'I was afraid to go looking for Caring, you know.'

'You, afraid? Harry Lighterman?'

'Caring's no joke. Oh, long grey hair like some queer old actor, but venom and aptitude. And, that much money, he could have a staff of trouble-shooters with him. I hung back, but then one day I hear some bugger might squeeze a stack out of him through the daughter. Well, I couldn't let that go unfought, could I?'

'I see what you mean.'

'So, I'm going to be around, Ralph. Self-respect dictates that. And then, leave aside the kidnapping, there's the wife. Patsy? That house could be full of money even if Caring's away.'

'Nobody can get near her now – so many police.' Christ, yes, how much was Patsy sitting on? She never gave any hint. Deceit he loathed, but with women you always had to expect it. Ember stood. 'We mustn't leave together. On no account.'

'What? Why?'

'I'll go first.'

'Listen, Ralph. I know where you are, remember. We've got a connection. Who's Anna, the one you thought you were talking to? What deal were you referring to?' He was still seated. He had always played it casual. 'I'll tell you, first thing I thought when I heard about that kid going was this was the kind of stroke old Ember could pull – experience back to Attila, good with kids, very money-friendly, probably likes girl-children, anyway, and so on.'

'Not Ralph.'

'Not Ralph? So, who's Anna? What was that about?'

'Look, I'm getting out now. I thought I heard something below. I've got these ears. Well, you know.' He was down the escape and over the wall before Harry appeared at the window. As Ember drove home, he saw no sign of him in the mirror, and he was really watching now. But Harry, like he said, knew where the Monty was and had no need to rush. He would be around.

Chapter 15

'It's the Chief's own idea, Ralph,' Harpur said.

'And how!' Iles declared. 'We were discussing ways to make our response to these Lynette phone calls at Caring's house more effective. Shall I give you Mr Lane's actual words? "I see here a job hand-made for Ralphy Ember." Yes, hand-made. There. We bring a plea on his behalf. The Chief would have come himself but there's something unavoidable in his diary. He insisted I accompany Colin in his place and ask for your help, Ralphy. To show due esteem.'

Ember knew he had no choice. These two got whatever they wanted. As usual, Iles had on a custom job navy blue suit and one of those dark ties with silver shields and other twinkles of class, signifying some Pall Mall London club, or a top school: very master race, anyway. Making a plea? Bollocks. They would drag him if he refused. Besides, there was something in Ember that yearned to respond to these men, to be on their side and part of their respectability. Until all this blew up, and he was drawn back into activities by Caring, he had been very much on the road to good citizenship, as a matter of fact, a true businessman. The way these two police walked was like conquerors. They did not have real money and never would, yet they believed in something: anyone who did not know Iles might even think it was law and order. 'I'll just pop upstairs and tell Margaret I'm going with you.'

'Great,' Iles said.

'I like to think I know my responsibilities as a member of the community,' Ember responded.

'Amen, Ralphy,' Iles said. 'Community. Yes.'

'I think Ralph prefers to be called Ralph, sir.'

'Oh, is that right, Ralph? Apologies.'

90

Ember gave a very slight nod of acknowledgement, no arse-crawling at this stage. It was fine to hear Iles being polite, but you also had to keep sharp. You never knew where you were when this one decided to go human for a while. It could feel like being strangled with treacle.

On the trip to Low Pastures, he sat in the back of the car with Harpur, while Iles drove. 'This brainwave hit the Chief only half an hour ago,' Harpur said.

'We came straight away, Ralph,' Iles told him. 'It's urgent.'

Harpur explained: 'The girl obviously reveres you, Ralph. We found that for ourselves, talking to kids and staff in her school at Cheltenham. And the local police say similar. So, the Chief decided that, if you could sit in with us up at Caring's place, and possibly speak to Lynette on the phone when she calls again, she might be so thrilled that she'd keep talking and we'll have time to trace. Now the reply is in the *Independent* these are key days.'

'Won't whoever's holding her make her put the phone down quickly, anyway?' Ember asked.

Iles gave a chuckle. 'The old brain's still ticking over. Yes, you're right, of course. It's just that the surprise of hearing you might cause a moment's confusion, not just to Lynette but the kidnapper. We need only a short time to make the trace. But it's still too brief when Patsy's answering.'

'I'll try,' Ember replied. 'Anything to help the girl.' He could not have meant it more.

'An outside chance, unquestionably. We've no others. And your link with the kid seems powerful. Apparently, she was boasting after you'd taken her back there – the Charlton Heston thing, Ralph,' Iles said, over his shoulder. 'I expect it bores you insensible by now, but a girl of that age would be knocked sideways, and the resemblance is indeed remarkable. She bragged to her friends she'd actually kissed you, Ralph, and even given you her precious monitor badge. Is that right? You had a triumph. Delightful, really.'

'Kissed on the cheek,' Ember said.

'Oh, obviously,' Iles replied. 'No tonsil-tongueing. Well, good Lord, you're a respected father of daughters yourself, aren't you, not Humbert Humbert?'

'Who?' Harpur said.

'Fuck off, Colin,' Iles replied.

Even so, Ember thought Iles did seem almost genuinely decent today. It was helpful of him to confirm the Charlton Heston, particularly after Lighterman, festering, envious sod.

The police had a man on Caring's gates and he let the car in. They parked out of sight from the road among a lot of other vehicles. As they walked to the mansion, Harpur said: 'You hear nothing around the club, Ralph?'

'Would that I did! A child's life in the balance.'

'And nothing about the unknowns in the Exeter bank raid?' Harpur asked. 'I'm very sorry to say we have to assume Caring was in on that. If there are disappointed accomplices prowling we must find them at once.'

'Caring part of that job?' Ember replied. 'Really? And now people trying to extract some of the gains?'

'Perfectly put, Ralph,' Iles said.

'What a world,' Ember replied. He felt worried going into the big drawing room to see Patsy. The trouble was, when you had been having a woman, it often warmed her retinas, and she could not keep that sparkling look of appreciation out of her eyes, even much later on. He was scared she would set up special signals now. People like Iles would notice that sort of thing. Ember could sense her staring at him, looking for glow signals in return, but he tried to ignore this, except to give a small wave of greeting when he came into the room and a sad smile to say how much he sympathised with her troubles.

If Lynette called, they would sit opposite each other with telephones at a big oval rosewood table, which must have cost Caring a packet of someone's money. Occasionally, when Ember's eyes did meet hers, he tried hard to read whether this suffering lady knew where upwards of another five hundred grand might be, but all he could make out were what he would have expected, the usual lovingness and fierce desire for him. These were all very well, but the thought that there might be big, extra funds somewhere around to her secret knowledge greatly pissed him off, and it would have even if she had been tastier.

There were police everywhere in this drawing room, Harpur's people and some from the Force that operated near the kid's school. He tried not to let it bother him. They could smell fear, like dogs, and they loved it. That was part of being conquerors. The only way to beat them was to keep saying to yourself that they knew nothing. They could strut but they knew nothing unless you told them. They could not get the other names for Exeter, and with luck Caring was eternally missing, like the Unknown Soldier, part of Nature.

'Ralph, you've lost a good customer with Oliver,' Iles said, while they waited.

'He's coming back. Everything will be all right.'

'Of course it will,' Iles replied.

Although Ember felt almost part of their team, he still kept his caution operating. As ever, you spent all your time listening to what these bastards seemed to be saying while trying to work out what they were really saying and planning. All right, this was similar throughout life, such as women or that Arafat, but with police it was worse, and with these two worse still, and worst of all with Desmond Iles. Such a brilliant comfort to know the other was knocking off Mrs Iles.

But, whatever this pair might be thinking underneath it all, and whatever they might be playing at, Ember was pleased to have the chance of talking to the girl again. He did feel a warm, innocent, living bond with her. Nobody else could do much: he had to bring that ugly kid back unharmed, if he could.

They all sat down. 'We heard you were thinking of moving on from the Monty, Ralph,' Harpur said. 'Buying something better, maybe London way.' Harpur had this big face that he could make look harmless and even kindly, like a boxer gone punchy.

'Leave the Monty? News to me,' Ember replied at once.

'A dream is it, Ralph?' Iles asked. 'Places up there are so pricey, yes? However well the Monty's doing, financing something like that would still be tough.'

'Right,' Ember replied.

'Unless you got a very special infusion of capital,' Iles said.

'Special? Infusion? That's like making tea, yes? I don't know where from,' Ember replied.

Iles had a nice chuckle. 'Oh, I meant backers. People who've seen what you've made of the Monty and would stake you.'

'Yes, that's how it would have to be. If I was interested,' Ember said. He added that quickly. These people, they led you on, tried to make you lower the drawbridge. Infusion, the bastard.

Ember sensed Patsy staring at him again. She said in a kind of moan: 'Move away, Ralph?'

'Obviously only a rumour,' Iles replied.

'Move where?' she asked.

'Nowhere,' Ember said, gazing at her, trying as hard as hell to seem believable and devoted. Jesus, she looked more worried about this than about Lynette. These two would be watching her, seeing all sorts.

'I hadn't heard anything of this,' she kept on. 'London? Why, Ralph?'

'This is gossip.' Ember thought she was going to cry.

'You'd miss him, would you, Patsy?' Iles asked.

Grief ripped her voice to pieces and she murmured: 'Oh, it would be so— '

'She and Oliver like to come down and see me at the club to chew the fat and so on,' Ember told them. 'They'd miss Ralph of the Monty, of course they would, and I'm big-headed enough to think many other customers would, too. If I was going. Which I'm not and never have been.'

'That is true, is it, Ralph? Is it?' she asked. She was making a bit of noise, booming away with suspicion and feelings, the way women could, and one of the police who was looking after the recording gear glanced up, very startled.

The telephone rang. For a moment she seemed uninterested in it. 'Patsy,' Harpur said. 'Your daughter? Ralph.'

Then she picked it up. She was weeping, already weeping, but at least it did not look so untoward now. Ember listened on his extension opposite.

'Mummy, you've done well with the notice in the newspaper,' Lynette said. 'But have you been in touch with daddy? If not, how will you get the money? I'm ringing to say that next time I call I must speak to daddy.'

Harpur pointed at Ember, obviously afraid the receiver was going down at the other end.

'Lynette, dear,' Ember said. 'Listen. This is Ralphy.'

'Who?'

'Ralphy Ember.'

'Ralphy? I think I recall.'

'You gave me your monitor badge?'

'Oh, that crap. You're in my house? Why?'

'Lynette,' he said, 'it's grand to hear— '

He was talking to the bleeps of a cut call.

Iles, on another extension, said: 'You did all you could, Ralphy.'

'Will you be able to trace?' he asked, putting the receiver back. He was shaking. It had hit him really hard to hear that child, so entirely helpless somewhere, her voice clear yet horribly strained. She did not remember him, but he would overlook it: she was still a kid in peril.

'A bit brief,' Harpur said. 'But not your fault.'

'Absolutely not,' Iles added.

'When would you move away if you moved, Ralph?' Patsy asked. She was wiping her face with a paper handkerchief, but looked just as bad.

'No, never.'

'It would really take enormous money you see, Patsy,' Iles said.

She went and sat down at a classy-looking little desk. 'I make a note of all these conversations with Lynette, while they're fresh in my mind,' she said, opening a pad.

'They're on tape,' Harpur told her.

'I like to write them as they seemed to me, if you don't mind,' she said. It sounded truly hurt and there was dignity.

'Entirely understandable,' Iles said. 'Harpur's not into delicacy.'

Ember would have waited, in case the child rang back but Iles said no, the shock value had gone. 'She didn't seem very impressed, anyway, Ralphy. You're not box office, old wanker.'

When Ember was leaving, Patsy shook his hand in thanks. She had almost recovered. In his palm she left the wet paper handkerchief, a tight ball.

As they drove to the club, Harpur said: 'Of course, the kidnapper knows police are listening. That's why it's so brief, and Lynette has a script. I don't think we're ever going to get anything concrete from the calls.'

'So, how do you find her?' Ember asked.

'Quite,' Iles replied.

Back at the Monty, Ember smoothed out the handkerchief and found a blurred note making what he deciphered as a full and touching message of love. God, he wanted to escape from this bloody place, now, today, leaving no tracks. He could afford it, of course he could, but what he could not afford was to show he could afford it. The money was useless, dead, like undiscovered gold. He felt enraged with that arrogant lout, Iles, in his high-flier's tie and suit, for suggesting he lacked the capital. And scared of him, in case he was really asking whether Ember had the capital, and, if he did, where from?

Chapter 16

They had a house surrounded, an abandoned farm cottage, on a deserted part of the coast called the Reens, about ten miles west of the defence post where he had met Lamb, and almost into the neighbouring Force's ground. Francis Garland had gone on ahead. Francis liked being ahead. By the time Harpur arrived there were twenty men and three women officers present, in a wide circle and keeping out of sight in the dark. So there would be no sound of a car or headlight beams, he had been stopped nearly a mile away and asked to walk the rest of the distance along a curving road, the sea on one side and flat fields bordered by the wide reen ditches on the other. You ran across strange people out this way, and mean crimes.

Garland briefed him. 'The farm family quit after two sea floodings in the last big storms. But somebody thinks there was an oil lamp burning upstairs a couple of nights ago. People assumed tramps or gypsies. Now a hiker says he might have glimpsed a girl through the window, a teenager. It's possible she even tried to wave to him for help.' Garland had come straight from some function at the police club and was in a dinner jacket and mauve bow tie and cummerbund. Another thing Francis liked was to cut a dash. Everyone said he would go far, but nobody said it to him. He knew. His black patent shoes were overlaid with mud.

'Any reports of a vehicle?'

'Birdwatchers' cars come out here, anyway, sir, so another wouldn't be noticed. We haven't located a vehicle near the cottage, but it was already dark when we arrived, and we're not using lights.'

Harpur studied the cottage through night glasses. No lights showed now, nor any other sign of occupation. Curtains hung at most windows and it would have been hard to tell the cottage was abandoned. So, local knowledge? Possibly, if they were here. 'The phone would have been disconnected, Francis. Can we believe she's been reading those bits under orders in a public booth?'

'It's possible.'

'Just about.' Then he forced himself to sound more positive. Rank was about being positive. 'Yes, of course it is.' Harpur longed for Lynette to be here, and to be reclaimable without injury, but would not risk optimism yet. In fact, before this call tonight, despair at the chances of bringing her back alive had begun to drain him. He feared that someone driven wild by Caring's playfulness with the Exeter money had been determined and clever enough to find Lynette's school and snatch her, then had no idea how to run things. In fact, no way to run things existed. Secrecy for a ransom payment was impossible: you could not lift a kid from school without the police knowing and moving in. The peril to Lynette became plain. The kidnapper might soon see that holding the child was useless and dangerous and decide to get rid of her. Yet, although things grew more and more urgent, what Harpur had told Lamb remained true: not all police could find it in themselves to fret about Oliver Leach's offspring – just a kid in the middle of routine loot war between villains.

'Who's in charge?' Harpur said.

'Mike Upton. He's talking of going in mob-handed in half an hour.'

'No.'

'I said you wouldn't want that. He's not inclined to be subtle over this girl. Do you know him? Field Marshal Montgomery type. Loves wielding numbers. He doesn't think much of me.'

'It's the mauve, Francis. Even in the dark.'

'You might do better, sir. He believes it's all balls, anyway, and we're not going to find her.'

'He could be right. But I think I'll go and look. Now.'

'You'll ask him?'

'Afterwards.'

'I'd better come, sir.'

Garland hated to miss anything front-line. He had that rosy future to think of. It would probably be his non-stop pushiness that had turned Mike Upton off. Upton was almost as young and bright and had his own pushiness to satisfy. 'No, Francis. I'll do it solo. Shit could fly afterwards, and flecks on your papers won't help. In any case, two's a crowd and noticeable.' They were talking inside a half-wrecked cow shed, with atmospheric views of the cottage through gaps in a collapsed wall. It was the decline of rural England. 'Go and keep Mike Upton occupied.'

Harpur moved off immediately. As he had told Garland, it was probably unforgivable, and later he might hear that it was, especially if things went wrong. About three quarters of his approach could be in the cover of some other farm buildings, but the last few yards would be over open ground. Before starting on that stretch he paused and took another long look at the house through his glasses. He half-expected to hear Upton yell at him to come back, but there was no sound except the sea mumbling mildly tonight, its King Kong performances off until the next heavy weather.

Harpur felt good. There had always been spells when he plunged into fierce fits of grandiosity: he saw himself at these times as the state's indispensable cleanser and miracle worker, someone born to undo evil on his own and rebuild perfect order. Megan called it his 'Hamlet mode' or sometimes 'Christ in the temple'. He recognised the absurdity, but did nothing to correct it. The point was, almost all rising police felt this juvenile, self-glorifying, purgative impulse. Thin blue mop. Comical, yes, but if it died you might as well pack up. Garland had shown it just now – was for ever brassily showing it. Iles had it. Dirty Harry had it. Mike Upton probably had it. Too bad. Galloping in solo to the rescue of a girl kid was irresistible, even a crook's girl kid. No, not galloping, slinking: if he was spotted too soon, Upton could still send a posse to halt him. Christ, if he was spotted too soon, what he wanted to stop happening to Lynette might happen before he reached her. Was he willing to put her at extra risk in the cause of kudos? This question he had no time to face up to.

He saw now that some of the windows had been broken, perhaps smashed by storm winds, perhaps by vandals, so possibly it was not so difficult after all to tell the cottage was derelict. The end of a light-coloured curtain flapped a little through one of the holes, as if beckoning. Or as if warning off. That was the trouble with many of life's signals: they could be read one way or their opposite. So rape judges said, anyway. Harpur wondered if it was this agitated curtain that the hiker had spotted and taken to be a message from someone inside. His shoes were as bad as Garland's now.

He crouched and now did try a bit of a gallop, making for the side of the cottage where he had identified a broken window. With any luck it would be out of sight of the main police party, though Upton would have them all round. He pulled out a couple of the worst upward pointing spears of glass and laid them quietly on the ground, then climbed in. What he noticed first was the smell of decay. The water and mud had got to quick work on the wood. Although there had been a smell in the old cow shed, too, it was by comparison good and healthy. He had his pencil light with him but did not dare put it on yet, partly because he feared alerting anyone here, but more on account of the siege contingent: they would see it and might decide to move in at once. The cottage could be swarming with saviours in a few minutes and he would be only one of a troupe.

He was in a room containing a couple of pieces of furniture which the family must have reasonably decided were not worth taking. Leaning in one corner on shaky legs stood a crude, small table, almost certainly home-made. In the middle of the floor on an old, decaying rug was one of those plump, round, stuffed cushion seats, what Harpur's mother in more innocent days used to call a pouffe, gashed on one side so that the curling innards spilled. It felt unnaturally heavy when he gave a jab with his shoe and immediately oozed a slow spread of sea water. On the walls Harpur thought he could make out in the darkness the up-and-down line where the water had reached. Coming into this place gave him none of the pleasure he usually took from penetrating strange property. Despite the bits of furniture, the house felt empty, and felt dead and hopeless.

As quickly as he could without light, he went through the rest of the ground floor, finding no other furniture and becoming even more oppressed by the odour of mud and rot. Above all, he wanted to see the kitchen, in case it revealed traces of recent food. Then he realised, though, that there would be no point in using this room more than any other to prepare food. It had nothing in it but a sink, with no water supply now. He found nothing there.

Through the front windows he looked for Mike Upton and his

people but could spot nobody. That meant he had them organised well, and also that they had not broken cover yet to get into the cottage. Harpur had a few more minutes. Swiftly, he climbed the bare stairs and at the top suddenly lost the feeling that the house was empty. For a few minutes he could not have said why and grew very excited, and also scared of what he might find. Up here, the flood odours were less strong and, instead, he thought he could pick up a hint of a recent fire, perhaps that distinctive sickly scent of burned paper. There seemed to be two bedrooms, no bathroom or inside lavatory. He abruptly opened one door and saw a bedroom that had been totally stripped. He tried the other and found it quite different. Newspapers had been spread in two places on the floor forming what might serve as a couple of basic mattresses, several sheets thick. With a couple of blankets they could make sleep possible here. He crouched down low, as though he might be able to detect the outlines of where people had lain. Stupidly, he even put his hand on the paper to check whether it was warm. None of that worked. He could have done with the flashlight now to check the newspaper dates. Instead, he searched for a headline big enough to make out in the dark, but found the papers were local, with reports that did not mean anything to him.

In a corner of the room near the window he could see what might be the source of the smell of smoke. There was a small, neat heap of ashes on the boards, as if a fire had been deliberately started there. He wondered if he was looking at the remains of the scripts the girl had used when telephoning, and real give-aways if found. Again he wanted to touch, and put his hand on the ashes. They were cold. Near were a couple of meal cartons, several soft drink cans and more newspaper, but rolled up and giving off another smell: fish and chips.

Descending the stairs quickly he went out through the window again and worked his way back to where he had left Francis Garland. He was not there any longer and Harpur began moving slowly around, seeking Mike Upton's position. When he reached there, Upton in police overalls was about to order his people in. Francis stood a little apart, talking intimately to one of the girl officers, the usual thing.

'I'm going to hit them with everything I've got, sir,' Upton said. He spoke as if expecting opposition after his argument with Garland.

'Good idea,' Harpur replied.

'Let's go then,' Upton said. He muttered into his hand radio.

Harpur and Garland followed them. 'Afterwards, get around local chip shops and take-aways would you, Francis.'

'I was going to suggest that, sir.'

'Good.'

'Nothing,' Upton said, when he had been through the cottage. 'Upstairs, newspapers that could be beds.'

'What date?' Harpur asked.

'This week and last,' Upton said.

'They've moved on,' Harpur replied.

'Vagrants? Newspaper beds is their style,' Upton said. 'Outside lavatory. Septic tank.'

'Some swear it's more healthy. Especially when there's no water laid on.'

'I was wondering about possible recent sanitary towels,' Upton replied. 'If it was the girl.'

'Right. Shall I leave you to root around then, Mike?' Harpur said.

'Here comes the Assistant Chief,' Upton replied. 'I expect he finds it tough getting out of bed when curled up with someone like Sarah Iles.' Upton went to meet him. The forensic and fingerprint people were arriving, too.

'Did that bruise you, sir?' Garland asked.

'What?'

'About the ACC being in body contact with Sarah.'

Iles, in a large-check, Scottish moors overcoat that almost touched the ground, said: 'I love this stretch of countryside – the flatness, the scruffy grass and shagged-out pond weed, as if God got tired round about here. So, you've let them slip away, Harpur? The Chief will really enjoy explaining to Gloucestershire how we missed them. Were you late – unreachable somewhere again? At least tonight I know one woman you weren't with.'

Mike Upton said: 'Bit of a fire in there, sir. My view, for what it's worth, is that— '

'I adore the whole idea of the sea taking slabs of the manmade back,' Iles stated. 'Some it terrifies, of course. They think apocalypse. Myself, I've always felt affinity with a storm-driven ocean.'

'I've heard others suggest the resemblance, sir,' Harpur replied.

'Which ocean?' Iles asked.

'Oh, one of the best, sir.'

They stood in the downstairs room. 'Yes, I see this salt-of-the-earth family, all grouped around their little non-Chippendale table there, eating scones, drinking stone ginger, sharing joints, and suddenly something at the front door. Who's there? Breakers. Marvellous. Elemental. You in here before the rest of them arrived, Harpur, stealing and fouling up evidence as usual, making your sodding deductions? You smell of smoke.'

'We've had the whole place very carefully encircled and monitored, sir,' Upton said.

'So, in here first, Harpur? Some of these footprints yours?' Iles climbed the stairs. Garland shone a light on the newspaper beds, if that was what they were. 'Well, I'd say so, wouldn't you, Col?'

'Certainly,' Harpur replied.

Upton said: 'In some respects, sir, I— '

'So we put out a call for sightings of two people with newsprint across their arses, do we?' Iles said. 'Especially the girl.'

'They might both be girls, sir,' Harpur told him.

Chapter 17

In the old days, if Ralph Ember wanted an anonymous gun it was easy. He would go to Piers Mills-Silver, put down half, promise the rest on delivery, and collect a week later. Despite the Court Circular names, Mills-Silver was nothing then, two-up two-down terraced house, eager for business and longing to be loved by anyone with true solidity. This was where the Baby Browning came from. Following that matter with Caring, though, it had to go. First act of hygiene after a shooting: lose the weapon.

Fine, but Ember suddenly felt he needed a replacement. Pressures had started to screw him: Lighterman, Anna, God knew who else – Fritzy, Leopold – but Lighterman above all. Lighterman obviously thought Ember might have Lynette, for God's sake, plus extra pickings. Hanging about every night in the club, Ember could not be more vulnerable, head up behind the bar, like a bloody coconut. Although his worries about the child still ravaged him, he had also to give a thought to looking after Ralph W. Ember, which at least was possible: what could he do for Lynette?

Of course, what he really wanted was to suitcase the beautiful riches and disappear, perhaps solo. He hesitated, though. That would be to write off the girl. In any case, if he did a runner, it would give the message to all sorts, including Harpur and Iles, that he had something to hide, such as half a million, plus insights on Caring. Too many fingers would point, all perilous. The funds were liberating, but not yet.

Although Leopold in Kew did very untraceable armament, Leopold might be one of the ones Ember wanted to protect himself from, so he would not be calling there. It had to be Piers Mills-Silver. Ember drove to see him. These days, Piers had moved up a rung or two, like Caring. Would he bother providing one weapon for someone he'd probably forgotten? Did he even handle that sort of work now? Some said Mills-Silver had gone totally above board, *The Times* delivered, teeth capped, nose hair clipped. Legality could strike anyone: think of dukes, or Ember himself, until lately.

'So what kind of piece do you want, Ralphy?'

'A stopper.'

Mills-Silver gazed at him, the bleak way Ember remembered from before. It meant you had just said something zombie, and piss off if you could not buck up fast. A gun was to stop, what else?

'The Baby Browning feeling its age, then?' Mills-Silver asked.

Christ, all those years, and that stuck in his tidy, dangerous head. 'Baby Browning?' Ember replied. 'A gun?'

'Nice little bugger. Nasty little bugger.'

'Oh, that one. It went long, long ago, Piers.' Did wonderman keep a written record?

'So, been dealing with someone else?'

'I didn't need one.'

'And now change? I heard real stress, Ralph. Some out of town job go wrong? Tiff over the split? And then Caring's kid.'

Ember blanked his face, the neither confirm nor deny rig, and tried to show no shock at what Mills-Silver knew. He was into fabrics, they said, and had moved from near Valencia Esplanade to a lumpy piece of detached mock on Border Grange, a new private estate: mock what, Ember was unsure, maybe Tudor, maybe Visigoth, but, anyway, black metal studs in the reinforced cardboard front door. Not in Caring's Low Pastures class, with grates bigger than a jeep, but still on the way to £400,000. It had given Ember true satisfaction to think as he drove on to Border Grange that he could slap down cash for any one of these places if he fancied. He did not fancy. He liked something from real history, instead of factory brick, with fake colour and fake wear.

'Good as gold, most of them at the Monty, Piers – but the odd psychopath I need to deter? Say a Barracuda.'

'That's a fierce demon, you know. Nine millimetres.'

'I want something thoroughly meaningful, Piers.'

'Well, I heard you had possible trouble.'

But, Jesus, how did it happen, this broadcast?

'One thing all our nannies told us over and over, Ralphy: someone monkey with a split and here comes endless pain.'

'You don't object to me dropping in? I hate phones.'

'Object? Object to Ralphy Ember? Of course I fucking object. You leave panic prints.'

Mills-Silver looked nearly good enough for the name, especially his haircut, which was in the Edward Heath class, but black, not grey, and definitely a West End mode. He must be on weights – big upper arms and shoulders in the white, Beach Bum T-shirt, and some decent tapering lower down, hardly any gut. Although he would be 50 or more his skin had some youth to it and he took care of his hands. His eyes were no joke, sometimes yellowy, sometimes worse.

'I can pay,' Ember said. 'The usual half and half?'

'I know you can pay. I've always been lucky with information. Ralphy, suppose I said a Barracuda, plus shells, no charge? Available the day after tomorrow. Look, I didn't invite you, but since you're here— '

Ember laughed. 'No charge? You're my uncle or something? You've got expenses.'

They were in a summer house in the garden, a happy smell of timber. Mills-Silver had taken him straight there. Perhaps he did not want Ember in the main property. Perhaps this was the office. He had a telephone in there – separate number, not just an extension, he said – and a barometer and chart of protected trees, plus a little stove for doing tea, though he did not do any now. He remarked: 'You're so lucky, Ralph. Business chances can spring out of nowhere. One thing I discovered.'

'I wouldn't mind putting the whole lot down now, in advance for the Barracuda, Piers. Or something else. Whatever's obtainable. Just a name in my head.'

'My kind of business could be your kind of business, Ralphy. I'm always trying to point meaty, spare capital towards sound development opportunities. Middle-man. I embrace that description.'

He had that basket furniture for the summer house, so any time your body tightened up with dread the chair rustled like rats in cellophane. Ember had come here looking for a way out of his worries, and had found more. 'Or if firearms and so on are not your line now, Piers, I'll try someone else.'

Ember stood up. 'Yes, I should have phoned. It's only a bloody superstition.'

'When I say a Barracuda no charge, it's self-interest: if I have a client, putting really heavy funds into an investment, I need him secure. A gun's only office furniture.'

'Or I could even be imagining. I might not need armament at all. Some call me Panicking, I know. Yes, I crack, occasionally.'

'Sit down, Ralphy. No rush. I hate to think of sums lying idle because of fear of attention. Tragic waste. The talents parable? So, deposit boxes: but can they take care of growth or Conservative inflation?'

Ember stayed on his feet. 'Come to that, would I have the nerve to pull a trigger these days? I'll get along then, Piers.'

'There's people up there in the house would really go hoity-toity about me entertaining someone off the street – that would be their words, not mine, Ralph – off the street, like you, even in this shack. Not my wife. She's learned what makes the wheels go round. But my thick, layabout son and his sodding layabout, coke-sniffing girl, all highs, puking and remorse. Now, though, I can say to them, this supposed item of dregs in suede boots is worth five hundred thousand plus – that about right, Ralph? – and, fair enough, he looks like Cardew the Cad, but with his head screwed on enough to know a prime investment when an old friend offers him the opening. That kind of answer would get through the smog, even to them. Come and sit down, Ralph. Yes, I'll have the Barracuda for you Friday and enough ammunition to take out all the evil you're ever likely to see. Do a few sums, will you? I'll need to know pretty exactly what you feel is committable. To within a grand, and obviously something fairly gorgeous or it's not worth the trouble for either of us.' He clapped his hands a couple of times. 'Oh, the more I think about it, the more I like this deal.'

Chapter 18

Anna Chitty, watching the Monty from a shop doorway across the street, saw Ember's wife and the two daughters wearing school uniform come out into the yard and drive away in a Fiesta. It must be the usual morning trip. Anna geared herself up to enter the club again for another confrontation with Ember. If it did not work this time she would quit. Once or twice she had been on the point of quitting anyway, and then the thought of someone enjoying the money that Peter was blown open for made her enraged and determined again. Pete always used to say she was great on determination. When he wanted to please or woo her he would list her assets, always exactly the same four: legs, determination, good taste in hats and what he called a cunt like Christmas Eve. All of it he meant well, which was one reason she had left him.

Ember could surely point her towards the funds, she knew it: all the inside gossip surfaced at the Monty. If she could catch him early in the day, before he had to start work in the club, she might have time to do some persuading. God, he had to see the justice of it, even someone like Panicking.

She was about to cross the road, when Ember appeared in the yard carrying two heavy-looking cases and with a suit in a plastic cover over one arm. He unlocked a Montego and put the suit on the back seat, then opened the boot and loaded the cases. He seemed hurried and anxious. Anna waited in the doorway. Ember turned and went back into the club through the rear door. Again she had an impression of rush, and fear. Panicking was panicking. Did it mean he was making a run? Why? This famous family man breaking out alone?

She did not understand, but realised suddenly that the next time he came out might be the last. Would he get in and drive away?

Although she had a car in the next street, by the time she reached it, he could be gone. In any case, she knew nothing about tailing. Quickly, she crossed the road to the yard, climbed into the front of the Montego and wriggled her way across to the passenger seat. She sank down, so as to be out of sight from behind. The boot lid was still up, which would give cover. She could have sworn she caught a smell of sweat near the car.

In a moment, she heard a door in the building slam shut and then the sound of Ember's footsteps. They were slow and heavy, as if he was once more carrying weighty items. She felt the Montego sink a little on its suspension as he increased the load in the boot. She tried to remember whether Pete had ever said Ember was liable to turn violent: people who lost control could lose control in all sorts of directions. Well, sod him. All she was here for was to ask questions, fair questions. It took him three attempts to force the boot lid closed.

He saw her before he opened the driver's door. As he stared in, full of shock, she had the notion for a moment that he was glad to see her, the craggy face alight. Crazy. Yet the scar on his jaw seemed to throb and take some colour – a pinkness that almost reached scarlet – like an isolated blush of excitement and pleasure. The surprise must have paralysed him and he had made no attempt yet to open the door. She leaned across and did it for him.

'In the film, does El Cid get a wound on the face, Ralph? I've never seen you looking so much like Charlton Heston.'

'Honestly? Some say I'm more like— '

'Why are you ejecting, Ralph?'

'Are you here for the money?' He climbed in to the car and closed the door. Like an entourage, the sweat smell came with him. He seemed to know it, and rolled down the window. 'Hellish stresses. Can't take it any longer. Now Mills-Silver.'

'Here for the money? Of course. Pete's entitled.'

'Where's the child? Oh, where? Yes, certainly entitled. I can see it from your angle. I wanted to find you. This can be sorted out.' He sounded frightened, and it was no longer that brick-wall, get-lost voice.

'Which child?' she asked, baffled. 'Tell me, do you know where the money is, Ralph? Why are you running?'

'Please. I've got to get out. All sorts of factors. But I'm still in agony about her. I'll do a reasonable deal, even now.'

'You're in no state to drive. Look at your hands.' He had his fingers laced together in his lap, trying to stop the shaking, but with no effect.

'Can you drive?' he said at once. 'Take me to wherever the child is and we can settle it there and then. I've got to get out of here, now, soon.'

'While your wife's away?'

'I won't be right otherwise. I'll see you properly treated and then disappear. Nothing to be afraid of. Say you will.'

He got out of the car and ran around to the passenger side. Pulling open the door, he waved a hand to her, telling her to get behind the wheel. 'Go,' he said. 'Take me there.'

She moved across and as soon as he was in drove from the yard. She had no idea where to go, but made for the edge of the town, and out towards the countryside.

'Ah,' he said, 'I wondered about this area.'

In a while, she pulled off the road on to a grass bank near an old water mill, empty for years. He looked around, as if searching.

'Tell me about the child,' she said.

He gave a giggle. '*Me* tell *you*?' I hardly know her, but I can't get her out of my head, that's all. A man doesn't just drop all responsibility. Not even Panicking Ralph.'

'I hate that name. Foul. You look so strong, all through.'

He shrugged, then made a gesture with both hands, indicating that she was driving his car because he couldn't. He stretched out his arms to show how much he still shook, and so she could see that his shirt cuffs were soaking.

'I don't know anything about a child,' she said. 'Except my own children. They're entitled.'

'Please. Why here?' Again he gazed around. 'The old mill? You don't need to bluff. Can we go in?'

She put out a hand and gently turned his face to look at her. 'Which child, Ralph? What's it about?' His skin was as cold as clay.

A change seemed to begin in Ember then. She felt him studying her face, really reading for signs. He sat like that for probably more than a minute. At the end, he had become more

110

composed. 'Why were you at the club again?' he said. 'Not to do the deal?'

'Which deal, Ralph? Just to find what I'm owed.'

'Oh, that,' he said.

'What else? Tell me what child you're talking about.'

'Oh, the child,' he replied, but his voice almost dismissive now. He was holding his hands out in front of him again. 'I'm nearly all right now. I'm like that.'

'Ralph, I've got to get to that money.' She made herself sound apologetic: 'Do you know, I actually had the notion when you came out of the club that one of those suitcases might be full of cash. Maybe my cash. You said you could settle up there and then. The money's actually here?'

'I could drive now, I think,' he replied.

'But where?'

He climbed out again and walked around to the driver's side and opened the door. 'A case full of bank loot?' He laughed, too. 'Do you want to have a look? Quite quiet here. And it's all unlocked.'

Jesus, was she being completely stupid, unbalanced by the obsession with her share? But she said: 'Well, yes, I would like to look. In all of them.'

He offered a hand to help her from the car. She climbed out and he stood back to let her go first. As she moved towards the rear, she heard the driver's door slam behind her, the engine start, and the car leapt away. She turned and managed to get a hand on the paintwork as the Montego left. Then she ran a few useless steps after it and screamed, 'Two-timing sod.' For a moment in the side mirror she could see Ember staring ahead as if she did not exist, his face full of misery. An old woman with a trowel in her hand stood up from behind a low wall in the front garden of a cottage near the mill and stared at her and the car for a moment, then went on with her work.

Chapter 19

So, standing in the middle of Sheepshitland, wearing her top-line town clothes – purple cloche hat, black culottes, bracelets, pearl grey shantung blouse, cornucopia ear-rings, the full, slam-bang ensemble – Anna wondered what the old woman would make of that episode. Girl ditched by man, an ancient tale? And the scene accompanied as ever by useless, female shouts of despair, plus this time the pathetic squeal of a manicure across high-tailing sheet metal, and that frantic little chase on clip-clop heels, spoiling the quiet. But, of course, whatever the lady in the garden thought, she could not get anywhere near the ultimate poison of things: this man had abandoned two women at once and almost certainly taken with him a plump fortune that was part theirs. Suddenly, Ember, a jibbering nobody, was somebody. He must have been in on the bank job, not just a gossip centre. For ever an asshole he had turned out more than an earhole. Panicking had cleaned up? It was unbelievable but she had to believe it.

What was salvageable? Anything? Ember, and all he was carrying, had irrecoverably disappeared. Perhaps this was the time to give up. She had done all she reasonably could to get her rights. If she phoned a taxi and went home she would arrive before the children returned from school. And she could settle thereafter to being a broke single parent of three, and no more fancy hats for a while, maybe a long while. The idea hit hard. She sat on a grass verge and took her shoes off. Thinking came easier out of heels. She could be not at all bad at thinking, if she was relaxed and able to take it at plodder's pace.

In one sense the situation had not changed. She had been looking for Caring Oliver, believing him to have cornered the money. Now, she suspected he might not have the whole load.

But he would still have some: Caring was not one to miss the lot. And that some was more than she had, despite a near-perfect proxy claim.

Though Ember would make himself very non-findable now, there might still be trails to Caring. He was the only chance. No trails would come from Patsy. But what if Anna went back to the Monty and talked to Ember's wife, woman to woman: conned woman to conned woman? Mrs Ember might know something from her husband about where Caring was. If Anna broke the news that Panicking had done a rich flit, it could make a bond between her and Mrs Ember, couldn't it? Couldn't it? They both had children. Surely she would see the injustice, feel some sympathy now? The shock of Anna's message might help.

She put her shoes back on and looked up the road for a public telephone, fearing a frigid answer if she asked the old gardener for help. But there was no phone booth and she walked over to the cottage. 'I wondered if I could call a taxi from your house,' Anna said.

The woman looked up and gazed for a few seconds in trembling rapture at the outfit: 'Of course, dear. Taxis, bangles, I used to be rackety myself, you know.'

'I've heard that.'

'Men? All cock and condescension – a phrase we had. Silly sods thought it was a pat on the back.'

When Anna reached Shield Terrace and the Monty she found the main doors were locked, although it must be getting close to lunchtime opening. She went to the rear and saw Mrs Ember's car in the yard now. The back door to the club had been pulled shut but was not locked. Entering past the cloakrooms, she emerged into the bar. From above in the building she heard a series of loud, heavy noises, like someone moving furniture or carrying out a violent, damaging search, possibly someone in a rage or in a rush. Occasionally she heard hurried footsteps, too. One person? More?

Although the curtains were across in the bar, a couple of lights burned and she saw at once the legs of a woman sticking out on the floor behind one of the pool tables. She could be sitting on the tatty carpet, her back against a table leg. Her ankles were together, her skirt tidy around her knees and her stockings or tights intact.

In the spells of silence between the noises from upstairs, Anna thought she made out the sound of intermittent quiet sobbing from where the woman sat or lay. Frightened and confused, Anna stood unmoving in the doorway for a couple of seconds. Occasionally the woman's sobbing changed to a gasping, wet sound, as if she were trying hard for breath through a blocked nose. Anna looked towards an open door behind the bar. She could just make out stairs leading up to what must be the living accommodation. The din came down through there and through the ceiling of the bar, making it shudder and the light fittings jangle. Tense, she watched for a while in case anyone appeared on the stairs. She had met very few of the men Peter used to work with, but those few she feared.

Without moving from her spot in the doorway, she lowered herself on to her haunches, trying to look beneath the pool table and see the upper half of the woman. There had been a moment when she thought again of quitting: turn, get to the car, home, shelter, Scrabble, motherhood. Things were happening faster than she could cope with, things with too much alarm built in. But then it struck her that to bolt now would be the kind of behaviour expected from Ralphy Ember: had she picked up a dose of yellow streak from the fabric and air of his Monty? She would not have that. Whoever saw a chicken glad-ragged like this?

The light was worse in the shadow of the pool table, but Anna could distinguish the back of the woman and see that her head hung forward. Was she properly conscious? Anna could also see that the woman's arms were pulled back behind her around the thick leg of the table, as if her hands might be lashed together, though the light was too poor to be certain. 'Mrs Ember?' she whispered. Anna had never met her, did not even know her first name, damn it, but who else would it be? Perhaps there was a tiny response: the head possibly lifted a little for half a second and even made a slight turn towards her. Upstairs, the noises had become less frequent and seemed further away, as if from higher in the building. The bar ceiling no longer shook. Normality, except for a haltered woman fighting for oxygen.

For some reason, when she moved towards Mrs Ember Anna went on to her hands and knees and crawled like the SAS, as if she might be spotted upright. But there was nobody to spot her.

When nearer she saw why the sound of breathing had seemed so laboured: blood was falling from the woman's face into her lap, probably from the nose and possibly a lip. Yes, her wrists were bound with a length of flex, and the lamp it had come from lay nearby. On her knees in front of her, Anna placed a hand on each side of Mrs Ember's head and gently raised it. The movement seemed to make her breathing problems worse and she gasped several times then coughed hugely twice, showering Anna with blood. She felt the drops spatter her face and go through her clothes to her neck and chest, a warm, thick shower. 'So be washable, shantung blouse,' she muttered. 'Oh God, you poor dear.'

She looked as if she had taken at least three heavy blows to the face, one of them possibly breaking her nose. It was hard to tell anything about her normal appearance, but her body was small and neat and Anna guessed her features would have been the same. Now, her nose lay flattened and shapeless and swellings disfigured her mouth and the right side of her face over the eye and on the cheek-bone.

'Who?' Anna said.

She did not look at Anna, and might not have been looking at anything. Her eyes were open, though the right one had been nearly blocked off by the bruising, and she stared towards the wall, but probably not seeing. There was no attempt to focus on Anna, even when she spoke. Mrs Ember's head felt slack between her hands, as though it would slump forward again if released. Perhaps she was moving in and out of consciousness, that tiny moment of response gone now, drowned.

'How many?' Anna asked. As if it mattered: one man able to do this to a woman could probably see off two. Fear still gripped her. She wanted to undo the woman's hands yet knew this would be a give-away. As things were, if someone, or more than one, came back downstairs, Anna could hide, and there would be no sign she had been in the bar. He – they – might leave, and she could emerge then and free Mrs Ember and get help. These were her calculations, full of caginess and good sense, but her feelings said to free her now and get her comfortable, end this degradation. She let the woman's head sink forward again until her chin rested on her chest and then Anna withdrew her hands. Crawling around behind the table leg, she unfastened the flex. Quickly, she moved back so she was in front of Mrs Ember and took hold of her in the armpits. Anna slowly tried to stand, lifting the woman with her. There would be more blood over the blouse and even the culottes. Mrs Ember's face was pressed against Anna's arm and breast as they rose together and she groaned a little. Perhaps the pressure on her nose and other injuries hurt her. Thank God she was not too big and heavy. Anna found she could manage. Perhaps Mrs Ember was providing a little help. She did not seem a total dead-weight.

The effort had made Anna almost forget the sounds from the upper floors, but now she heard what seemed like renewed shifting of big items, with an occasional heavy crash, though still from a long way off. Did the Monty have a loft? The purple hat went askew and then fell off and rolled away, as she shuffled with the woman towards a padded Monty bench, like a couple of wrestlers. That sweet hat would never feel the same after the greasy underfoot of this crud dump. She laid Mrs Ember on the bench, putting her on her side, so she would not choke on blood. One of the pool tables had a cloth cover over it and she brought that as a blanket to help against shock. Anna went behind the bar and found a bottle of armagnac. She poured a little into a glass and took a good pull from the bottle herself. Returning to Mrs Ember, she gently put the glass to her damaged lips and eased a little of the brandy into her. That started her coughing again for a moment and more of the blood spattered Anna's face and hair and clothes. In a little while, the woman was able to swallow the armagnac without trouble. Some flickers of intelligence came back to her eyes and now she did look at Anna and seemed to try to identify her. She even pulled a hand up from under the covering and rubbed some of the blood away from around her nose.

Anna was bent over, holding the glass to the woman's mouth, and thought she heard somebody on the stairs behind. Urgently, she turned but saw nothing. It occurred to her suddenly that the living quarters would probably have another exit, a private staircase. For a second, the thought comforted her: there might be no need for anyone to come back through the bar. Then, though, she wondered, Why the search, anyway? It was obvious. Hadn't she walked into a try by one of the Exeter team to find Ralph –

one or more of the team? The idea must be around that he had cornered a healthy share, and Mrs Ember had been beaten to make her say where her husband and the funds were. On neither could she help. Prudent Ralphy was gone, with the totality. This search would find nobody and nothing, and whoever was up there might return in a rage soon and attempt again to pulverise information out of Mrs Ember.

Part of the population, far and away the biggest part, would have picked up the telephone and called the police now. Anna was no part of that part. Among all her uncertainties, she felt sure of this. Peter's teaching in those rough years had gone deep: it was a way of life, jungle credentials. In any case, if you were hunting a legacy from a bank raid you did not ask Harpur Inc. for help.

Mrs Ember whispered something unintelligible. Anna crouched lower and put her ear close to her lips. 'Try again,' Anna said.

'Warn Ralph.'

You've got a gem here, Ember, wherever you are, you stocked-up, galloping shit.

Perhaps the best protection would be to open the club and let customers in. She gave the woman another drop of the brandy. On the wall just above where she lay were framed photographs of what seemed to be club outings abroad, and Anna caught a reflection of herself in the glass of one, her face streaked with blood and a wide stain across her blouse. She had a brief smile. She could be advertising a horror movie. This day had been some disaster: no money, plenty of mess.

'Who are you?' the woman whispered.

'A friend.'

'Yes, you're that.' She reached up and drew Anna's head even closer and kissed her on the forehead, a light, brushing kiss, perhaps to spare her mouth.

'Well, I am here for my money,' Anna replied.

Behind her a man repeated the question: 'Who are you?'

When Anna turned she saw a very small, bald figure of about forty with the face of a boy, an unpleasant, perky boy, and one who was letting his teeth go. He emerged from the door leading to the accommodation stairs.

'Who are *you*?' Anna replied.

'Ralph's done a bunk, has he? With everything?' He had on a brown suede jacket that looked about big enough for a fattish, spoiled dachshund, and black platform shoes with gold buckles which almost brought him up to stunted.

'Did you do this?' Anna asked, pointing at the woman's face.

'I was in a hurry.'

'I heard you. You turd.'

'I'm not just acting for myself. I have a duty.' He came over and looked down at the woman's injuries. 'Listen, get her help when I've gone. I'm metropolitan, yes, but humane.'

Mrs Ember raised her head a fraction from the bench. A sagging cable of blood stretched between her face and the upholstery. 'Ralph will kill you,' she muttered.

'Who, Ralphy?' He showed all the dud teeth in a smile, an unbeatable range of greens and blacks, like some golfer's trousers. Turning to Anna he asked: 'You're here for the split, too, then? So, let me think, were you Pete Chitty's? I'm still choked about him.'

'I'm going to open the club, so don't try anything.'

'Would I get evil with Pete's widow, for God's sake? Anyway, what's the point now? You're going to let people see her like that? And here? Even Monty people? You'll kill business, blossom.'

'How did you reach her nose?'

'You know, I'm sweaty after all the effort,' he said, and walked towards the cloakrooms.

'Can we get out of here?' Mrs Ember said as soon as he had gone. She still whispered but her voice was better now.

'He won't try anything more.'

'Get me out of here.'

'All right. Try. See if you can walk.' Anna pulled the cover off and helped her swing her feet from the bench and on to the floor. She tried to stand, Anna holding her arm, but it seemed too much for her, still. Mrs Ember swayed and sat down on the bench. As she did, Anna heard a door open on the other side of the bar and turned, expecting to see the little piece of violence on his way back, but it was Ember, coming in from the yard.

His wife saw him at once and pointed urgently at the men's room, signalling the warning she had asked for, but not one he could possibly understand. The blood and the presence of Anna

118

would tell Ember something was wrong, though, and he stood still in the doorway, as Anna had. She quickly crossed the bar to him.

'You'd gone,' she said.

'I found I couldn't. Bale out? I'm a family person. What's happened? Margaret's face? There's a stain like kissing lips on your forehead.'

They were standing close to the door of the men's cloakroom. 'He's in here,' Anna said.

'Who?'

She put a hand out to show his height. 'Bald. Eyes like mildew.'

'Leopold? From the Botanical Gardens vicinity?'

'Metropolitan.' She lowered her voice a bit further. 'You could take the sod now, in there. He'll be off guard.'

'Yes.' He did not move, though.

'Quick.'

'Yes.' He reached up and drew a finger along the scar on his jaw. 'Armed?'

'Well, I don't know.'

'I'm still without, you see. Takes time. Would he come that distance unequipped?'

'Jesus, Ralph, he's broken your wife up, broken your place up.'

Ember glanced towards the door of the cloakroom, then back. 'This Leopold, he's – well, as you said, metropolitan. In the Gents, or anywhere, they're always exceptionally poised. That's well known.' He began to walk over to his wife. 'It will be all right, Maggie, love.'

Leopold came out of the cloakroom. 'Of course it will, Ralph.' Comradeship throbbed. 'This was a very serious misunderstanding on my part. I'm happy to admit it. She's looking better already. The damage upstairs can be put right. No harm to the pianola.'

Ember said carefully: 'This causes me a hell of a rage, you know, Leopold. It would any husband. Contusions.'

'Of course,' Leopold replied. 'I don't hold that against you in the least. It's spirit.'

'Fuck you,' Anna said.

'And why is this one here, Ralph?'

'Search me,' Ember replied. 'And the state of her!' He was sitting alongside Margaret, holding her hand, examining the wounds. She kept herself very upright on the bench, as if not wanting added contact with Ralph. Anna went and sat on her other side.

Leopold leaned against a pool table facing them. He wore first-class jeans and an amber roll-top sweater. Anna would have said chic, except for the scale of it all. 'You can see why I'd be edgy, I hope, Ralph,' Leopold declared. 'Even to the point of violence, foolish violence: people are generally surprised at my strength. Up in Kew, I'm getting imperfect versions of what goes on here. Little alliances, carve-ups. Look, I supplied you boys honestly and my associate, Winston, did good work for you. We deserve proper treatment. Winston's locked up now, yes, but I can act on his behalf, can't I? Are you in touch with Caring Oliver's Patsy at all? That's what I wondered, especially. Forgive me, but women are your currency. And have I been working on the right end? Then I make the trip and find this one.' He nodded the gleaming, toffee-apple head at Anna. 'Ralph, the point is, I could feel shut out, and more important, that Winston's shut out. He can't use it just now, but there's got to be a handful for him, Ralph. Yes, I do have obligations.'

'Of course.'

'I knew you'd see it.' Leopold gave a big, curly, murky smile.

Full of reason and deference, Ember replied: 'But can I help? It's the aforementioned Caring, isn't it? What I keep telling everyone, Leopold. Of course I can understand you've got nerves. Of course you've got your doubts and suspicions. Do I smell armagnac? I think I could do with one of those, too.' Unlinking his fingers from Margaret's he stood. Instantly, Leopold tensed and stood straight himself, and seemed about to stop Ember, then changed his mind. 'You want one, as well, Leopold? Decent stuff.'

'Only if it seals no hard feelings.'

'Certainly it does,' Ember said. 'Oh, I felt aggrieved on first sight of Margaret, and if you've upset the pianola machinery, yet I can appreciate how situations could be misread, by yourself – or even myself, come to that.'

'Thanks, Ralph.'

120

'Let's forget it, shall we, Leo?' As he skirted the uncovered pool table on his way to the brandy Ember suddenly grabbed one of the cues that were lying there and swinging it from the narrow end brought the butt around in a great, powerful arc to crash into the side of Leopold's head. Leopold had never stopped watching Ember, so saw it coming and tried to get underneath.

'That pianola's a bloody heirloom,' Ember hissed.

The blow caught Leopold high, above his right ear. Maybe Ember had been aiming for the temple. If he had hit him there one contact might have done, but this was on a tougher part of the miniature skull. Leopold staggered back against the table and was reaching under his jacket up near the shoulder when Ember used the cue again, two-handed, lower this time, and took the side of Leopold's jaw. Anna found the doughy sound sickening, even though it was Leopold. He still did not go down, but looked very dazed and his hand dropped away from under his jacket, as if his strength had left. Ember, scarlet with rage and fear and effort, had the cue moving once more and now it did take Leopold in the proper spot just below the forehead, splitting the skin wide in a bubbling wound, and he fell at once, folding against the pool table leg where Margaret had been bound. Ember skipped quickly around to him, the cue raised again. Leopold did not move, though. Ember kicked him hard in the ribs, then twice meditatively in the face. He looked down with disappointment at his suede shoes: 'Not cutting him at all. I should slip into something a little less comfortable.'

'I knew you'd see to him, Ralph. Regardless,' Margaret said.

'Well, responsibilities.' He bent down and pulled a large pistol from a shoulder holster under Leopold's jacket. He put it in his own pocket, then went and sat by Margaret again, shaking visibly but with a good grip on the cue still. Slack like an off-duty puppet, Leopold snored and grunted from the far depths of high-grade concussion. Ember said to Anna: 'If you want surprise, kid, never go for anyone in a cloakroom. Mirrors everywhere.'

'Ah, sorry. Did you bring the cases back?'

'Cases?'

'In the car.'

'Oh, those cases.' He laughed for a time.

121

'Ralph, what was he saying about you and Patsy?' Margaret asked.

'What was he saying about anything? Little made sense, love. I'll dump him somewhere. He'll find his way home, eventually, or die of exposure, if we're lucky. He can have a bit more clobbering before I leave him. It's got to stick in the memory and help him later when he's in London, like Nature with William Wordsworth, the poet. No weight there, but I'll back the car right up to the yard door for him in a minute.'

'The boot's full, isn't it?' Anna said.

He laughed again. 'You're really interested in luggage.' He gazed down at Leopold. 'The thing about Ralph Ember, which not all recognise, is he can switch it on.' He frowned, maybe waylaid by the past and honesty. 'Sometimes.'

'Almost always, Ralph,' Margaret said.

'Sometimes,' Ember replied.

Anna crouched down near the little man on the ground. 'Are you sure he's going to come out of this? Such a colour.'

'He should have thought of that before brutalities towards the wife and property of Ralph W. Ember. Admittedly, skulls are very problematical.'

The barman arrived for the midday opening.

'We've had a crisis or two,' Ember told him. 'Give me a couple of minutes, then let them in. There's a bit of blood around here, Clive, if you could get a mop and bucket.'

'Who's your flat friend? Someone's been knocking the armagnac,' the barman replied.

'That's an idea. Pour me one, will you,' Ember said, bending to wipe blood from the heavy end of the cue on Leopold's suede jacket. 'A shambles upstairs, I bet.'

'You'll be all right now, Ralph – I mean having his gun,' Anna remarked, straightening up from the small body.

Ember stared at her, hurt. 'Never, ever, keep someone else's firearm. You don't know where it's been. You had no education?'

Chapter 20

Harpur and Iles drew into the Monty yard, the ACC driving his Orion. This sort of visit lay far outside Iles's proper run of duties, but Harpur knew he exulted in coming to the club and chilling the customers. 'We bring news, Ralphy,' Iles said. 'Port and lemon for me, a taste I picked up *inter alia* from whores. Harpur, a gin and cider, simply because he's coarse.'

'News?' Ember asked, preparing the drinks. He moved down to one end of the bar to talk to them, leaving the part-timer to serve.

'And how's the lady of the house?' Iles replied.

'She wouldn't grumble,' Ember said.

Iles picked up his glass and walked around the club, having a good gape at the people in this evening. 'Keeping up the quality, I'm glad to see. It could be bingo night at All Souls.'

Harpur said: 'Ralph, the Chief Constable's decided to go public on the Lynette Leach matter – Press, television, radio. We're going to be releasing a lot of the detail. That will involve some mentions of you: the fact that you took her back to school, and were present when the head announced her disappearance. The point is, if we didn't give it, the reporters would find out for themselves, anyway. Obviously, they'll interview the school staff.'

'So we're here to tell you you could get some attention, Ralphy,' Iles explained. 'Visitors.'

'I see.'

'Not just media attention,' Harpur said.

'I don't understand,' Ember replied.

'To some degree, the finger's going to be put on you, isn't it, Ralph?' Iles said. 'People looking for this Exeter loot will gather that you and Caring must have been damn close. Surrogate daddy.'

'Just be reasonably on your guard, Ralph,' Harpur told him. 'Naturally, we'll keep an eye. But make sure you take care of yourself, too.'

'Look, get your wife down, will you, Ralphy?' Iles said. 'I very much feel she should be warned.'

'I don't want her frightened, Mr Iles. I can break this to her, carefully.'

'Sweet,' Iles said. 'You're delightfully considerate, Ralph. Just bring her, will you? I'd like to know if she's heard any talk here – things that might seem very casual, but which could easily turn out significant. That's detection, you know.'

'She's resting at the moment.'

'Ah, I'm so glad,' Iles replied. 'She deserves it. But bring her. You've never done anything with Lynette, have you? Or have I already asked? Youth's a stuff and you're one of the ones who stuffs it, I hear.'

'This whole thing will really distress Margaret,' Ember replied. 'As a matter of fact she's not too well.'

'There's a hell of a lot of it about,' Iles replied.

'An accident.'

'What I said,' Iles went on. 'Which areas damaged?'

'Well, the face.'

'The worst,' Iles said.

'She's self-conscious,' Ember explained.

'Nothing more understandable,' Iles replied. 'You'll find this hard to credit, but I've had facial damage myself now and then, and I'd stay in a darkened room, keening. So pop up and bring your wife down now. Or we'll go up to the flat, if she wants privacy.'

'No, it's all right, I expect,' Ember said at once.

'What's the trouble? Some untidiness up there? Don't worry. Harpur's place is always in squalor.'

'I'll fetch her,' Ember replied. 'A little outing among people might do her good.'

'She's got one of the very best in you, Ralph,' Iles said.

When Ember came back down with her the four of them went and sat at a table in a corner where the lighting was especially subdued. Harpur felt sickened by her bruising and the ruin of her nose.

'I've given Margaret the bad news about Lynette, and she says she's heard no gossip in the bar, Mr Iles,' Ember said.

'It's appalling,' Margaret Ember murmured.

'Tell us about this accident, Mrs Ember,' Iles replied.

'A door. Walked into a door,' Ember said.

'So stupid,' Margaret Ember added.

'This is always happening now,' Iles remarked. 'Do you remember the old days, when a door really was a door?'

Harpur said: 'Caring's missing, of course, and I feel that if anyone were searching for him, anyone wanting to put pressure on through the kidnapping, this is one of the places they'd come – looking for rumour, gossip, a lead to him. Same as ourselves. The Monty's a sort of social centre, yes, Ralph? One of the club's great strengths.'

'Thank you,' Ember replied. 'But, if I may say, not a centre for talk about kidnapping.' He gave a small, sad laugh.

'And no out-of-town visitors? London hard nuts, on a quest?' Harpur asked.

'None I've seen,' Ember replied.

'Mrs Ember?' Harpur asked.

'Not at all,' she said.

'You weren't letting one of them in when the door turned nasty?' Iles inquired.

'Ralph, we've got to find Caring,' Harpur said. 'Whoever's got Lynette has obviously decided there's nobody to deal with at present – no source of funds and ransom. So, things have gone silent. It's why we've decided on publicity: news about Lynette might reach Caring, even abroad, and make him break cover.'

'I quite see the point of that,' Ember replied.

'Knowing him, would you say he might respond?' Harpur asked.

'Oh, yes indeed. Immediately.'

'Poor Patsy Leach,' Mrs Ember replied.

'Margaret and I would know something of what she feels, Mr Iles, speaking as parents of girls,' Ember stated.

Iles said: 'I'm one myself, you know. They're a worry. Think of the Hearst woman.' Last time Harpur had heard Iles on this line it was Eva Braun. 'I hope you're seeing someone good about these injuries, Mrs Ember, not some old back-street, struck-off relic recommended by Ralphy here. Your hubbie cuts corners.'

'If she takes things easy it will all clear up nicely,' Ember suggested.

'Stupid cunt,' Iles replied. He took a notebook from his pocket and wrote a name and telephone number on it. Tearing the page out, he gave it to Mrs Ember. 'This is a good cosmetic treatment boy. In the Lodge. Mention my name. He owes me infinitely and will see you right, no charge. Do it soon. Noses can be a sod. Look at Harpur's.'

'If you come across any pointers to Caring – the slightest thing – we'd like to hear,' Harpur said.

'Absolutely,' Ember replied.

'We really want to help on this,' Margaret Ember said. The swellings around her mouth made the words indistinct.

Iles said: 'Is it you who's been knocking her about, Ralphy?'

'Knocking her about?' Ember cried.

'What's behind it?' Iles snarled.

'No,' she said, her voice suddenly high enough to draw attention: a couple of men playing pool turned for a moment, until they met Iles's eyes. 'Ralph isn't like that.'

'So who?' the ACC asked. 'And the place wrecked upstairs? Really turned over? Someone thinks you're sitting on a prize chunk of the loot, Ralphy?'

'I'm going to really listen out for anything on Oliver Leach,' Ember replied. 'He has his unfortunate aspects, yes – I'm referring to alleged criminality – but to give Patsy and him this sort of agony is beyond.'

As Harpur and Iles walked to the car in the Monty yard, the ACC said: 'Duplicity can be near to an art form.'

'Ember's developing skills in his maturity.'

'Like most of us, Col.'

Later in the evening Harpur was meeting Sarah Iles, who had recently enrolled for night classes in French and occasionally went. About Sarah's love-making there was a wonderful, relaxed, joyfulness that had at first amazed Harpur. She rarely spoke and never closed her eyes, watching him all the time when their heads were level, a smile that was near to a grin on her face, her mouth ready to kiss or be kissed, rubbing lightly across his cheeks, his neck, his chin. Clothes, no clothes, she did not care. If they were half dressed she would force her hand up under his shirt, fingering his ribs or his nipples, and, when they were near the ultimate, spreading both her hands on his back, no great pressure but talking to him through them instead of words, as if gently, subtly, holding his body to her and making sure the position of it was precise. Even cramped in the rear of a car it was like that: violent enough, careful enough, gorgeously tender.

They were in Harpur's car tonight, back near the concrete defence post at the foreshore. Luckily, the ancient unmarked Viva which he previously drove had lately coughed itself to death, and these days he took what he liked to think was an anonymous old Senator from the headquarters pool. It gave a lot more room. What had surprised and delighted Harpur was the contrast between this brilliantly warm, cheery woman who would be under him or over him or head-to-toe with him, and the aggressive toughy Sarah had always seemed when she was simply a friend, and the beautiful wife of a boss. Even then, Harpur had always been fond of her – possibly sensed that what he saw was not the whole picture. These brief evenings with her, and a very occasional afternoon, had transformed not just his view of Sarah but his life. He told her he had never known anything like it and, although he was not sure she believed him, she had the courtesy to behave as if she did: consideration like that really counted as you grew older. Harpur was a great yeller during cums, which he thought must be a pain to her, especially as she always remained pretty quiet. But she said she liked to hear him, and that had to be more evidence of her good nature. 'There are no words, but I hear words, Col,' she said tonight, 'and they tell me we're linked.'

'I can say that in clear. We're linked, all right.'

The Volvo estate where he had seen the woman's hand pressed against the steamy window the other night was here again, in the same place. As he and Sarah lay still for a while now in the few minutes before she had to get back home he glanced towards the other car occasionally, but although he could make out vague movement in it through the darkness, he did not see the clawing fingers. Oddly, he felt as if he had lost contact. For a moment, he thought he heard a voice from the Volvo, a woman's voice, calling something, though it was impossible to tell what: perhaps only the same kind of cries as he made. Then, very briefly, he thought he glimpsed someone on foot close to the estate car, a man, perhaps even trying to see into it. Almost at once the figure disappeared among the trees. Christ, peeping Toms down here? It would be just the place.

'What's wrong?' Sarah asked.

'One day we might be together,' he said. 'Not just linked. Together.'

'Yes, one day.'

They were on the rear seat of the Senator. Suddenly, the front passenger door was pulled open and Francis Garland put his head in. 'Oh,' he said, 'I'm sorry, sir. And Sarah. This is one hell of a mistake. I thought you were alone.' Harpur had never heard him off balance before. 'Shall I wait outside?'

'Well, yes.'

Garland closed the door. Harpur and Sarah sat up, hurriedly putting their clothes right. 'Jesus,' she muttered, 'sometimes the earth moves, sometimes the car door.'

Once before Harpur had been interrupted by police when making love in a vehicle. That time, though, he had been beaten up by friends of the woman's husband. He climbed out of the Senator and he and Garland stood where they would be hidden from the Volvo. Garland said: 'I saw your Senator, and assumed you'd had word and made it here ahead of us. Did I hear you call?'

'Had word of what?'

'It's Patsy Leach in the Volvo. We managed to follow her this time from Low Pastures. She's with Ember. Sordi— ' He did not quite finish the word, as if suddenly realising it could apply not just to Patsy and Ember. Skilfully he adapted: 'Swordsman extraordinary is Ralphy. Always was.'

'I noticed someone snooping.'

'Erogenous Jones, sir. He'll be cut up you rumbled him. Even you.'

'Does Patsy know you tailed her?'

'No.'

'Keep it like that.'

'Of course. Well, I'll bid you good night now, sir. There's no need for me to infringe further on your evening. Obviously I'll tell the rest of our people you were doing an observation, privately.'

Infringe further on your evening. You could tell he was a high flier. 'I'll give your best to Sarah,' Harpur said.

'All that was a long time ago.'

'Don't you miss her?'

'Yes, sometimes I do. She's a marvellous girl. But why am I telling you, sir?'

Chapter 21

Ember, naked again in the Volvo with Patsy, suddenly realised that he had begun to find her sex shouting no longer irksome but deeply exciting, almost too exciting. They were front to front tonight, so he could fix his mouth on to hers to keep her quiet for a while, or he feared he would come off early like a schoolboy. She gnawed at his lips, but not too severely, and this was something other women had accustomed him to, anyway. During this little intermission of silence in the Volvo, he thought he heard a man yell hoarsely, wildly, wordlessly, not far away, perhaps from that old Senator parked on the other side of the clearing: the noise would be coming through two layers of glass, so precision was difficult. Ember wondered if he should have a shout or two himself one of these nights. Patsy might expect it and regard him as short of passion otherwise. Caring used to shout?

For a moment then, he had a foul vision of Oliver, his mouth open wide as if in ecstasy, but filled with bright brown mud. Ember groaned through the kiss, almost retched. Patsy groaned in thrilled reply and their mouths vibrated. This was her kind of language. Ember pulled his lips clear so he could gulp more air, and she at once began a loud commentary: 'Cock king, prince prick, ram rod, you seek me, reach me, you delve and soothe. Oh, yes, soothe.'

He was glad her thoughts reached that final gentleness. It helped him get control again, eased the ferocious, accumulating pace. There had to be some simple comfort in these things, as well as the screaming and roughness and fanging. She had her troubles and needed that comfort, and Ember still felt it was only charitable to respond and put up with the foul language.

'Tell me you hate Oliver for having me before you, Ralph.'

'Yes, I hate him for that.'

'You could kill him for that.'

'Yes, I could kill him for that.'

'Might one day.'

'Might one day.'

'And others. Some others.'

'And others,' he said.

'Not shag-happy, you understand, but some others.' She wrapped her legs hard around him contentedly. 'Split these earlier men apart. Wipe them out. That notion makes me feel so happy, as if I were virginal again when I came to you.'

'I can see that, Patsy,' he stated. He had heard some woman comedian on television the other night talking about the day she became a virgin.

Patsy began to call out further instructions, all crude and brilliant. God, if only she was beautiful and, or, much younger, she would have been one of the most sumptuous fucks he ever had. 'What was that?'

'What?'

'I thought I heard footsteps outside.'

'No. How can you be thinking of such things now?'

'You're sure you got out from Low Pastures unseen again?'

'It's a doddle.'

'Well, only an idea. But you're right. It's nobody.'

When they were dressing he said: 'I'm going to London overnight. About Lynette. At home, I've said a business trip.'

'Oliver's in London?'

'Lynette. Maybe.'

'Why do you say that?'

The Senator pulled away at speed. Evidently someone had to get home in a hurry or an alibi would crash.

'We had a visitor at the club today. Something he said.'

'What?'

Leopold's words which had alerted Ember were, 'And have I been working on the right end?' Strange, mysterious. 'He seemed to suggest the ransom demands had been going to the wrong person,' Ember told her.

'Which wrong person?'

'Obviously, you. On the phone, through Lynette.'

'So, who's the right person, then?'

'God knows,' he declared immediately. 'Whoever's got big money.'

'What's all the "seems" and "suggest"? Aren't you sure?'

'It's a guess, Patsy. But if he's been working for the ransom he must have your daughter.'

'If, if. Didn't you ask him? You actually had him there and didn't ask?'

'He got so he was in no condition to reply, that was the trouble. It definitely couldn't be helped.'

She turned and glanced at him. Then she said: 'It's nonsense. Lynette's far away with Oliver, I tell you.'

'Perhaps. I'll just have a look at his house, in case. I've been there before. At Kew.'

'So who?'

'You wouldn't know him.'

She combed her hair, which was certainly one of her strongest points, soft and no grey, not even masked grey that he could tell. 'Ralph, this sounds dangerous. He'll be at home?'

They were in the front seats now.

'I don't think so.'

'His house, and holding a prisoner – surely he must be there.'

'No. I'm sure he won't be. As a matter of fact.'

Again Patsy took a glance at him. Then she turned the car and drove out to the road. Ember looked all around in the darkness, but saw nobody on foot, only closed up cars – private islands.

'Your obsession with Lynette, Ralph. Is it because—?'

'A child kidnapped and in great danger, Patsy, that's all. I can't rest. I'm bound to feel a duty. It's through you, as much as anything.'

'What does that mean, "as much as anything"?'

'Has he really got it wrong, about the ransom? Or would you be able to pay? Darling, are you holding exceptionally good funds?'

'I might understand your damned interest in her if Lynette was in any way pretty or had a brisk body,' she replied.

He hardly understood his unflagging concern over the child himself: just that he was responsible for her. 'It was lovely tonight,' he told her.

132

'Yes. You know what I continue to want, though, Ralph, don't you?'

He thought he did, but gave no answer, hoping he didn't.

'I still long for you to take me back to where we first made love,' she said. 'The woods, the solitude, the springy soil. It would be a re-dedication, if that's not pompous.'

'I will take you,' he replied. 'Soon. But tell me, Patsy – you didn't answer: could you provide the big money ransom, if it came to that?'

'Quite often I dream of that spot in the woods, you know, in amazing detail. I see it as so special.'

They came to a junction where a right turn would take her towards Low Pastures and the spot where Ember had left his car. She went left. They would be on the motorway in a couple of minutes. He felt sick again. She whooped and laughed: 'Damn it, I'll drive there now,' she said happily. 'Your wife thinks you're on a business thing, so that's OK. Our little wood, our own corner of countryside. Then you won't have to bother pilgrimaging to bloody London.'

'Patsy, love, it's crazy,' he replied as gently as he could. 'In the darkness we'll never find the spot.' He thought of switching off the engine, or of risking a small accident while still on B-roads and smashing his elbow into her face two or three times.

'Ralph, I can't take it when you talk to me only about Lynette and about money,' she replied. 'And both so cruelly tied in your mind.' She made her voice whine: '"Could you pay the ransom?" "Exactly how much have you got, Patsy?" It's just not you, Ralph – calculating, footling, the very opposite of that awesome sexuality.'

'Oh, look, I only— '

'Together we're beyond all that, surely. Surely. Yes, the trees, the bushes, will gloriously re-affirm it.'

He sat back in his seat as they drove on to the motorway. He could postpone the Kew trip, though it must not be for long. 'Won't they notice your absence at Low Pastures?'

'Up theirs.'

Chapter 22

'It was raining by now but that didn't seem to make any difference to her, sir,' Erogenous Jones said. 'Everything came off, and fast – a bit like one of those fertility things, splashing and cavorting et cetera? – and Ralphy had to do the same. She was pulling at his buttons. I don't think he went for it much.'

'She's been reading *Lady Chatterley*,' Iles remarked.

Harpur said: 'Drive all that way for a— ?'

'And this was the second time in the night?' the Chief asked. They were in his room. Lane had on uniform today, because of a Press conference due soon. He looked comparatively tidy, Harpur thought. 'Have I got that right?' the Chief said.

'Oh, yes, sir,' Garland said. 'The second at least.'

'It's obviously been a very trying session,' Lane told him and Jones. The Chief had sent out for tea and sandwiches for them.

'I'm sorry about the dirt and so on, sir,' Garland replied, 'but we had to get as close as we could, and the ground was pretty wet.' Their clothes were streaked with mud and both had removed their shoes and left them near Lane's door.

'Some stress, yes, sir,' Erogenous added. 'We're motoring without lights on the minor roads or we'd have been spotted.' Erogenous – otherwise Jeremy Stanislaus Jones – was probably the best tail Harpur had ever known, in a car or on foot. Although he had his long service medal and was getting old for lying in muck to watch love-making, he had an everlasting, bubbling curiosity in people's behaviour, and seemed as intrigued by this outing as Harpur was.

He said: 'This can't be all that far from where the girl was at school.'

134

'A wood, four or five miles from Cheltenham,' Erogenous replied.

'Myself, I dote on that Cotswold area,' the Chief remarked.

'And Panicking couldn't get it up, you say?' Iles asked.

'Not at first,' Garland replied. 'He seemed off colour – almost as if thrown in some mysterious way by the place? Sad to watch, really. I think he wept. Erogenous believes so, too. Turned away from her for a little while, his face in his hands, rain streaming down his shoulders and back, like a statue in the park.'

'This is the second time in a night and after a long drive remember,' the Chief said.

'From all we hear about Panicking that wouldn't normally rule him out, sir,' Iles replied.

Jones said: 'Anyway, eventually it's all right. Ralphy's restored and active and she's shouting to the trees and greenery in a sort of triumph – I think that would be the word, Chief. Like a . . . proclamation? It was moving, in its way.' His neat, lineless face brightened. Erogenous loved evidence of vitality.

'Anything we need to know about in what she said?' Harpur asked.

'Generally not, sir. Obscenities, though original and heartfelt,' Garland replied. 'Phallus worship to a high degree.'

'Thank God some of them still have it,' Iles said. 'Utterly reasonable, yet there's this damned anti-lobby, much stronger than the vivisection lot.'

'Then some references to their being bound to each other and this spot bearing benign, leafy witness,' Garland continued. 'Forcefully yelled. Note of reproach, as if Ralphy might have let her down somehow? It was around dawn by now and she set the birds going.'

'That starling tumult is wondrous with a hard-on,' Iles commented. 'Isn't sex a full-time job, though? Rain? She wouldn't feel it. Where were they earlier in the night?'

'The foreshore, sir, near the defence post,' Jones replied.

'Carnality Strand?' Iles asked.

'Right, sir,' Jones replied. 'A bit along from Sewage Strand. Mr Harpur will confirm. He was there observing, too.'

'Harpur? How?' Iles said, turning that slim, grey head sharply towards him, like a greyhound spotting the hare.

'That was exceptionally alert, Colin,' Mark Lane said. 'You had information?'

'One of my tipsters, yes, sir,' Harpur replied.

'Yes, exceptionally alert, sir,' Iles remarked. 'Which tipster would that be, Col? How on earth do they hear these things?'

'I never ask,' Harpur said. 'First rule of the game.'

But you could not flatten Iles. 'Which tipster would it be, then, Col?'

'Well, we're due to meet the newspapers and broadcasters now, Desmond, Colin,' Lane said, 'to tell them they can publish on Lynette, and exactly what they can publish.' He stood up and straightened out his tunic, then deliberately undid a button, still fighting military smartness.

'Could you find this spot in the woods again, Francis?' Iles asked.

'I think so.'

'Is that important, Desmond?' the Chief asked.

'If it has a mystical, therapeutic influence, sir,' Iles said. 'I adore overtones. My mother used to say, "Desmond, leave those overtones alone. Why can't you play with your dick like other lads?" '

Chapter 23

Ember left for Kew early next afternoon. 'Resolution!' he told himself, once or twice. He could not delay or the trip would make no sense: if the child was imprisoned somewhere in Leopold's house she might have been without food and drink since his departure and, by now, that could be a long time. Perhaps she was tied up – Leopold went in for that. Ember sometimes wished he could stop thinking that he alone had to save her, if she was savable. These bouts of nobility, part-time El Cidness, were a fucking mystery and mostly a pain. The burden pressed harder on him than ever.

He knew his suit showed it had just come out of a case, but too bad: he was on his way to reclaim a kidnapped girl, not get the OBE. Almost as soon as those two police left after the post-Leopold quizzing at the club, and while Margaret was out of the way lying down again, he had unloaded the clothes luggage from the car. Not the money luggage. Because of Leopold, he decided it was too risky to leave big stock in the loft. It had been lucky, too, that he had put Caring's clothes and the monitor badge in the car when he did his little run. He had junked them now in the incinerator: junked the idea of laying false trails, too. Although Leopold himself would certainly not be doing any more rummaging or menacing, the same grab-all idea could come to Harry Lighterman, wherever he might be, and then there was that lad called Fritzy to worry about, wherever *he* might be, too. Ember would have preferred to put the whole quantity deep into false-name deposit boxes. But at any moment he might still need to pay out a slab on the spot, to buy his life, and he required a big bag of cash very close, permanently. His mother always used to say, 'You're twice the man with a ten pound note in your pocket.' Multiply it by about ten thousand and she had a point.

There had even been a couple of minutes in the club when he thought of trying to pay off Leopold. But this bugger would not have been satisfied with what Ember had in readies, that was certain: metropolitan scale, metropolitan tastes – and he would have wanted enough for two, even though Winston could not spend at present. As it turned out, the thick end of the pool cue paid off so much sweeter. Pool cue but golf swing. Ember had a minor smile at the thought as he drove towards London now, the back of his neck seeming to feel warmed by the presence of extensive cash in the boot, like a sun lamp. That had been some operation with Leopold's head – cool and jaunty. Panicking Ralph? Cardew the Cad? People wouldn't think so if they had seen Leopold dropped. Well, Chitty's ex-woman did see it, and he had probably been wise to promise her straight out yesterday a fair lump of entitlement, which should help with her silence. At some stage, he certainly meant to think about this promise. She was not a bad kid, getting a ruination of blood across her gear through helping Margaret, and very lustrous legs and tits, plus features: obviously a hundred points up on Patsy as to flesh, yet no secret heavy funds, this was the drawback. If he could only have had that twenty-five grand returned from the dead bank manager's stupid wife, he might have handed Anna some of it there and bloody then. Naturally, she would have shouted for more while accepting, but deep down she would know she was lucky. This after all was a widow merely, and a widow who had been living apart.

When he reached Kew, he parked near the underground station and then went and had a good look at the house before doing anything. It was a risk leaving a boot full of cash, but he saw no alternative. Ember approached the house very discreetly: Leopold was never going to be lording it there again like the king of Lilliput, but he might have associates, even a staff. When Ember visited before, to pick up armament for the Exeter project, the place had struck him as much more than living quarters. Think of the White House. It was still daylight now and he walked past, trying to look environmental, such as a bark groupie on his way to the Botanical Gardens. Then he turned and did another inspection. The house stood a good way back up a gravel drive, so it was hard to see much from the street. He thought he made out some movement across a room on the first floor, perhaps a woman, perhaps elderly, yet with a modern hair-style, although grey. He was afraid to loiter and afraid to go up the drive for a closer inspection. If that new pistol had arrived from Mills-Silver he might have felt more valid. Perhaps he should have asked for something simpler to get than a Barracuda. It would be easier later at the house though, in the dark. He took one more walk past, as slow as he could make it without being conspicuous, but this time spotted nothing at all behind the windows. It might be a half-witted mistake to have come here, one of those long-shots that never had any hope, a plan hatched from scorching guilt, not sense.

This was the sort of area he would like to move to, if he could hold on to the money, and perhaps shake a really worthwhile sliver more out of Patsy. Prices for a house and club up here were sure to be fierce. You had to be talking about a million. Goodbye Shield Terrace and the Monty and its gang of snivelling little-people crooks. Don't call on Ralph W. Ember when you're up on a day-trip. Margaret would like London, and there would be a stack of good private schools. It was a fine distance from Patsy, and further still from that heartbreaking spot in the woods. Good job they could not identify people from bare arse prints in the soil, because Patsy's would be there. Waiting for darkness, he walked to a small group of shops – good quality shops, such as antiques and fabrics – and studied property pictures on an estate agent's display. The thing about these photographs, you could really feel a stately aspect in the rich yellow brickwork and big windows with lead in.

'Word of mouth.' When he looked to see who had spoken, Ember found that a couple of men, early twenties or less, had come and stood near him at the display. This kind of encounter nobody wanted, it was untoward. But they stayed together, on his right. If they had taken positions each side of him he might have been straight into collapse. 'Anything that finishes up on these boards is a dud, mate. All that's worthwhile goes word of mouth in these parts. You from these parts? You looking seriously?'

'To me you look like you're looking seriously.'

'We could show you a place or two, places about to reach the market. It's the only way. Primacy.'

Ember said with quite a rounded chuckle: 'Well, window-shopping's my limit at this time.'

'See this?' One of them pointed at a lovely tree-shaded place that Ember had been greatly taken with, advertised at *£650,000, but try offer.* 'Total shit heap.'

' "Try offer," ' the other said. 'How estate agents spell death-watch beetle.' Now he did move quickly around and stood on Ember's left, but it could be to see another part of the display. Could it?

'These we're talking about are all walking distance.'

Although Ember felt that old numbness in his legs, he knew from previous times he was all right and that his feet would definitely still be there if he glanced down. He felt pleased he could control that urge and said: 'I'm not totally sure about Kew. A taste for St Albans, too.'

'Come on, we'll give you a mini-tour.' He took Ember's arm just above the wrist, not a hard grip, almost like a friend. There was a smell of Imperial Leather soap coming from him, again a friendly, cheerful smell. Ember knew he had to go. He also knew which house they would be making for. 'Call me Maskrey, would you? He's Potter, or as near as makes no difference. I've done no checks.'

'Ember.'

'No first name?'

'Ralph.'

'One thing I'm sure of – you wouldn't want to be called Ralphy, Ralph,' Potter said, 'not someone looking seriously at property in this bracket.'

Ember found he could walk and a few minutes later Maskrey remarked: 'We always call her Mother. In some ways it's lighthearted – a joke, and yet there's respect present too.' The three of them were in Leopold's place now, a ramshackle kitchen on the first floor, and a woman over seventy wearing jeans, and with her grey hair cut punk, had joined them, the coiffure that had mystified him from the street. They sat in a line at the breakfast bar, facing a pine-boarded wall, the woman, Potter, Ember, Maskrey.

140

'We could see that this was the house you were really interested in,' Potter remarked, turning to smile in comradely style at Ember.

'It is very lovely,' Ember said. 'Genuine period is so winning.'

'Pacing outside.'

'You've been here before, I think,' the woman remarked, looking along the bar and also smiling. 'This would be to see Leopold. Possibly Winston, too.'

'I'll fetch the paper. You can read the whole thing, Ember,' Maskrey said, standing. He was in a baggy, grey-green suit, and had very clean-looking dark hair resting on his collar. His shirt was white and he wore a plain yellow tie, not a mark on it, like a TV presenter. He came back with the *Daily Mail* and spread it in front of Ember at an inside page. There was a picture of Lynette and another showing Iles and Harpur and that Chief Constable, Lane, seated behind a table on a platform addressing reporters. The headline read: 'Police seek girl kidnapped from private school.'

The woman said: 'Leopold's disappeared. In a nutshell. No, I'm not his mother, nor theirs, and I'm past child-bearing. Still I feel for them. Leopold could not be more capable, and that's the guts of it. If he doesn't keep in touch it's because something's wrong.'

'No, he's not mentioned in that news report, though you are,' Potter went on. 'That's just background for you, Ralph. We're bloody worried. He can be taken advantage of, Leopold, owing to his stature and a trusting nature.'

'This place is nothing without Leopold,' Maskray said. 'Well, if you called on him, I expect you could feel that. Kitchen on the first floor, yes, for Mother, but another below, and nobody but Leopold allowed anywhere near it. Herbs in jars.'

'I remember from conversation about the Exeter outing that you're the one who sweats, Ralph,' Potter remarked. 'Yes.' Thin and stooped, Potter wore baggy, floral trousers and a mauve roll-top jersey. His face was Social Security: a lovely calmness because the Post Office would always have enough to cash the cheque, even if you were last in the queue.

'I looked in Leopold's diary and he's got no appointments here today,' Maskrey said.

141

'Very much on the off-chance, this visit,' Ember replied. 'I happened to be in these parts.' In any moments of silence he tried to listen for sounds of the girl somewhere in the house.

'Mother and I said you're not tooled up. Potter disagrees.' Maskrey had sat down again at the breakfast bar and leaned over and felt around Ember. 'We win.'

'Yet I don't account myself an expert on armament,' the woman said. 'How would I be, a career in confetti manufacture? I look at faces.' Her own was long and close to beautiful, what Ember thought of as churchy: lines of sadness for mankind, though with some joy lying beneath, as if mankind might make it after all. It was hard to think she could be part of anything deleterious, yet here she was, and offering dark suggestions about Leopold. She had on a pink Frying Tonight, global warming T-shirt with the jeans, and a thin, reddish scarf tied in a big bow in the front, maybe because her neck wanted to tell the world about ageing. Ember thought of making a run for it, which was always one of his first ideas when trouble came. But Potter and Maskrey looked so casual you knew they were ready for anything and had a system for smashing him on the way to whichever exit, or worse than smashing him.

'Leopold talks about you a lot, Ember,' Maskrey said, 'not just the sweats and the panic. This long, good past, and all kinds of rare values.'

'Plus dick activity,' the woman added.

'All right, Mother. But Leopold exaggerates all that aspect in everyone,' Potter said, 'because he doesn't get much. It's an unhealthy obsession of his.'

'Since the Falklands I can take it or leave it alone,' the woman told Ember, 'so don't feel stud-doomed.'

'Is it to do with this?' Maskrey asked, pointing at the Lynette report again.

'What?' Ember asked.

'You hanging about this property.'

'How would it be?' Ember replied. 'What's the connection?'

'Motored?' Potter asked.

'No, train,' Ember said. He did not want these two into the car, not at this stage. If it came to a liberty deal later, that could be different, might have to be different.

'I'm glad,' the woman said. 'I knew you weren't in the drive and because of the Gardens they're hellish about parking. As you're going to be here for a long while you could have suffered.'

'If there's a blank page in the diary, perhaps Leopold was going somewhere,' Ember said.

'In your direction, as a matter of fact,' Maskrey replied.

'Really?' Ember said.

'Leopold tells me nothing,' the woman added.

'That's why we all call you Mother, Mother,' Potter said.

'When you say in my direction you mean generally in my direction – that general part of the world?'

'Generally, general. Nervy? He mentioned your name,' Maskrey replied. 'For a call. Didn't he make any contact?'

'I wish I'd known he was coming. It would have saved me a trip.'

'Fair point, Ralph,' Potter remarked.

Chapter 24

Nut calls teemed, as Harpur had expected. Once the kidnapping was news the special telephones at Lower Pastures never stopped. There were people who knew they had seen her, and men and women who said they were holding her, and men who said they were Caring Oliver, and girls who said they were Lynette and desperate, and girls who said they were Lynette and loving it. Police answered them all now, because Harpur thought it might be too distressing for Patsy: she acted cool, but who really knew? Most calls were obvious rubbish. Some had to be followed up, though, either by Harpur's people or by the police at Cheltenham. It was hard on manpower and womanpower.

As a result, when Patsy did another of her secret night exits from the house, only Harpur was available to follow. He did not rate himself as a tail, and thanked God she seemed to be making for Carnality Strand again at the foreshore. Even if he lost her he knew where to finish up, and when he drew into the spot he had occupied with Sarah the other night, the Volvo was in its usual place, too. Probably he should have recognised some of the other cars dotted about: irregular lives liked regular geography.

Presumably, Ember would leave his car at a distance and walk the last stretch for discretion's sake. Harpur waited and watched for him. This was not the most elegant sort of police work. Why was he here, anyway? They had established she was having Ember and it was not vital to Kinsey log every time she had him. Harpur had been bothered about Peeping Toms the last time, and now felt like one himself. He could see her behind the wheel, hardly moving, apparently staring ahead towards the sea wall and the defence post on top. In the bad light she looked sad and almost pretty. Odd to think how much of his life centred on this bleak

144

spot – the hours or half-hours with Sarah, the briefings from Jack Lamb, this surveillance. About every one of these attendances was there something deeply sordid, to take the word that Garland almost used the other night? In fact, was there something deeply sordid about Harpur himself? Very likely. His wife often said so, especially in company and at full volume, and she did not even know of Sarah. His children echoed their mother. Harpur could not see any great changes coming up, though, not in the sort of work he did, nor in the sort of love life he had. He needed both. Harpur realised Sarah Iles would have totally failed to understand his frantic quest for squeamishness: if you wanted something you took the conditions. He loved that clarity in her but could not match it.

In the Volvo, Patsy was starting to show anxiety. She glanced around now from time to time and adjusted the driving mirror, as if wanting to catch the earliest possible sight of Ember. He did not appear, though. She had been here almost an hour. Anybody tied up with someone else's spouse might get jumpy at long waits, and he could see it could be especially bad when the someone was as shifty as Ralph Ember.

At just before midnight he heard an approaching din and a load of yelling and singing kids arrived with a howl of tyres in what Harpur guessed would be a stolen van. There were six of them, four boys, two girls, none over seventeen, all high on something, all in party mood, all in scruff fashions. Instead of lurk parking like everyone else in the extra shadow of the trees or sea wall, they left the van in the middle of the clearing. Its radio boomed rap crap through wide open doors, and outside the kids did their bit of strut and shuffle dancing and passed a couple of bottles of Newcastle Brown between them. Harpur's daughters were into rap, and rag-tag clothes and maybe Newcastle Brown and whatever else. He found himself almost fearfully studying the girls and felt relieved not to recognise either. His children were still a bit young for this kind of carry-on, but it would not be long. And after that, adultery down here or somewhere like it, eventually? Life's little circles. Some of the love cars moved off hurriedly, and Harpur wondered whether there might be a choicer venue for Sarah and him in future. Turning, Patsy watched the youngsters but sat tight. She obviously needed to see Ralphy, and, in any case, if you had lived with Caring you did not take fright at a handful of pissed joy-riders.

In a while they brought out a can of petrol from the back of the van and with plenty of ritualistic arm waving gave it a good soaking. One of them threw a lighted ball of paper and the fire boomed and torched. That lost them the arsehole music, which was one big plus, but they continued to caper and whoop as the flames soared, like night riot shop burners having a rhythm break. Another car pulled out and away in a panic. Harpur thought of the bug scramble if you lifted a stone in the garden. Light from the blaze made it clear that Patsy was a woman alone in the Volvo and the gang moved over towards her slowly, still hearing some beat in their upended minds and moving their feet to it. They looked menacing – tribal – and Harpur prepared to get out and bite them if they messed Patsy around. Goodbye secrecy, but even a villain's wife waiting to fuck another probable villain had a right to the law's good offices.

The kids, though, seemed to mean no harm: occasionally, very occasionally, Harpur wondered if he was too hard on unreconstructed youth. Patsy wound down the window and talked to them. Then she sat back a moment, obviously took a decision, opened the door and came out of the Volvo to join in the fire dance. She might not be lovely but she was game. Perhaps that had been part of what Caring went for. She seemed to pick up the steps fast, if they needed any picking up. Harpur fractionally lowered a window himself and heard one of the men saying that this lady's guy had stood her up and it was a raw pity, so everyone had to make a fuss of her and help her forget. They asked her name and made sounds of sympathy. Perhaps it really would buck her up.

It struck Harpur suddenly that if they felt like inviting all solitaries into their little party, he might be next. That would not do. Quickly, he rolled the window back up, then climbed into the rear of the car, took his jacket off, pushed down his trousers and lay out on the rear seat, face down, hoping that if they came close the standard view would convince them there was someone underneath and that he needed no consolation or extra company. This would be his first ghost affair. Yes, he had to admit that he and his work did occasionally touch the sordid. He thought he heard them approach – a mounting volume of

146

rap chatter, like that arts *Late Show* Megan had on television sometimes, and then quickly move away. They had tact as well as sympathy.

When he sat up and looked again, Patsy was returning to her car, waving. The youngsters ran in a strung-out group towards the trees, also waving, still full of merriment. Harpur could hear sirens in the distance. It would be at least the fire brigade and possibly the police. The Volvo drew away. She had been there for two hours, and no lover could ask for more patience. Harpur followed.

She did not make for Low Pastures but drove to near the Monty and stopped at the far end of Shield Terrace. After watching for a few minutes she left the car and walked down to look in the Monty yard, obviously checking whether Ember's car was there. The club would still be open, but she made no attempt to enter. Instead, she returned to the Volvo and drove off. He thought that now she would take the car back and go home.

Harpur looked into the yard, too, and could not see Ember's Montego. Then he went quickly to Low Pastures and was sitting in shirt-sleeves when Patsy appeared in the drawing room wearing her dressing gown. She came and took a chair near him. Harpur picked up a slight smell of pyre. Patsy looked hurt and yet exhilarated: it would be the youth sequence around the blaze. Harpur almost envied her that. The job tonight, the self-examination, and his play-acting, had made him feel low. He must get back to superiority – what policing was all about: there might be a chance to squeeze some revelations out of Patsy in her present state.

'I shall try to sleep soon,' she said.

'Yes, good. You can leave things here to us. How have you spent the evening?' It was late, but at the other end of the room the bells still summoned the duty listeners to a flow of lies and inanities.

'Mr Harpur, you might regard this as foolish – but in private prayer in my room,' she said. 'I'm afraid it's a very long time since I spoke to God. But tonight, I— What else is there for me to do?'

'Not foolish at all,' Harpur replied. 'Many draw great solace from it. Would you like to see a minister in the morning? Might it help?'

'Stuff that,' she said. 'I'm having no vicars in this house, at least not until I'm dead.' Her dark eyes shone for a moment in anger and then grew impenetrable again.

All the same, Harpur pushed on: 'I've been wondering about Ralph Ember.'

'In what respect?' It was deadpan.

'This connection with your daughter.'

'Connection? Which connection?' she said. They had been talking quietly, so that the conversation did not reach the other police in the room, but her voice went up suddenly, and she was snarling. Once more her eyes became lively. Rage suited her. Her heavy face grew formidable, not just jowly. Rage did suit her, but for a harsh second he thought of Charles Laughton as Captain Bligh.

'Oh, I mean taking her back to school and acting as proxy for Oliver,' he said.

'Exactly. That's as far as it goes. Representing her father, because he was abroad. I don't see that as a connection, as you call it.'

'Perhaps it was the wrong word,' Harpur said.

'Entirely.'

'I think about them making that journey alone together.'

'Which journey alone? What the hell are you talking about, Harpur?'

'Well, when he took her back to school. Overnight? They were alone, yes?'

She stared at him, her face white, her lips trembling slightly. For a second she seemed about to say something to shut him up, then switched to questions: 'What point are you making? Is this some filthy suggestion about my Lynette? This is a child of fourteen we're talking about.'

'No reflection on her. But you know Ralphy Ember. Or perhaps you don't very well.'

'He's a colleague of my husband. I met him once or twice at the club, that's all.'

'Ralph can be as good as gold. A free spirit.'

'Yes? What does that mean, for God's sake? Should I care?'

'He's popular with women, Patsy. The Charlton Heston thing?'

'And what does *that* mean?'

'He looks like him.'

'Does he? Yes, perhaps a bit. So?'

Harpur grew even more confidential and played even rougher: 'I don't want to say anything that might be construed as blame, Patsy, but not all mothers would allow Ralph Ember to take their pretty daughter of fourteen on a long motor trip to school through the night.'

'Pretty? Nonsense,' she replied. 'She's hopelessly plain and always has been. Oliver's genes are strong. She takes after him. I sometimes wish she'd been a boy.' She stood up, still excited-looking, still fierce: 'What's the purpose of this conversation? What are you saying about Ralph Ember? What did you mean, "a free spirit"? This is police bluff.'

'He does pretty much what he likes. Comes and goes as he pleases. No very discernible loyalties, except to himself. Oh, yes, he does look after himself.'

She sat down again and put her face close to him for privacy again: 'I don't believe it,' she said, 'you tricky sod. Won't believe it.' He thought she would resume shouting. Instead, she leaned back in the chair for a moment and then went on in a relaxed tone: 'What I mean is that Oliver thought highly of him, trusted him utterly.'

'Ember?' Harpur replied. 'He could fool anyone.'

At the telephones a sergeant said into the receiver: 'Yes, love, so your name's Lynette Leach. This is great. We're looking for you. What's your second name? No, not Leach. What's your other Christian name, the one in the middle, like Margaret *Hilda* Thatcher? That's it. So what's yours? Yes, I know it, but do you?' In a moment he put the phone down. 'Just another dud, Mrs Leach, I'm afraid.'

'The little devil's living like a queen somewhere,' she replied.

Chapter 25

Jack Lamb rang Harpur at home wanting a meeting, but somewhere other than the foreshore. 'There could be activity: they had a blaze.' Lamb said.

'Yes?'

'I thought you'd have heard.'

'They don't tell me everything, Jack.'

Lamb suggested a launderette they sometimes used and Harpur loaded up in the house with washing. Megan knew the drill and silently watched him. Always, she re-did any clothes he took, as if they must be tainted by association with Lamb or with informing or with the job: for her, the launderette had become a perverse symbol – not of cleansing but contamination, and Harpur feared she saw most police activity other than traffic direction the same. A part of Harpur admired this eternal toughness in her and her eternal wholesome clarities and certainties. They made Megan Megan and always had. They were also almost impossible for him to live with now, though, and impossible to work with. These attitudes were bits of her family past and student past and he had learned to turn his back on them. They did not make for a great marriage.

The launderette was a venue Harpur disliked, anyway: too much window on to the street, too many dubious people in and out: steady folk had washing machines. But he always let Jack choose. The tipster was the one at risk.

Huge and cheerful-looking as ever, Lamb was already there, feeding a tub, when Harpur arrived. They sat in a corner with coffee from the machine, shielded a bit by other customers. 'Yes, a vehicle cindered near the defence post,' Lamb said. 'I know because a kid who drops me good insights now and then was involved, I'm sorry to say. One of those nights of excess and violence we're all liable to, Col.'

Christ. 'Yes?'

'And yet a fortunate aspect emerges, too.'

Christ. 'Yes?'

'Try and restrain yourself. Do you know who happened to be down there, Col?'

'Who's that, then?'

'This kid's very clued up. Obviously, or I wouldn't use him. He recognises a significant face.'

'Yes?'

'Patsy Leach.'

'That right?'

'Alone.'

'Yes?'

'Waiting, Col.'

'Yes?'

'They all got friendly. The kid asked waiting who for.'

'Yes?'

'Well, he got no answer – except "Oh, just Mr Money Bags." A sort of joke? Like Mr Right?'

'That's how it sounds, Jack.'

Lamb was in what looked like a hand-made, lavender, light-weight suit and heavy silver-striped silk tie, plus what could be Gucci pale grey shoes. Always he went in for a bewildering mixture of flamboyance and extreme caution. There were not too many dressed like this who used the launderette. Things in his art business must be bright. But, then, they almost always were. Harpur never asked too many questions about it. Megan said he could ask no questions at all, gagged by what she called 'terminal dependence'. Lamb went on: 'There's some real oddities following their tastes down there, Col.'

'Yes?'

'A bloke in a car having it off with himself on the back seat. Bit desperate? *The Looking Glass Whore*? Voyeur?'

'Could be.'

'This kid's good on faces but he had only buttocks to look at here, so I don't know who.'

'It's probably not too important, Jack.'

151

'I'm not sure. They were going to pull him out in disgust, but Patsy Leach said no, that everyone was entitled to his own kicks – or her own kicks.'

'Patsy was always progressive. Is this what you got me down here in the steam to tell me, Jack?'

He laughed in that big way of his. 'This is mostly just conversation so far, Col – a wry glance at humanity.'

'What then?'

'It embarrasses you? All right.' He grew businesslike: 'Piers Mills-Silver? A meaningful name?'

'One-time purveyor of untraceable arms, now supposedly gone legit. Fabrics?' Harpur replied. 'We look at him occasionally. Not much success.'

'The fabrics bit is real, but what does it front? He still does some armament, for special customers, I hear. He's been chasing a Barracuda lately. And, Col, he's into a property thing at the marina, how bent I don't know. Probably no more than routine bent – for the marina, for all marinas, everywhere. He had to commit himself to putting up half a million very soon, maybe this week, maybe next. And the tale I get is, he had it all in hand, gave his cast-iron promises to some very rough and formidable people, and then suddenly loses track of his supposed backer, which was obviously not Barclays Bank. People are pressing him. Piers looks so unwell.'

'You're saying there's a spare £500,000 floating around for investment?'

'Apparently. Or there was. Where from, you ask. Could it be Exeter?'

'It's interesting,' Harpur replied. 'So who gave you the tip, Jack? This youth?'

Lamb nodded, but not as an answer. It was an acknowledgement that he knew Harpur had to ask these questions and would, naturally, expect no reply. Jack stood up to help an old woman unload her clothes from a drier. Returning, he said: 'So, I hear of a Mr Money Bags missing, failing to keep the date with Patsy Leach. Colin, she knows what big cash is and if she says Money Bags, even in a quip, she means a lot. Then I hear of Mills-Silver's supplier disappearing, too. I have to ask, is this the same substantial character? If we're talking about half a million, cash, how many people of that rank around the place, after all?'

'You, for a start.'

'You're kind, Col.'

'Jack, intuition's leaping a bit here? But, yes, it's possibly one and the same man.'

'Don't you think it would be very useful to know whom she was waiting for?'

'Could be.'

'Carnality Strand – it attracts a year-in, year-out clientèle, yes? A faithful clientèle, you could say.'

'I believe so.'

'If Patsy and her friend have been there before, someone like that voyeur might have seen him and could help identify.'

'Yes.'

'Find the auto-auto fuck and you could be going somewhere.'

'Right. But you've only got a description of the behind. It'll make a great photo-fit.'

'Well, and the car, Col, of course. I told you, this kid is professional and tutored by me. Our solitary friend's in an old Senator.' Lamb pulled out a hotel match packet and passed it over. 'The number's on there, Col. Get the Vehicle Licence Centre into action. You might even find a link with the kidnapping, which is the bit that interests me. Anything to find the child.'

This afternoon Harpur had parked the Senator a couple of streets away from the launderette, thank God. Scrapyard next. 'This could be useful, Jack.'

'You always erupt with enthusiasm, Col,' Lamb said, gathering in his own wash and leaving. 'I have to go and look at a couple of Tissots.'

'Where from?' Harpur forced himself to ask.

'Late nineteenth century.'

Chapter 26

'Myself, I think you came looking for the Leach child, Ralph.'

'Lynette? How would she be in Kew for heaven's sake, Mother?'
It seemed terrible to be calling her that, but she insisted.

'It's nice in you – the concern over this girl,' she replied. 'Even
Maskrey says that. You accepted risk for her sake, and so you're
a prisoner. Behind that scar you're a very feeling person.'

'Leopold was the one I came to see.'

'You have grace and nobility, Ralph.'

These big places in London were built with their own wine
cellars and they had fixed up a bed for Ember among the old,
empty racks by putting a mattress on the floor and giving him a
couple of blankets. These were good blankets, obviously from a
prestige shop in the West End. Up here, even when they buried
you in a stone pit, there was a lavish touch. The cellar had
electricity for light and a fire and yesterday Potter brought him
a couple of books, the usual stiff-covered shit by Charles Dickens
and Thomas Hardy that looked as old as the house, but he had
opened one of the buggers called *The Return of the Native*, in case
Potter asked. Mother was lying naked under the blankets with
Ember. He had kept a singlet on: somehow it seemed untoward
to strip off totally with a woman of this age, especially known as
Mother. Of course, she had wanted the light on when they made
love, because she enjoyed looking at his face. So many were like
that with him. He could understand. Ember was tender with her
altogether, not just the matter of the singlet: plenty of gentle finger
tracing and stroking on her arms and thighs. Mother seemed full of
sweetness and joy, pulling his head fondly down so that her spiky
hair-do could rub gently under his chin. He did not mind that.
Women were entitled to express themselves, old or not. 'Lynette?

So, now you mention her, is she here?' he said, as if the idea had just hit him.

'These houses have double cellars, one on each side. The other for coal, originally, of course. But it's been cleaned up a treat. And dry.'

He lay still and listened, trying to pick up any vestige of sound coming from elsewhere at the same depth in the house.

'The cellars are secure,' Mother said. 'Well look at the door of this one. It would stop Panzers.'

'But, Mother, if— '

'What's to be done with her? Well, of course. It's a hell of a situation. If she's traded eventually for ransom, she could talk afterwards, couldn't she? Pinpoint us. Or if no ransom, come to that, which looks more and more likely to me. It wasn't thought right through. Now, these kids, Potter and Maskrey, are left with the problem, and they can't handle it. Well, there is no way to handle it, except the brutally obvious.'

He did not ask what that meant. It could apply to him, also. He began to sweat.

'That's why they're desperate to find Leopold. He's the thinker. If you look like that you have to have something. He knows what he intended when it all started.' Mother rolled out of the bed and, taking her clothes from where they had been draped on the racks, began to dress. This was a body that went back to the parting of the Red Sea, yet she had the bravery to show it, the rounded shoulders and poor blue knees. She was in multi-coloured Bermudas and a dark red angora sweater tonight. 'Those two lads have been very good with Lynette – no flesh infringements. Leopold, I'm less sure about. He gets so little of it, as was said. Who'd fuck that set of teeth? He feels loveless. That's basic to Leopold's personality. Maskrey and I had something very intermittent going for a while – well, he's just a kid – and this really got to Leopold, seemed to make him even dwarfier?'

'But she's all right?'

'Lynette? That's what I mean about you being nice at heart, Ralph. You're troubled, genuinely. Oh, she's getting decent grub and Radio 1. Potter's gone down to your place, the Monty, to see if he can pick up a line on Leopold.'

'Still no trace?'

'Potter's pretty sharp and thorough.' Blowing Ember a kiss, she walked up the cellar to the heavy oak door. She shook the handle and in a moment a key turned on the other side and Maskrey let her out. Ember noticed her touch his hand fondly, which must be for old time's sake. He hoped to God there was not going to be jealousy and ill-will over Mother. Obviously, she was the last thing in the world he had wanted fondling from, but she had come to him, shy and smiling, probably her own teeth, which explained why she had spoken badly of Leopold's, and carrying a 20p-off pack of six barley wines. Well, Maskrey himself had let her in, so how could he turn sour now?

He and Mother stood in the doorway looking down at Ember on the mattress. 'Shall I switch out the light before I lock up, Ralph?' he asked. 'It's late.'

'No, I'll read a bit.'

'Reading can be one hell of a comfort for some,' Maskrey said. 'I can't cotton on to it myself.' He took a couple of steps into the cellar and picked up *The Return of the Native* from the floor and read the title. 'This to do with what Enoch Powell wanted?'

'Books I'm very much in favour of. Always have been,' Ember said.

'I suppose your wife will be fretting,' Maskrey replied, putting the book down. 'Did you do disappearances before – women and so on? You can see now what Mother meant when she said you were lucky you didn't leave a car parked, can't you, especially if anything of value in it?'

'Yes, very lucky. If I could give my wife a call, to say I'm all right? No geography or anything.'

'You really are so considerate, Ralph,' Mother said.

'Potter and I don't want any contact from you with the outside for the moment, Ralph. He'd like to arrive at the club out of the blue. I wouldn't be surprised to see him back with Leopold tomorrow, so there'll be a chance for a re-think.'

After Maskrey shut the door, Ember looked at the first page of *The Return of the Native* again and then threw the book at the wall. He picked up another one, called *Barnaby Rudge*, and hurled it as well, but without opening it. Charles Dickens and Thomas Hardy were calibre figures, unquestionably, and great for schools, but some books seemed at their best when they stayed shut. He sat on the mattress and tried once more to hear anything from Lynette.

Chapter 27

Megan was away in London once more on some literary weekend and whatever went with it, so Harpur had to ferry the children around to judo and a skateboard shop, then a disco in the evening. When these duties were over he thought he might slip down to the Monty again and check whether Ralph Ember really was missing. Jack Lamb did not usually go in for speculation, but even his speculation tended to be prime. They would be getting tired of Harpur at the Club.

'So what happened to the disgusting old Senator?' Hazel asked on their way to the skateboard shop.

'I needed a change.'

'This is even mouldier,' Jill said.

He had taken a once-silver Cortina from the pool. 'Anonymity is my middle name,' he replied.

'But does it help you find the kidnapped kid who's in all the papers?' Jill said.

'It will.'

'Shouldn't you be giving that your total snoop effort, not chauffering middle-class respectables to social trivia?' Hazel asked.

'Possibly.'

'Can she be still alive, anyway?' Hazel said.

'Of course,' Harpur snarled. 'We have to believe that, for God's sake.'

'Oh, for fuzz morale? Team talks?' Hazel replied. 'I meant realistically.'

'Leave him alone, can't you?' Jill told her. 'Third degreeing. Who do you think you are, West Midlands? He has to play mother and drive us, hasn't he, if the real one's not here? "Fictionality and

Historicity in *Mary* fart-arsing *Barton*." Is that Micky Spillane? Does she really have to dodge off to such things all the time, Dad? I suppose there's more to it, on the side.'

'Lubricious,' Hazel remarked.

'You shouldn't speak of your mother as she,' Harpur said. 'Twice.'

'Why?' Jill asked.

'I don't know,' Harpur said. 'Isn't it supposed to be disrespectful?'

'I speak of you as he.'

'Men can take it.'

He reached the Monty at what would be the early part of the evening for the club, after leaving the girls at their disco: he was forbidden to go too near that, or to pick them up afterwards, which always fretted him. Margaret Ember was behind the bar, her face still marked but beginning to recover, though her nose looked bad. Harpur's arrival caused the usual moments of resentful silence and tension, but nothing comparable to the effect Iles would have had: Harpur was treated as a manageable pest, the ACC as a raging plague, and Iles always said Harpur would be kept for ever at middling rank by a pathetic lack of core malice. Many of the faces in the club this evening were familiar to Harpur from cells or interrogation rooms or Lord Mayor's banquets or red-light areas. He gave a friendly nod here and there, with few responses: Iles would at least have raised a grin of recognition from some of the girls he commissioned now and then when he was low, or high.

Harpur went to the bar. 'Running the shop, Mrs Ember?'

'Briefly.'

'I know the feeling. Ralph's away?'

'Briefly.'

'I know the feeling. Could we talk somewhere?'

'Ralph prefers to be here if it's talk with people like you. Because it's so fascinating.'

'Give him a ring. Ask him to come.'

'I told you, he's away.'

'Could you ring him if you wanted to?'

'I don't follow.'

'Do you know where he is?'

'Of course.'

159

'It's not another Caring-style disappearance?'

'I don't know anything about that.'

The bar help arrived. 'Come and sit at a table again, Margaret,' Harpur said. He took a drink over to behind the one-armed bandit and after a while she joined him, carrying a cup of tea. 'Has Mills-Silver been in hunting him?' Harpur asked.

'Piers Mills-Silver? Fabrics king?'

'There's another?'

'No, why should he?'

'Sometimes I think of putting non-stop police protection on this place, you know. It's a vortex.'

'I'll mention that to Ralph. Sexier name than the Monty.'

'No other ungovernable visitors? A few people here tonight I don't recognise.'

'All properly signed in. Ralph's very fussy. "Ungovernable visitors"? I don't get it.'

'You haven't walked into any more doors?' he explained. To show concern, Harpur touched her arm. She withdrew it immediately, then glanced about the club, obviously ashamed, making certain nobody had witnessed the contact.

She stood up. 'It might be better if we went somewhere private.' She took him into a store room at the end of the bar and they sat at opposite ends on metal barrels.

Harpur said: 'Well, look, Mrs Ember, would you give Ralph a phone call now, just so I can talk to him and be sure he's in touch and all right?'

'He wouldn't like that.'

'I don't want to know where you're dialling. Just to hear his voice.'

'It would be the principle of it, Mr Harpur. Why can't he go where he wishes? He's free. I hear your wife, for instance, goes where she likes. Do I ask you where?'

'My fear is he's done a permanent flit, with a fair whack of prize money.'

She stared at him out of her bright, endlessly hostile, dark eyes, in that bright, scarred face, showing next to nothing he could read, then lifted the cup and drank some tea. Although she drank daintily and silently, Harpur heard 'Fuck off, copper.' Panicking Ralph had done well to land this woman. Did he realise how well?

'Was he holding a lot of cash?' Harpur asked.

'We haven't been doing too brilliantly. Look at it now, and this is a Saturday night. Big deal. We bank our takings immediately, anyway.'

'Some think Ralph's a bit of a banker himself. Deposits from Exeter?'

'What does that mean?'

'What's he doing away?'

'He wouldn't want me to discuss that.'

'A woman?' Harpur had to give a bit of pressure. 'Ralph's regarded as a looker, apparently. I don't see it, but I'm not a girl.'

'Your wife's a looker, I believe. And brainy?'

'I'm thinking of two points, really – trying to weigh this situation from your point of view, Margaret. He could be lavishing all this cash on some bird, birds, rather than you and the children. We're possibly talking about hundreds of thousands.'

'And what's the other point?'

'He might be in peril, obviously.'

She smiled a smile of goodbye and stood up again. 'I'll be in peril myself if he comes back and finds me neglecting the bar.'

'Come back when?'

'Oh, any time. You know Ralph.'

'I'm not sure.' Banker? Wanker? 'Are you taking up the ACC's suggestion on the cosmetic surgeon?'

'I've seen him. I'll be going in soon for work on my hooter.'

'Mr Iles will be glad he can help, sometimes.'

'I'm glad he can help, sometimes.'

He gave up then. Nothing else would come. Nothing else? What had come at all?

The Chief and Iles were at some formal, inter-Force sports dinner over in the county tonight and Harpur drove to near the ACC's house, *Idylls*, in Rougement Place, walking the last couple of hundred yards. Whenever he went there, Sarah would open the front door with a great flourish, holding it wide, the light streaming all over him, as if he belonged, and then her arms would be wide, too, to embrace and welcome him. It was like coming home from the war. They would kiss on the doorstep, a long kiss, a reclaiming and victorious kiss. She said she hated secretiveness. On the other

161

hand, Harpur quite liked secretiveness, largely lived by it. There was a big, tree-lined drive that probably hid the greeting from the road and Rougement Place neighbours, but Harpur worried all the same. He tried never to show it, either in words or physical tension. Life threw enough cold water on love affairs, without his adding to it.

One of her other tastes when they were in the house was for them to undress each other downstairs in the grubby living room, or drawing room, as Harpur had heard Iles call it once when off guard. This added up to another of her assertions that things between them were above board and glorious and almost domestic. Himself, he was not too keen on the domestic tinge, but again he made no objection, because it seemed important to her. Sometimes they would begin their love-making in this room, on an armchair where discarded sweet packets or old copies of *Radio Times* might rustle under the weight, or standing against book shelves or a wall. Tonight it was against a wall, alongside a Victorian portrait in oil of some woman Iles said was an ancestor and could be, judging by her look of cheerful insolence. Sarah's head knocked against it a couple of times now, pushing the forebear askew: was Harpur bringing crude chaos to this dynasty? Sarah hardly seemed to notice. At such times she did not seem to notice much at all, except what they were doing. He held her under her bottom and she took her feet off the ground and gripped him around the hips with her legs, moving back and forth on him like on a swing, muttering her love.

It was a treat to go upstairs behind her then, recalling times as a kid when he had tried to gaze at women's knickers on bus stairs, only now there were no knickers, just the gleaming skin, and lovely blurred blue hint of veins in her thighs and behind, and the thick line of fair hair between her legs. What growing older gave you was perspective.

In the big bed she said: 'Just lie still there for a minute, as if we were sleeping together, husband, wife. I mean, really sleeping.'

'What, now?'

'Like people who live together.'

'It's difficult.'

'I know. Try. Hold me close.' In a moment she said: 'That'll do. Now, closer. Have you heard of this new non-penetrative sex? No? Nor me.' The telephone rang. 'I'll have to answer. It will wake the baby. And it could be Des.' She rolled away and picked up the receiver. In a while she said: 'He's not here now. Who is it? Luke who? I see. Of course.' She turned back towards Harpur and waved a hand urgently in what he took to be a signal to get to the other extension. Leaving the bed he went quickly downstairs without dressing and gingerly picked up the phone in the room they had recently left.

A man was speaking, local accent, a kind of whine, falling at times to a whisper. 'And Mr Iles says always let him know, confidential, when anything out of the ordinary comes up. This is the established basis of my work.'

'I see,' Sarah said.

Harpur moved over to straighten the oil painting of the woman. The end of his cock touched the leafy wallpaper and left a damp mark, which he tried to rub out with his fist, spreading it.

'I wouldn't trouble you with this, Mrs Iles, but it's happening now, while I'm speaking, that's the thing. It's something Mr Iles might want to get to personally right away.'

'I expect headquarters could radio reach him if I gave them a call, though he's probably an hour's driving away. Or they could easily send someone else.'

The voice grew strained, even angry. 'No, please, not through headquarters. Not someone else, either. That's not how it works. A source is what I'm known as – like on TV about Stalker and so on? Sources have to be private, never referred to on a switchboard. Nor over radio or car phones. It's hairy, my activity. We deal only one to one – a trade phrase. You know that word umbilical, at all? How it is.'

'Yes. What is it that's happening, Luke?'

'Not my real name, naturally. A disciple. The beloved physician, Mr Iles said. What's called a code ID, between me and him.'

'What is it that's happening, Luke?'

'Even telling you, Mrs Iles – well, I have to be careful. His wife, I know, but— '

'He may come in at any moment. So I can tell him immediately.'

Harpur gave up rubbing the wall and hoped the mark would dry out. He found himself listening almost as intently for the sound of a car in the drive as he was to the telephone voice. He tried to imagine, and then not to imagine, someone coming home and finding a man bollock naked, apparently answering his phone. Not just someone, Iles. There was a pause at the other end of the line and then, as if he saw no choice, the beloved physician said: 'Yes, well someone in the Monty club, someone there now at this moment asking around if we've seen or heard a guy called Leopold. Don't ask me Leopold What. Well, that's the point, really. This boy closes up if you ask him his own name or what this Leopold's other name is, or where they come from. But he's really worried about Leopold, anyone can see. This is what made me think, ring Mr Iles. All I know, this Leopold came down from somewhere and was going to look for Mr Monty, that's Ralphy Ember, and it seems Leopold has disappeared. Traceless. Very small. Bald. Brass buckle shoes. So Mr Iles said always to let him know on the quiet about anything that came up re Ralph. Ralph's on the edge of so much, or more than the edge. I got to a phone box.'

'You might run out of money.'

'A pound in. Don't worry about business expenses. Mr Iles sees me right.'

'Good. Luke, I could tell one of his most trusted colleagues. Not headquarters. No switchboard. He'd get over there right away.'

'Not Harpur?'

'Well, yes. I might be able to reach him, as a matter of fact.'

'Most trusted? Mr Iles always says tell Harpur total nothing. Especially not Harpur. Mr Iles likes to have these matters first. That's how it works, Mrs Iles. Private. Like a toothbrush? Or a belly-button. As I said, umbilical? To be frank, Mr Iles said he would make a big grief for me if I ever told Mr Harpur anything, and Mr Iles could. He knows certain unfavourable matters. Do you understand?'

'Certainly.'

'Harpur quite kosher? He was up the Monty tonight earlier, putting his hand on Mrs Ember's arm. Then they go into a private room in a hurry, door closed. Something crafty, of intimacy, between those two? I'm walking on ice. In this profession I have to know exactly where I am.'

'Interesting.'

'What I thought, if Mr Iles could get here now, corner this lad who's asking the questions, it could lead on, couldn't it? Where does he come from? Where did this Leopold come from? Will you tell Mr Iles that? It could lead to – well, there's a bank robbery outstanding and talk about loot floating, people scouring for it from all over, maybe this Leopold, and then this terrible kidnapping. It could be all mixed in, all important. Information's a commodity, Mrs Iles.'

'I'll tell him at once.'

'But not that trusted colleague.'

'No, not that trusted colleague. Will you go back there now?'

'Sources disappear once they've performed their role.'

'But so as to point the man out.'

'Those who point out point themselves out. It's been nice talking to you. I don't suppose it will happen again.'

When Harpur went back to the bedroom, Sarah said: 'Should you go?'

'Well, yes, I should.'

'I was afraid of that.'

'But perhaps not at once.'

'I was hoping that.'

'The picture's straight again,' he said.

'*Inter alia.*'

He climbed back into the bed. After a time she said: 'You're a very loving policeman.'

'Can't think of a better citation.'

'You might need it. Why would Desmond try to cut you out like that?'

'Oh, just the way our noble game's always played, Sarah. I never even knew he had tipsters. An ACC! Your husband's very gifted, the sod.'

'Yes? So tell me about Mrs Ember – fondling her arm, a private room.'

'It was work. I'd better get over there,' he replied.

When Harpur arrived, at around midnight, the Monty was heaving. It would be tough finding anyone in this scrum. He made for the bar once more and Margaret Ember. She looked sickened to see him. 'Again, for heaven's sake?' she said.

'Someone here looking for a man called Leopold?'

'Leopold? Who's Leopold?'

'A visitor.'

'I can't help. And now here's the other bugger, in colour.' She began to shout, almost: 'Are you trying to kill the club – drive everyone away?'

He turned to see Iles pushing through the mob towards him, still wearing his dark blue and gold formal uniform, though no hat, and looking majestic.

'What the fuck are you doing here, Harpur?' he inquired.

'I had a tip.'

'What tip?'

A huge, half-drunk fair-haired customer of about fifty in a white summer suit came up alongside Iles, saw the uniform and said something Harpur did not hear, then laughed tumultuously and repeated whatever it was to a couple of slags with him. Turning, Iles quickly took him by the throat with one hand and threw him across the room so that he knocked over two tables and a dozen glasses. People leapt up cursing to avoid the cascading drink. The man fell limbs adrift among the wreckage, his outfit blotched top to toe by rum.

'What tip would that be, Col?' the ACC asked.

'Someone searching for a man called Leopold.'

'Leopold?' Iles asked. 'This is a new one on us, isn't it?'

'Well, yes, sir. Why are you here? Have you been home?' How else would the bugger know he should come here.

'Home? Why do you ask?'

'And Ember's certainly missing,' Harpur replied.

'I was just passing.' The ACC knew the most basic rule of them all: protect your source. 'One likes to look in and see things are as civilised as ever here. I've a soft spot for the Monty, that's always my trouble. Where did your tip come from, Col?'

'I was going to drift around the crowd and see if I could trace this stranger.'

'Where did this tip reach you, Col?'

'I don't know whether you'd mind helping me on this trawl, sir.'

'It doesn't sound too difficult. I usually find people here exceptionally accommodating.'

The crowd had already started to thin very fast. Harpur located nobody who could help. By the time he and Iles had finished looking the club was more or less cleared.

In the car park afterwards, the fair-haired hulk in the decorated sun gear came rushing at Iles, screaming about bringing the posse and flashing wide fists. The ACC hit him once under the right eye and the man sat down hard. Iles swung back his foot and simulated a powerful kick, letting his patent shoe pass beautifully close to the left ear. Then Iles picked up a dog turd from the ground and rubbed it first into the man's coiffure and afterwards the shoulders and lapels of the East of Suez jacket, making quite a thing of cleaning his hand. 'You've got some good finger-prints there, sonny. Treasure them.'

He turned back to Harpur. 'Your tip said this character was actually in the club? And you came at once? Your house is not too far from here, either.'

'But we missed him, sir. Possibly you scared him off. That gold on the shoulders panics people.'

At home, Harpur's daughters had not arrived back. He resisted the urge to go looking for them and went to bed but did not sleep. At around 3 a.m. he heard the front door click and then lay awake for another hour. He went quietly and checked that both were in their beds, flat out: sometimes they pulled the ploy of first one home to make a noise opening and closing the two bedroom doors, cover for the girl still not back. After this, he dozed pretty well for almost four hours.

Chapter 28

On Saturday nights, Anna Chitty's older daughter, who had turned fifteen, usually went to a disco in the town and came home late. Anna was not allowed to meet her afterwards. That she understood, but the waiting always made her very anxious and she rarely slept until the girl was in. Tonight, at a time she preferred not to check on, Anna heard the front door open and close and then footsteps on the stairs. She turned over and began to relax. A moment later, her bedroom door was opened and the beam of a flashlight found the bed and her face. She sat up, very afraid, sure it was some echo from the past.

A man's voice whispered: 'Take it easy. This is only a search for information. The name wouldn't mean anything. Connection with your late hub, though at a bit of a remove, true.'

'There are children here,' she replied, and then thought how feeble this was. 'You're in my house with no right. Get out. Get out. All that's finished. I'm somebody else now.'

'We'd all like to be that.' He closed the door behind him, switched on the light and put the torch into his pocket. About twenty, he was thin, and stooped, his face long, pale, not showing much. He had on a navy jersey and black cords. In the old days, there had been people like this around Peter all the time, people who had never worked and would never work, who could see a chance of easy money as soon as it gave a hint, but knew how to keep the excitement out of their face, in case others picked up the signs and wanted some, too.

'Oh, look, you could pull a sheet up over yourself?' he said. She slept naked. 'I can be out of here in no time absolutely no bother. I came down from elsewhere on behalf of friends with two names for calling on: that rat-hole, the Monty Club, and, clearly, Mrs

Anna Chitty, wife of the late Pete. The club's a dead loss. And it's dicey. I think I've been spotted. So, here we are.'

She did what he said and covered herself.

'We all knew of Peter, though no meeting. You were estranged, but still a real sadness, I'm sure. That boy had a reputation, and to finish up as he did was such a sickener. None of us regarded it as equitable, not anyone in my circle. But now it's one of this circle, a lad called Leopold, who is himself the worry. I've been sent to find him. We're nothing without Leopold. He's been around this area, no question. The woman in the club's badly marked on the face. Leopold likes to make a point.'

Anna heard the front door again. The visitor heard it, too, and switched off the light. She was aware of him crossing the room to stand very close to her. In the dark, she could not make out whether he had a pistol in his hand or the flashlight again.

'My daughter,' Anna muttered.

'Daughter? Three in the morning? Our notes say the eldest's fifteen.'

'Only once a week.'

They listened to her come up the stairs, go into the bathroom, then close her own door. He sat on the bed in the darkness. 'Look, we're in a spot, Anna. There are two lives that could depend on all this – on finding Leopold, finding him intact. Otherwise, we might be forced to cut our losses. Put it this way: your kid does come home, eventually, yes? Try and think of a girl not coming home, ever.'

The words hit her astonishingly hard. At once she guessed he had to be talking about Caring and Patsy's child – the girl's life, plus another, he said. To think of people like this holding a girl made her shake with anger or dread.

'You ought to wear something in bed,' he said.

She tried to imagine it, a girl never coming home. It was an intolerable idea, and, in the middle of her fear of this man she suddenly found a wish to help the girl, Lynette, if she could. Once or twice in the old days, when Anna was still with Peter, she had met the girl. She remembered little about her, and nothing very attractive, but a kidnapped child was a kidnapped child. Whatever you could do you did, surely to God.

He said: 'I'm here to locate Leopold, that's all. I can be away

169

in no time. We thought he might make contact – you, at least your husband, being on our books from way back.'

'Yes,' she said.

'Leopold came to see you?'

'Yes.'

He leaned forward and she found herself pulling the sheet tighter around herself. 'Ever hear that line from *The Cruel Sea*, "I'm a tit man myself"? Well, I'm a leg man myself. I expect you're used to very rough people in your time, Mrs Chitty. Me, I can enjoy just the conversation. Now, excuse me, but to be sure we have the right person.'

'Small, bald, good clothes, bad teeth. Some charm, but muted.'

'Came to your place, here?'

'Here.' She reasoned that if she said it had been the Monty he might go back there and scratch about until he discovered the whole story on Leopold. That could be dangerous.

'How did he find it? I had a job and I'm good at that sort of game.'

'He seemed pretty bright to me.'

'Yes, he's bright, but broad-stroke bright.'

'He was wanting news of Caring. Whereabouts. I was a sort of last hope, I think.' She managed a laugh.

'That's right. What we all want, his whereabouts.'

'I couldn't help, still can't. But I told him Caring might make contact. Now and then he does. Old time's sake.'

'Ah.' She was aware of him staring at her in the darkness.

'He said to let him know if that happened.'

'Let him know? Leopold gave you somewhere to contact?'

She laughed again. 'Oh, no, that's not likely is it? Advertise your own place? Hardly.'

'Hardly.'

'He's going to keep in touch with me here. Give me a call now and then, or oftener.' She wanted this man out of the place, and yet must not lose him if she was to help the child.

'Is that right?' he said. 'Leopold will be in contact with you?'

'That was his plan,' she said.

'And?'

'And?'

'Well, what happened next? He's missing, Anna. Where was he going?'

'He was looking for Caring.'

'Looking where?'

'He didn't say. Would he tell me? Hardly.'

'Look, is this right, Anna?'

'It's not much, is it? What there is of it is right.'

'It's good. It's as much as we have. So, listen, I'll keep in touch, too. I'll give you a call now and then.'

'Good.' Great.

'When I do, I'll just say my name is Three A.M., to mark this occasion. He hasn't called yet, has he? We're all very concerned.'

'Not yet.'

'You'll tell him we're concerned? To get in touch?'

'Of course. You said two lives.'

'Right.'

'Who else?'

'Else? I've said no names at all.'

'Do you need to?'

'Of course not, you're a sharp one. You've been with track record people, and you read the papers, watch the television. Yes, she's one of them – those lives.'

'And— ?'

'You get down in the warm now and sleep. I'll let myself out.'

Chapter 29

Under a purple and ochre wall tapestry in the big lounge at Kew, Ember listened with everything he had to each of the words, trying to work out if what he was hearing was all he should be hearing. Had Anna Chitty said more than he was being told, and how much more? Did this lot know what had happened to Leopold?

Potter explained, the scrounger's face as blank and calm as ever: 'Anna gave me some load of shit about Leopold having been there, to her place, and intending to phone her soon. Oh, I don't doubt she's seen him – a real description – but not there. That didn't sound right at all. And, beside, Leopold would never have found it. Maybe she witnessed something sensitive and final at the club? I played along. There was a fifteen-year-old kid possibly awake in one of the bedrooms and other kids around the house, so a lot of tumult and notice if anything went wrong. I had to get out as soon as I could. Mother, I saw pretty soon I'd done it all wrong. I asked her to imagine her own child being missing, and it got to her, put her against me, I could tell at once from her voice. I should have talked straight out about the money. I'm one who can admit a mistake now.'

'Children are an emotional minefield,' Mother said forgivingly.

'She'll go to the police, no doubt of it. This is the one-time wife of a really seasoned boy like Peter Chitty, but she's going to tell the police and they'll tap her line for when I ring her and do a trace. She guessed we have Lynette.'

'That wouldn't be too difficult,' Mother remarked. She had on a camouflage combat jacket and khaki trousers this afternoon.

'Or if I come back they'll be waiting. So, obviously, no more contact there. She was clever even at 3 a.m. – didn't push it too hard and ask for a number to call. She's been around, knows what's on and what's not.'

'Kidnapping's special. It upsets some people,' Mother replied.

Ember said: 'She wouldn't contact police, not Anna Chitty, regardless.'

'In your club, was she, and Leopold there, too? Who knocked your wife about, for Christ's sake, if it wasn't Leopold?'

'I haven't seen him,' Ember replied. He tried a joke to show he could – to show himself he could: 'He's memorable enough.'

'This makes things very poor for you,' Maskrey told him, 'and the kid, obviously. I don't see how either of you can live, to put it basically. And then you fucking our Mother.'

'For God's sake, there was barley wine,' Ember replied. 'She came to me.' He felt more trapped and scared in this big room now than at any time locked up in the cellar.

'Leopold would greatly disapprove of interfering with Mother,' Maskrey said.

'And then blaming it on the lady and ale,' Potter added.

'I confirm I made some of the running,' Mother told them. 'Ralph's a genuine draw.'

'Leopold's never going to show, that's the fact of it,' Potter said.

'Look, don't despair, you weed,' Maskrey replied. He was probably younger than Potter, maybe less than twenty, yet had the edge. It was not just clothes, though the pinstripe suit he had today looked good enough for the High Court, a lawyer in the High Court.

'So who knocked your wife about, Ralphy?' Potter asked again.

'She flirts over the bar. I got mad.'

'Not in you, Ralphy,' Potter replied. 'You're a gent.'

'Now, do you want to tell us where Leopold is? And if he's coming back?' Maskrey asked.

'I don't know, boys,' Ember told them. 'But of course he'll be back. Look, of course he will be.' Jesus, to finish up cornered among bric-a-brac by a couple of juveniles and an old woman. Where was all that great past now?

Potter made himself sound like a general, that down-grade face so solemn: 'Here's my scenario, based on what I picked up and, I must admit, on instinct. The basic element is – Ralphy here and Caring Oliver are in close and constant touch somehow, or were until we took Ralphy.'

'Tell us news,' Mother said.

This was the room where, all that time ago, Ember had come to collect weapons on Caring's behalf for the Exeter job, a high-taste room, with the tapestries, antiques, a *chaise longue* and thick, heavy curtains the subtle colour of status. They had brought Ember up from the cellar for what was called this 're-appraisal of key matters'. Ember had known it was not good, even before Potter started talking. They had defeat and agony all over them, these two, Potter and even Maskrey. Kids of this make, you didn't know what they could do in such a state, but it would not be sweet or kind or selfless. Ember thought again about making a run. He felt pinned here, yes, but once he was back in the cellar he would have no chance at all. At least this room had three doors and four windows. He could see the street. He even saw a blue-lamp police car drift past. But Maskrey and Potter had Ember nicely in an alcove and sat facing him, pretty close. This house was probably full of armament still, and they both looked a bit bulky up at shoulder holster level. Now and then he thought Mother might help somehow – might talk for him, or help him get out on the quiet, risk-free. Yet she was not saying much for him now. She seemed relaxed, but maybe she feared these two as much as he did, and the way they might tumble into mad savagery, as modern youth so often did.

Potter went on: 'Yes, Caring and Ralph in alliance, an enduring part of the old Exeter bank team: Caring maybe still abroad, maybe not. Anyway, a distance. So Ralphy comes up to reconnoitre this place in case the kid's here: Ralphy's had a visit from Leopold and puts two and two together about the girl's whereabouts. Ralphy could seem harmless enough, compared with Caring looking around here himself. Everyone would know why Caring had come, if he got spotted, like Ralphy was spotted. This is cat's paw work, the kind the dossier says Ralphy often used to get.'

'Sounds right,' Maskrey commented.

174

'No, excuse me, but not right at all,' Ember gasped.

'So the real point is, Caring could be here next, if we've been targetted?' Maskrey said. He sounded near to break-down.

Potter looked towards the windows: 'Caring and God knows who else. He can afford to hire.'

'Could very well be,' Mother remarked.

Jesus, some gratitude for prolonged loving attention in that cellar bed, when all she should really be expecting was a catheter in an eventide home. She was standing with her elbow resting on a mahogany chest, looking burly in her commando gear, and yet still womanly and warm.

'We've got to disappear,' Potter said. 'Fast.'

'Finish things here and go,' Maskrey added. 'This whole enterprise is disaster. It's been wrong from the start. Taking that cottage at the Reens – supposed to be close to the ransom funds – was the first mistake, and it's got worse and worse.'

Mother turned her head and gazed with real fondness at Ember: 'Look, Ralph, whatever happens here, it wouldn't be revenge. I'd hate you to think of it like that, never mind what you might have pulled against Leopold down there.'

'Pulled nothing,' Ember declared. 'I'd always regard him as a distinguished friend.'

'This is something inevitable, because of the way events have turned out,' she went on. 'It's our survival package, nothing else. You know how priorities operate.'

'So we'll go back down to the cellar, right, Ralph?' Potter said. 'Here's the same Smith and Wesson K-frame as you had in Exeter, but silenced, so if you make trouble in this room it's of not much odds, except defacing the tapestry, and that's all right now, because we're getting out.' He brought out a pistol from under his anorak.

'Ralph goes along with orderly government, don't you, Ralph?' Mother remarked.

Maskrey stood.

Ember, on a beautiful old straight chair against the wall, decided he had better speak and offer while his voice could still get around the words: 'Look, I can put you in touch with really first-class money.'

Maskrey kept moving towards the kitchen and the door down

to the cellar. 'My impression, my information, is Caring's holding all the big stuff – the way Caring always does,' Maskrey said.

'Some in my car, and then a lot more at the club,' Ember said. 'It's a fact.'

'Car?' Mother asked.

'Well, yes. I didn't want to say at first. I'm sorry. Things are different now.'

'Car where?' she said.

'A street by the station.'

'You think it's still going to be there after how many days, you hallucinating jerk?' she said.

'Maybe stolen, maybe towed to the police pound,' Maskrey said.

'I could go and get it from the pound.'

Maskrey suddenly turned back, grabbed Ember by the hair and pulled him up out of his chair, screaming into his face: 'We're likely to let you near police, aren't we? That car could have interest now, if the Chitty woman has started talking. They'll have gone through it.'

'How much?' Mother asked.

'One hundred and twenty or thirty grand,' Ember replied.

'It's not worth the risk,' she said.

'Just a matter of opening the boot, perhaps,' Ember replied.

Maskrey let him go and turned again towards the kitchen. 'Forget it.'

'Yes, if it's where you left it, it's because they know there's something wrong and they're waiting for one of us to show,' Mother said.

'They'd have been knocking front doors already if that was so,' Ember told her. His brain could keep going even in heavy stress sometimes.

'He could be right,' Potter said.

'This is forty grand each for you, maybe no bother,' Ember told them. 'I'd let my own share go.' He gave them a hurt smile to show he knew they would take it, anyway.

'We'll need something to help a disappearance, Mother,' Potter said. He bent that thin, weak-looking body towards her, as a way of pushing the argument. You could see the bugger specialised in leaning over counters to pick up hand-out cheques. Forty thousand was a very big hand-out, and he would be the one of these three to realise it first.

Mother thought about this and straightened up alongside the mahogany. 'Handcuff him then,' she said. 'We come straight back if the car's gone, or any sign of a watch.'

They manacled him to Potter's skinny wrist and hid the metal with their sleeves. Ember took the three of them to where he had left the Montego. In a way he was grateful for the handcuffs because Potter took some of his weight and kept him upright despite that wobble in his legs. The car was not there. 'I could have it wrong,' he said. They tried three or four more streets without success and then went back to the house. Taking him straight down to the cellar, they closed the door behind them.

'You did come by train, didn't you? You're pissing us about,' Maskrey said. 'Delaying, looking for a chance to make a break.'

'No, but listen, there's a ton of money in my club,' he told them. He was hoarse with terror and spoke in a sort of shouted whisper, which would have made even the truth sound like lies.

'Balls, Ralph,' Mother said.

Potter undid the cuff from his own wrist and fixed Ember's arms behind his back. The metal skidded on the sweat. Then Maskrey pushed him against the wine racks.

'I can show you,' Ember said.

'Oh, fine. We all go to the club and you pull something,' Maskrey replied. 'We know you've got skills from the old days, Ralph. Or the police are there, because of Anna. They were crawling everywhere already. Now, really all over the place.'

'In any case, Caring's holding all the real cash,' Mother said. 'We've heard of Caring's magic touch.'

And so Ember came clean. 'Caring's dead,' he whispered.

Mother did not even pause: 'God, come on, Ralph. This is going to happen because it's got to happen. I hate to see you wriggle.'

'It's true,' Ember said.

'Do it now, boys,' she told Maskrey and Potter. 'This is sickening. I've conferred my body on this man, and listen to him whimper.'

'I can take you to Caring. Show you,' Ember said.

Again it was Potter who wanted to believe. 'Yes? So where is he, then? Another spot where police are waiting?'

177

'Nobody knows, except me.'

'This is crap, from top to toe,' Mother said. 'I want us to proceed.' She was like Fidel Castro, that outfit, that know-all voice. 'And then the child. We've got to go. Caring will be here. Caring, plus an army.'

'He won't,' Ember said. 'Don't you think he would have shown with funds before now? He loved that child.'

'I nearly believe him,' Potter said. 'Somehow.'

'Somehow?' Mother replied. 'You smell easy cash again, that's all.'

'Something wrong with that?' Potter asked.

'You're telling us you've got Caring's share tucked up?' Maskrey asked.

'A lot of it,' Ember said.

'This would change things, wouldn't it?' Potter asked.

'It's rubbish. Like the car,' Mother said.

'Where's Caring?' Maskrey asked.

'This is a wood. No danger.' Ember had remained against the wine racks, watching their faces, searching for any happy sign of sympathy or greed.

Maskrey paced about a bit. 'I want to see. If it's true, this is real funds. The club gets to be worth thinking about. What I mean, it's still what this operation was all about. Something for all, including a welcome back for Winston from jail, eventually. Like Leopold used to say, a duty. Is this half a million, more?'

'That direction. A few hours' driving,' Ember said. 'We'll need spades.'

Mother muttered: 'This is so much— '

'Potter can stay with the kid. If Ralphy tries anything, we're on the phone to him here, and the child – I think you're concerned about Lynette, Ralph.'

'Yes, of course.'

'So you understand?' Maskrey said. 'This child's on your plate.'

'I'm used to it.'

'And we leave the cuffs on,' Maskrey said.

'This you will not regret,' Ember told them. 'This is true vision. Something I was always sure you had.'

Mother drove and Ember, his arms still fixed behind him, sat in the back with Maskrey. On the way Maskrey bought a pick and spade. It was twilight when they reached the spot near Cheltenham. Maskrey undid the handcuffs and gave Ember the tools. Maskrey sat on the passenger seat of the Escort, with the door open and a K-frame on his lap. Ember began to dig. In a while he came to Caring's head, just discernible in the near dark. 'How well did you know Oliver?' Ember asked, taking a rest. 'Would you recognise the quiff, soiled?'

'Never met him. I've heard descriptions.' He came and looked down into the pit. 'You'd better keep going a while longer. I don't call this conclusive by any stretch. It wouldn't satisfy a court of law.'

'How is it?' Mother called, from the car.

'Looks very sound indeed, I must admit,' Maskrey said.

'Have I done you an injustice, Ralph?' she called.

'I understand caution,' he replied. 'I didn't take offence.' Swinging the spade down to uncover what might be left of Caring's face, he suddenly changed the direction and caught Maskrey's shins, not far above the ankles. Maskrey staggered and slid on the soft mud, toppling leftwards but still upright, fighting for balance, his legs momentarily astride the grave. The gun went off firing anywhere as Ember struck again, catching him slightly higher now, hips and a hand. Maskrey dropped the gun so that it lay on the rim of the grave, out of Ember's reach on the far side, and with the next spade blow he knocked it away, out of Maskrey's reach, too. Maskrey was sliding, half into the pit, half standing, half kneeling, crippled for a minute and groaning. Ember could have hit him again, reached Maskrey's face and head now, like Leopold with the pool cue, but made for the pistol and picked it up as Mother started the Escort. Ember dashed over the soil before she could draw away. He dragged her out of the car by her combat jacket and put the keys in his pocket.

With the Smith and Wesson in his hand, Ember went back to Maskrey and made him get out of the grave, crawling because his legs were bad. Then Ember handcuffed him with his arms around a sapling. Ember repacked the soil feelingly in the grave. Mother watched, blending with the foliage. 'We'll all go back to Kew in a minute for the child,' Ember said. 'This time I won't be the one with the cuffs on.'

Chapter 30

'I've got something to tell you both. You might as well hear it straight,' Patsy Leach cried out, coming suddenly into the room, her voice rich in venom and injury. 'It's to do with Oliver. I haven't been wholly honest with you.'

Harpur was up at Low Pastures again late at night with Iles, still waiting for calls from the girl, or Caring, or anyone else, now the story had made the media. Harpur thought it was hopeless, but Lane insisted that someone very senior had to be here at all times. Once the papers and broadcasters were involved the Chief liked to keep matters watertight: despite everything, Lane took the media seriously. Gazing inquiringly at Harpur, Iles had been talking about the solidity and joy his baby daughter brought to his marriage. 'I've never seen such contentment in a woman as in Sarah now, Col.'

'Great, sir.'

'What's that mean, you glib ponce?'

'Well, just great, sir.'

Iles stared at him for a while in that meditative, evil way of his. 'All right, great. Yes. I ask myself why Sarah and I didn't start sooner? The meaning of marriage – the meaning of a relationship between two people – it all falls into line when a child comes.'

'I know how you feel, sir.'

'Of course you do, Col. Megan still giving her all to literature, and so on? Myself, I'm rediscovering Thomas Love Peacock.'

'She may be doing a bit with one of those three.'

Both men stood when Patsy entered and Iles did up the button of his navy blazer and made what came out as almost a small bow to her, his hair falling forward. The ACC believed in such courtesies, even to someone like Patsy. Once, he had explained his thinking to Harpur: you never knew which woman you might be driven to making the best of one day, given the decline of offers with age, and a bit of charm invested early could turn out crucial. 'How do the Scriptures put it?' Iles used to ask: 'Cast your bread upon the daughters, but be ready to settle for mum.'

'Oliver came back for a weekend recently,' Patsy said. 'In fact, he was with Ralph Ember when he took Lynette to school.'

Iles sat down. 'And why are you telling us now, Patsy?'

'It's obvious, isn't it? – that two-timing bastard Ralph.' Her heavy face grew immeasurably heavier with pain and rage. She was leaning against the flock-papered wall, glancing from one of them to the other, obviously needing sympathy.

Iles responded. 'He's failed you somehow?'

'You know he's done a runner?' she replied.

'He's away for a while, yes,' Harpur said.

'Don't make me laugh. He's gone, for good. And with no word to me.'

'And he'd been leg-overing – in Caring's absence?' Iles inquired gently. 'On a nicely established basis?'

'We had something lovely going, full of trust and warmth. Or so I thought.'

'I hate to see you upset,' Iles replied. 'Things of the heart can be so unspeakably painful.'

'Those three, all joined up somewhere together now, it's obvious.'

'Which three?' Harpur asked.

'Oh, come on.' She was wearing a purple-striped football shirt and baggy white trousers. Harpur thought the combination did something for her, despite the sadness – made her look a little younger, showed off her good sturdy body. He could remember when there had been a faint touch of glamour to Patsy, years ago, and once in a while she seemed able to get it back. It was encouraging. She said: 'The three: Oliver, Ralph, Lynette. Don't you see, they've had this planned from the start? That swine, Ralph, he was always on about Lynette. We had such sweet times, in the countryside, at the coast, yet his mind was always on her. Mind! Lip-smacking. Plus they've got a cartload of funds, of course.'

'From?' Iles said.

'Oh, business profits, obviously.'

'Quite,' Iles said.

'But some of it due to me. This is a wife's fair entitlement, surely. I feel betrayed three ways. Can you understand?'

'Vile,' Iles said.

'Why we'll never hear another squeak from Lynette on the telephone,' she added. 'That was all a game. The kidnap is a game. That damn mock-up in the cottage on the Reens. I've said throughout that this was to throw the search away from Oliver himself – give him and her time to settle, wherever it is. And now Ralph can join them. Immaculate, in a foul, treacherous, male way.'

'You're understandably harsh, Patsy,' Iles remarked.

'Oh, I'm grateful – people of your rank giving hours to tiresome duty here for the sake of Lynette, but can you really believe we're going to hear more ransom demands? You're chasing supposed kidnappers and the three of them are living a gorgeous life, laughing at you and above all laughing at me, and at the way I've been used.' Patsy began to weep.

She had sat down now in a big, winged armchair and Iles went and put an arm tenderly around her shoulders. He spoke very softly, consolingly: 'Ember's appallingly at fault, Patsy, but at least, if you're right, the child is safe.'

'The child,' she sobbed. 'The child, the child. Always the child. Yes, important, but what about me?'

Iles said: 'I think of Ember very much as a family man. Are you sure he'd quit?'

'Family man?' she screamed, 'my God, he— '

'Oh, of course, everyone knows he'd shag anything that moves, absolutely no reflection intended,' Iles replied. 'But he always went home afterwards. Home was holy to him.'

'Has there been contact of any sort with Oliver since this trip to the school?' Harpur asked. 'Is that the last time he was seen or heard from?'

'What? What are you asking?' Patsy said.

'Yes, what *is* this, Harpur?'

'Only that, if he went down to Cheltenham with Ralph and— '

The telephone rang and Iles moved quickly to it. He listened. 'Right,' he said, replacing the receiver.

182

'Is it something good?' Patsy whispered, her hand anxiously to her lips, as if fearful of the answer. 'Ralph's come back?'

'Someone's arsoned Piers Mills-Silver's house at Border Grange. He escaped by jumping from the bedroom window. Fractured pelvis, at least,' Iles said.

'These marinas look superb when they're complete,' Harpur replied, 'but the early stages can be so costly.'

Garland arrived to take over the telephones not long afterwards. Sergeant Jane Bish was also working tonight. Perhaps Garland had fixed the rota. Another scandal in the making? Police adultery on kidnap duty would be a fairly ripe situation, and there were a lot of Press about. Who could control the urge behind these alliances, though?

Harpur decided to go home. Iles said he would stay and talk to Patsy for as long as she wanted. 'It comes under the *noblesse oblige* clause, Harpur,' he muttered. 'You're all right to leave. Nobody would accuse you of *noblesse*. Perhaps I'll reminisce with her about those antics she had with Ralph in the wood. I don't think I'm ever going to get down and see that favoured site for myself.'

As Harpur drove out from Low Pastures at about 2.30 a.m. a car parked close to the gates flashed its lights several times. He pulled up, slipped a wrench into his pocket and walked back. It was not a vehicle he recognised. When he looked inside he saw Anna Chitty. She pushed the door open for him and he climbed in and sat alongside her.

'I went to the nick to get them to ring your house, Harpur, but they said you'd be up here.' She became silent for a few moments. 'Look, one thing above all others that Peter taught me, never talk to police, even if someone's broken in and buggered your granny.'

'Ah, Pete was really one of the old school. But he won't be at the next reunion.'

'A kidnapping is different,' she replied.

If it was one. He said, though: 'It's been a kidnapping for a long time.'

'This is information that's only just come my way. Do you want it or not, Harpur?' She looked away from him while she spoke, obviously intent on keeping the contact to a minimum.

He waited.

'I've got a daughter who stays out till all hours,' she said.

'I know how you feel.'

'Last night when she was coming home she spotted a man leave a car and enter our house. At first, she thought it was a burglary, but then she saw the light go on in my room and heard him and me talking when she came in.'

'A friend? You'd let him in? Well, you've got a life to lead, too. Why not? But what's in this for us, Anna?'

'Not a friend. A visitor. He used a credit card on the front door. My daughter's like you – she thought it was mother with a boyfriend and didn't interrupt. Then, tonight, she was very late again. It's not supposed to happen twice a week. So, a big row, and while I'm slagging her off, she screams – What about me, receiving men in my room in the small hours?'

Harpur, trying to make sense of it all, asked: 'Who was this man?'

'Someone looking for one of his mates, called Leopold. And he spoke as if he knew about Caring Oliver's child.'

'Who, though? Leopold? Do you know him? Why come to you?'

'I knew nothing,' she said. 'Nothing about Leopold, nothing about anything.'

He waited again, but she did not add to it. 'I see. Where was this visitor from?'

'Well, he didn't say, did he? Would he?' She still stared ahead through the windscreen.

'Jesus, Anna, this is interesting, maybe vital, but what do you— '

'During this barney tonight my daughter wants to prove she knows and has recorded every damned incriminating detail about my young, stud caller, as she thinks – how he looks, what he was wearing, his hair, make of his car and— '

'She took the number?' he asked, hardly able to get the words out.

'She thought he was a burglar, you see.'

'This is a very bright kid indeed.'

'A bright, ungovernable kid.' Anna Chitty produced a piece of paper and handed it to him. It made a change from being handed his own number by Lamb, anyway. Patterns could be spotted in this case. Youth was coming out of it well, as far as vehicle identification went. He might have to revise his views of teenagers. 'You can do a trace right away, can't you?' she said. 'You needn't wait until morning? This might be a girl's life.'

'I'll do it over the car radio. Now. It will take a couple of minutes.'

He opened the door and climbed out. Before he could close it she said: 'Harpur, I don't want it ever known I was in touch with you.'

'If it saves her life?'

'Didn't I tell you, I don't ever talk to police?' Pulling the door shut she drove away.

Chapter 31

As they came near to Kew, Ember grew jumpy. Could he handle matters from now on? The journey had been fine. After turning things around in the wood, he had felt great anyway – an operation as triumphant as the one that saw off dear Leopold. When you thought about it, they were rubbish, these people: no polish, no training, no calibre. Because they were so smug, their concentration fell apart. Had they ever seen real old hands at work? Somehow, they had picked up a big place in Kew with antiques and cellars and a boot-scraper, but it was a living miracle. They thought everyone outside London was a push-over. Who'd volunteer to show they had it wrong? Ralph W. Ember.

Mother drove and he sat alongside her, the pistol on his lap. He had Maskrey in the back, with his wrists handcuffed behind him. If he tried anything it had to be with his head and Ember reckoned he could deal with that.

At the house, though, he would have to unlock Maskrey and go in with him and Mother, so Potter would imagine everything normal. He was sure to be alert, waiting for news of what they had found. Ember wanted a nice, quiet, deceptive approach, and then a sudden move and Potter made safe, too. Although he thought mostly about what those two, Maskrey and Potter, might pull, he did not forget Mother. He had the idea she could make problems, even if she was a grey old woman. For instance, she had been almost fast enough to get clear in the Escort at Caring's last resting place. All the way Ember had kept a good eye, in case she tried anything fancy with the driving, and he had one hand ready to grab her or the wheel. It still amazed and hurt him that you could take a woman into your bed, give the full loving kindness regardless of age and hair-do, yet she might have

186

poison for you. Nothing must go wrong at the house, not just for his own safety but Lynette's. It was the situation pretty well as it had always been: these three, Mother, Maskrey, Potter, knew that if Lynette was freed she would talk and pinpoint.

Mother said: 'I admire you, Ralph, that's a fact.'

No time ago in the cellar bed she had been groaning and cooing her gratitude and nearly eating his lips and scar, so a word such as admire seemed ordinary, but he let it go. 'To see off Caring and then Leopold. This is some stature.'

'Leopold? That's a real mystery,' he replied. Admit nothing unless you could not help it or there was possible gain. Basic lore.

'But obviously you're not afraid he might be at the house now?'

'Who knows what Leopold can do?'

'You've got all your own share and Caring's?' Mother asked. 'Remarkable, even for someone with your pedigree.'

'So Leopold had it right?' Maskrey said. He must have tumbled that Mother wanted Ember pleased with himself, and off guard.

'Had what right?' Ember replied.

'Coming to see you – searching your place.'

'I've a soft spot for Leopold as well as limitless respect,' Ember said. 'I'd hate to think anything untoward has happened to him.' That was the way to reply when you meant to scare the shit out of people and make sure they behaved – quaint, vicar's words like 'untoward'. It had the feel of refined conversation but something terrible was hidden there, and the best of it was, they knew. Oh, they knew. This was control. Also it was referred to as style, and came only with experience. This was the way to keep them tame during the drive. Yes, Mother wanted to get him relaxed, so up came the slab of flattery. He could see through that and deal with it: stay mild and talk the lies they saw were lies. They would have a very good idea that 'untoward' signified Leopold's shiny little head took a meaty battering. It was called reading between the lines which people like diplomats were always having to do. These people saw now that he could be ruthless. What grey hair in stacked mud was was ruthless. And a pool cue across the temple was ruthless, though they did not know the details of that. Ember had always yearned to be known as ruthless, up to a point.

Now they were getting near the house, he could not rely on style any longer. This had to be planned. He started to sweat and his eyes swam. Jesus, he might have dropped these two somewhere deep in the country, gone to try to find his own car, then taken off for home or wherever, no trouble: more likely wherever than home, not wanting any more tangle and bother from Patsy. Why couldn't he fight free from his link to this ugly child, Lynette? He was not ruthless, but sloppy. But if he was not ruthless, still only Panicking Ralph, why the hell couldn't he just panic, and get clear? Where had this bloody goodness and courage come from and why did they stick?

He made his voice brisk and hard. 'Pull in, Mother.' She drove to a side-street and stopped. Ember turned around, with the pistol low in his left hand pointing at Maskrey through the gap between the two front seats. Why didn't they have first names, these two sods? They called him Ralph, like the butler. The gun would be hidden by Ember's own body and Mother's from people in the houses or passing. He told Maskrey to get down briefly on his knees in the back, and with his right hand Ember undid the cuffs. Then he made Maskrey sit on the seat again, still covered by the pistol. If this boy had ever seen or heard a biggish gun go off in a car and knew the way blood and so on could display their message all over the windows he might have guessed Ember would never fire. This was an advantage when you dealt with infants. It was Caring who made the other gun go off in a car, Ember would always believe that.

'All right, Mother. We go to the house. You take us nice and quietly up the drive, no light flashing or horn stuff to signal anything to Potter. We're back from a successful expedition, right?'

Mother turned in the street and Ember stayed looking backwards and kept his eyes on Maskrey's face. Of course, it was the face of a scared kid, a youngster who had been in a bad way even before, but, all the same, there was a brain still at work behind those worried eyes. They had some light in them, still some metropolitan fizz and bull-shit. You could not ignore these or you were getting as dozey as they were. All right, this was a youth, but if Leopold picked him he must have more than O-level Arts and Crafts.

Mother turned into the drive and they stopped. Ember had not been able to work out how he would manage it from here. His mind kept dodging away from dealing with the hard little problems of what to do when the three of them climbed out of the car, then took the few steps together to the porch, opened the front door, went in and waited for Potter to appear. Often when there was pressure he could not make his thoughts take a grip on detail – to see in advance the layout of buildings, get into his head the place of corners and doors and stairs. What his thoughts did was drift and bolt and reach only big, general notions, like fear of the future and permanent escape. Sometimes he thought he should have been a marquee evangelist.

Ember would have to leave the car first, wouldn't he, and then shepherd the other two ahead of him. Did he keep the Smith and Wesson out, in sight? Did he put it in his pocket and stand with his hand around the butt, like some heavy in an old film, threatening them through the material? Wouldn't Potter read that just as fast as if the thing was on view in the open?

So Ember tried hard with the exactitudes. 'I'll get out first,' he told Maskrey, 'then Mother, then you. The two of you stand together on this side of the car and then, when I say, we move towards the front door.' It came out all right, strong, clear. He was whispering, anyway, as if for security, though he knew he would have had no hope of finding a proper voice.

'There won't be trouble,' Maskrey replied, and for the first time Ember realised that this kid might be more frightened than himself. These two must be wondering as much as Ember was why he had come back. They would see in him the ruthlessness but also bravery, hardness, resolution, no matter what they might have heard about a soft centre. Or they could even think some craziness had struck him, and that could make them very scared of the gun.

'Absolutely no trouble,' Mother said.

'I take the child and disappear,' Ember replied. 'You can do what you like.' He wanted to make it sound as if a deal had been agreed. With deals, he felt at home. He was a businessman: Ralph W. Ember, who sometimes had letters in the local Press. Although he still whispered, he reckoned it was a firm whisper.

Ember left the car. Mother climbed out and came around to his side. Then Maskrey opened the rear door near where they

189

were standing and put his feet on the ground. He winced. His legs were probably still not too good after the spade blows. Ember stepped back a pace. He had kept the pistol out so far, against his thigh and pointed downwards, not visible from the house, he hoped. You stayed very awake when people did theatricals about an injury. This was the moment they could leap on you like bloody Tarzan. 'Just get out, will you,' he told Maskrey. 'The pain will pass.' If Potter saw him hobbling he would know things had not gone perfectly.

They moved towards the front door, Ember last, the gun still at his side. As they took those few steps, Ember's brain did pick up a fraction and he realised that if Potter saw them from a window he could tell instantly that matters had changed, never mind the pistol or Maskrey's limp or Mother's frowning face. When Ember left he was a prisoner, someone to be watched. They would never have let him walk behind.

Mother turned the key and opened the door. They all stepped into the hall. Ember kept close to Maskrey's back, to hide the gun and let him feel it was close. Almost at once, Potter appeared at the top of the stairs and came slowly down. He stopped about halfway, like Ingrid Bergman in some drama to do with intrigue. Ember could not see the faces of Mother or Maskrey and did not know whether any signals were passing. Potter stood with a hand on the polished banister rail: 'Well, was it right about Oliver? What's wrong with you two?'

Nobody spoke for a few moments. 'Yes, it was right,' Mother replied.

'Caring's body?'

'Right,' Mother said.

'Jesus.' Potter stared at Ember for a moment, then came down a couple more stairs and stopped again. 'So, where does that leave us, Mother? Better or worse? Is the money easier?'

Ember raised the pistol one-handed, pointing it at Potter between the other two. 'Keep coming,' he said. 'I want the three of you close together.' Most of it was whisper, with his full voice breaking in for half a word now and then, fighting up from somewhere. It would do.

Potter remained where he was, looking urgently from Mother to Maskrey and then back again.

'Come down,' Ember said. 'These two will tell you I can be utterly ruthless, but it will be all right. Everything's agreed.'

'What's agreed?' Potter replied.

'Come down, Potter,' Ember said. 'So, haven't you got a fucking first name? Mother, tell him to come down.'

She did not speak.

'Tell him.' Ember tried to shout, but very little came out.

Instead, it was Potter who shouted. 'Panicking Ralph? Taken over? What happened?' He suddenly let go of the banister, crouched and, turning swiftly, ran back up the stairs. He veered out into the middle and then back to the rail then out again, making himself less a target. Ember quickly went to a two-handed grip to stop himself shaking and fired twice. He saw one bullet tear into the banister rail and heard the other hit a wall on the first landing. Potter kept going and went out of sight round a bend at the top.

For a second, Ember thought of going after him. If not, there would be someone loose in the house, and probably able to get himself armed, if he was not armed already. But there was a choice – one of them free upstairs or two of them free here. This was the kind of problem that could bring on the worst of his panic seizures, taking not just his brain out but his legs and all his physical strength. At different times in his life there had been moments like this, decision moments where he could see no answer, and always his reaction had been to get clear, forget whatever he was supposed to be doing, forget the people who depended on him. He could convince himself he had no option. What use would he be, unable to think, hardly able to move, except running?

But today he somehow held to his purpose. 'Get me to Lynette,' he said. He and the child could be out and away, maybe before Potter had equipped himself.

'Potter's got the key,' she replied.

'You're lying, Mother.'

'He was in charge here, while we were away.'

'But another set?'

'No,' she said.

'Take me down there. We can break in.'

'We?' she said.

He almost struck her with the pistol barrel. That was her getting on top again, the sarcastic way she said it – almost a grin on. Maskrey had straightened up a bit, too, not that shagged-out look any longer, which had come from getting hammered in a grave.

'You've seen those doors,' Mother said.

'Maskrey had a key.'

'Yours only. Love-locked in,' Maskrey replied. This was how far this bastard had come back – he could be jokey.

'Try it.' Ember waved the gun at the two of them and looked back up the stairs for any sign of Potter. He thought he could hear him moving somewhere, maybe at the rear of the house, but could not be sure. There must be a chance that Potter would take fright and get clear. He was only a kid, too. Being shot at could take the vim out of people much older and heavier than Potter. But Ember did not really believe it. That boy had shown no dread just now. For him, Ember remained Panicking Ralph, a nobody. That was one reason he had almost gone after him up the stairs, to squash that slur, which it must be, must be, for God's sake.

And then Mother changed her tone. For a while, Ember did not understand. 'Yes, come on, Maskrey, we'll take him there,' she said. 'Ultimately, Ralph's a good man.' Perhaps it did mean something to her, then, the bed contact, the things he had managed to say to her and do, just as if she had been the youngest flesh. They could mystify him, women, yet he believed that basically many of them had good feelings and often an idea of loyalty, somewhere.

'Maybe we can do something with the door. Why keep her now?' Mother added.

'I'll tell her to play dumb about where she was held,' Ember said.

'There you are, Maskrey. It will be all right.'

'Hurry,' Ember said.

'Potter? Don't worry. You've destroyed him, Ralph. He knows he had it all wrong about you and weakness. He's on his bike.'

She turned and made for the kitchen. Maskrey followed, then Ember. She opened a door, switched on a light and began to descend some stone steps. Again Maskrey and Ember followed. From the top of the steps he could see a short, brick-walled passage leading to another door, the same sort of solid, heavy barrier as had kept him in. When they reached the door, Mother called out: 'Lynette, love? Here's a visitor.'

Ember looked back up the steps. 'Not so loud.' Suddenly, he thought he saw why Mother had turned co-operative and brought him down here. It could make a perfect trap. There was no way forward. If Potter appeared, Ember would have three of them to deal with in this tiny tunnel, and Potter might cut the light. Even such a nothing kid would have heard of that as a gambit. Had Mother realised all at once that the only money available must be held by Ember? Had she seen that he might call off the rescue effort, escape and disappear? And so this offer, to get him enclosed here?

'Lynette?' Mother called again. 'He's come to bring you out.'

'What visitor?' The voice from behind the door was small and wary. 'Is it my dad? Dad, have you paid? I want to go home.'

'It's Ralphy,' Mother said.

'Ralphy? Ralphy Ember?'

'It's me, Ralph Ember, Lynette. You'll be fine,' he said.

'I remember you. You look like Charlton Heston?'

'A bit, yes.'

'Where's my dad?'

'Don't worry. Your dad sent me. He couldn't come.'

'But who'll pay them? Have you paid them?'

'Try your key,' Ember told Maskrey.

'Yes, try,' Mother told him.

It was an old-style mortice lock. They looked easy, but could be as tough as buggery and, in any case, he was not going to be able to get down and give it attention, with these two standing here and Potter liable to arrive.

'Are you on their side, then, Ralphy?' Lynette called through the wood.

'I'm trying to get you out.'

'I thought you were a friend of my dad, a real friend.'

'Yes.'

Maskrey selected a key and tried but it failed to turn. Ember could see another, similar key in the bunch. 'That one,' he said.

Maskrey turned and tried again. 'No go,' he said.

But Ember had been obscured, and unable to see whether Maskrey had really used the second one. He did not even know whether Maskrey was genuinely trying with either of them. He snatched at the keys and in his anger bent down himself with them. Almost as soon as he made the move he knew that it was a disaster, dead against the little bit of planning he had been able to work out. Maskrey must have hit him with some kind of karate blow on the back of the neck, driving his head hard against the door. Ember stayed conscious and kept hold of the pistol. He was just going to straighten and swing around with it when he was thrown against the door by a body charge, so the gun was pressed to the wood by his stomach. He fought to release himself but realised all at once that there were two people holding him, not just Maskrey, and from the weight and strength he realised it must be two men, not Maskrey and Mother. Potter had found them.

'I'm going to reach up and take the pistol, Ralph,' Mother said. 'Be very careful. If it goes off it will damage the woodwork or your gut.'

'What was that noise, that noise against the door?' Lynette said. 'Ralph, are you still there? Who's with you?'

'In any case, if that one doesn't go off, this one will, Ralphy,' Potter said. Ember felt the muzzle of a handgun against the side of his head. 'Nothing will be heard from down here.'

'You be careful, too, Potter,' Mother said. 'Ralph has to talk to us about funds.'

Ember felt her arm go around him gently, like a lover's, and her hand took his right arm and followed it between his body and the door until she reached his wrist and then the pistol. There was something disgusting and pitiful about it, the dry, old feel of her fingers spidering over him, the disgrace of being jammed helpless against this door by a couple of yobs, the sudden uselessness of the fine gun. And then the faint, hopeful, hopeless sounds from the child on the other side of the door, depending on him, but not knowing that he and his face were shoved into this timber so hard that he would not be looking like anyone human, let alone Charlton Heston. For a couple of seconds he feared he would weep. That had happened to him before in a crisis. 'Now, let go, Ralph,' she said. 'You've done damn well for someone of your make, but let go now. God, you're sweating a bit.' She was picking his fingers one by one away from the trigger guard, like

194

somebody lifting dog hairs from a coat. He did not resist. How could he resist? 'Here we go,' Mother said, and drew the gun away from under him.

The weight against him slackened. Only one man seemed to be holding him now. 'Stay there, Ralphy,' Potter said. One of them felt over him slowly for other armament.

'All right?' Mother asked. 'I think we'll go into the cellar and take stock. How does that grab you, Ralphy?'

He was no longer held. 'You can stand against the wall,' Maskrey said.

Ember moved from the door and faced them. Potter had the pistol in his right hand and in the other a metal pipe cosh which he must have used to imitate a gun muzzle against Ember's head.

'Well, I certainly owe you a few, Ralphy,' Maskrey remarked.

'There's ups and there's downs, Maskrey,' Potter said. 'Stay contained.'

For a second it looked as if Maskrey would turn on him. Maskrey had been the top one, and now he was getting instructions. But then he replied: 'Point taken. I agree with Mother: the main object is to locate the funds.' He bent down and opened the door with one of his keys.

'And locate Leopold,' Potter added.

'Oh, Leopold,' Mother said.

'What!' Potter cried, 'you're not saying he's done Leopold as well as— '

'Here's Lynette,' Maskrey said. 'We don't want her upset, Potter.'

'Of course not,' Potter replied.

'So here's Uncle Ralph, Lynette,' Maskrey said. 'He's been bothered about you.'

The child was standing back in the middle of the cellar but now suddenly ran forward as if she meant to try to escape and Ember was afraid someone would forcibly stop her. But then he realised she was making for him, smiling, crying a little, her arms open to embrace him. Nobody tried to prevent her. She leapt up and clasped him around the neck and he lowered his head and kissed her on the cheek. She held him fiercely, her feet off the ground. 'Ralph, Ralph,' she sobbed, 'thank you. You're not one of them, are you?'

'Are you all right?' he said. She looked dirty and thin, her hair all over the place and she smelt a bit, but he knew he wasn't the one to complain about that. She had on what must be bits of her school uniform, a grimy pink blouse and a navy skirt.

'No, not on our side at all,' Mother said. 'Ralph's a real fan of yours. You're a lucky kid. In a way.'

The girl was trying to whisper to him, her mouth close to his ear. He heard: 'Leopold. Don't let Leopold— '

'No trouble from Leopold,' Maskrey told her. 'Ralphy's dealt with that.'

The child looked no prettier, probably worse, her doughy skin seeming to hang looser and her eyes very bloodshot, but none of that mattered. She was just a kid in great peril. Her face was touching his and her legs and small breasts pressed against him, yet he had no sexual response. This he felt proud of. He wanted nothing like that. For God's sake, Lynette was an imprisoned schoolgirl, abused and desperate. He would think of her like a daughter.

'Can we all come into your little nest, then, Lynette?' Mother said.

Ember had his arms around the girl and when she slowly released her hold on his neck he placed her gently back on the ground. Even had she been pretty he felt really confident he would not have given way to a hard-on through clasping her. She stood for a moment in front of him, then reached up again and pulled his head down, so she could speak in his ear once more: 'Look after me, Ralph,' she whispered.

He took her hand and they all went in. Although this cellar had been well cleaned and turned into what was almost a reasonable room, perhaps he still detected a vague, sweet, gritty smell of coal. He looked up to see if there was a trapdoor where the loads had been tipped from the drive, but it must have been blocked off and plastered over. They had put in a proper single bed, a couple of chairs and a table which had a ghetto blaster radio on it, and a television set with video and what looked like a stack of films.

'You take a chair, Ralphy,' Maskrey said. 'Lynette and Mother can sit on the bed.' Maskrey himself perched on the edge of the table. Potter, the gun in his hand, pulled one of the chairs around so he could sit opposite Ember.

196

'You see, Lynette understands completely about the financial side,' Mother said. 'Obviously. She did the telephone calls.'

'How it looks, Lynette, is that Ralph is holding very large funds on your father's behalf, your father being abroad,' Maskrey added. He leaned forward to address her, like a teacher. 'We think some of this money could have been lost through carelessness, left in a parked car, would you believe! That's spilt milk, anyway. As for the rest of it, I believe Ralphy has got it tucked away somewhere, maybe at his club, maybe in banks, maybe who knows where? The point is, I think he should tell us where and then help us get it, if we need help. That would be possible if, for instance, it was in a bank and needed to be signed for and collected.'

He was talking to the girl, but really talking to Ember. In its crude, cruel way it was clever.

'Do you think he should tell us and help us, Lynette?' Maskrey asked.

The child gazed at Ember but did not speak. She seemed to know what was happening. In the days and nights since they took her she had probably learned very fast.

Ember said: 'Yes, there's some money.'

'Ah, grand,' Mother replied.

If he denied it or tried to delay they would tell the girl what had happened to her father and say Ember had done it. The threat had never been made, but there was no need for it to be made. They knew he understood. The notion sickened him. He could not bear to have her hear that. In a way, this dread was absurd. Far worse threats shadowed him and her – also unspoken, also real.

'I hold money for and on behalf of her father,' Ember said.

'Oh, good, Ralph.' The child beamed at him, her face alight, despite the pallor from being locked up, and despite the fear and alarm that never really left her eyes.

Potter said: 'Ralph *is* good. He wanted to give a whack of money away to a lady whose husband was killed. That's what I heard.'

'So where, then, Ralph?' Maskrey asked.

'Deposit boxes.'

'I was afraid you were going to say that,' Mother replied. 'This means visits.'

'And me?' Lynette shouted at once. 'Can I come? Oh, don't leave me here again.' The joy had gone from her. 'I'd never give trouble. No calling attention. That's what you're afraid of, isn't it – calling attention?'

'Banks in your area?' Potter asked.

'Yes.'

'This is a pain. We've already had a journey, and it nearly turned out bad,' Mother said.

'What journey?' Lynette asked. 'Where did you go when you left me here?'

'This is going to be the same drill then,' Maskrey said. 'Lynette will have to stay behind.'

'No,' she screamed. She was going to jump up from the bed, but Mother held her arm, not hard, but held it.

Potter said: 'In the old days, Lynette, there was always gold in the bank to cover the amount out in bank notes. You're our gold. We'll go to other banks, but this is our own bank, with you in it.'

Ember watched her think about that. This child was clever: no wise-cracks now, because of the situation, but a mind that worked. In a while she said: 'So, when you've got the money, there'll be no need for you to keep me, will there?' The words should have sounded bright with hope, but her voice was shaking.

'That's right. That's what a ransom is for,' Potter answered.

'You needn't keep me, and you can't let me go, either, because you'll be afraid of police.'

'I've told them you'll never talk, Lynette,' Ember said quickly.

'That's right,' Maskrey said.

She gazed at Ember. 'And you think they believe you? Ralph, you know they can't.'

'Yes, they will,' he said.

Her head dropped. She did not look at him when she spoke next: 'Are you trying to save yourself, Ralph? You're like everyone used to say? You're Panicking? Oh, no, please, please.'

Mother said: 'Ralph's just Ralph. He does what he can, like all of us, Lynette.'

'Well, I'll never get out of here,' the child said, her head still lowered.

Ember lowered his own head, as if ashamed, perhaps as if weeping, and then drove his feet down hard and launched himself head first at Potter's face. But maybe Potter saw it coming a second too soon. He still had the pistol in his right hand and the length of pipe in his other. He swung to the side in his chair so that Ember hit him only in the shoulder. At the same time, Potter struck down at Ember's scalp with the piping and then struck again. Ember, struggling to keep on his feet and struggling to keep something of his brain still operating through the pain and haze, realised that Potter could not fire because Ember was indispensable at the banks.

He tried to gather himself for another attempt and saw Potter standing now, waiting, the cosh raised, the pistol ready to be used as a club. 'Sunk, Ralph,' he said. From the edge of his eye, Ember glimpsed Maskrey approaching him, but in no hurry, sure that Potter would do all the damage necessary. Potter hit him again, this time on the side of the neck, wanting to hurt him and stop him, not risk anything more serious.

Mother and the child had stood up, Mother holding Lynette by the hand now. Lynette stared at him again, maybe trying to will him to win, and maybe knowing he couldn't. And then, from the edge of his eye once more, Ember saw Maskrey shoved fiercely aside into a corner of the cellar. Potter turned, raising the pistol now, but as he did was hit in the face by the video machine, which had been flung at him with great force, and when he tried to recover, was smashed twice in the face and head by the ghetto blaster being wielded like a club, once across, then back. The contact set it going, and Ember heard a line from a rap song his kids played over and over: 'Police, police, who said they necessary?'

Chapter 32

The Chief said: 'Triumph, yes, but, Colin, before Desmond and so on get here, I really must broach one matter with you.' Lane, standing at the window of his office in shirt sleeves, his trousers held up by what appeared to be a length of rope, gazed out into the car park away from Harpur, and shook his big, sandy head a couple of times in sadness. 'After all, I'm running a police force here, aren't I?'

Lane was not like Iles, who expected answers to all his questions, but Harpur replied: 'Only one of the very best, sir.'

The Chief raised a hand, to signify he knew when he was being buttered and could do without it: 'This is rumour, I admit. I might be about to fall into some gross impertinence. If so, I will ask you in advance to forgive me.' He did turn around and squarely faced Harpur for this, the fat, sallow features showing some agony, but resolute. He moved to his desk and sat down, as if some formality were needed, though he had on no shoes and shuffled the distance in loose-fitting, heavy, khaki socks. Lane rarely wore shoes around the office. He seemed to have become deliberately even more scruffy since people started talking about bringing in ex-military officers to head-up the police.

Harpur said: 'I know you would not speak hastily, sir.'

'This is to do with – well, I'm sure you can guess – the portentousness, the hesitancies – this is about— '

'Sarah Iles?'

'I want to make it clear from the outset, I regard her as nothing but a wonderful woman. And I speak for my wife, also, in this.'

'She is, sir.'

'Sarah, a wife and now a mother, and motherhood, one thought, would – well, in the past she has been unsettled, apparently.'

'She dotes on the baby, sir.'

'Of course.'

He continued to gaze at Harpur, possibly expecting him to talk unprompted. Harpur stayed quiet. Not only crooks had the right to silence. Eventually, Lane said: 'And then your own very fine wife, Megan. And family. Megan – so active in all sorts of ways.'

'Yes, very.'

'Her literary club? Still booming?'

'Oh, certainly, sir.'

'You yourself – you can't get interested in all that?' His tone announced that he wished Harpur would, to keep him respectable.

'Megan says I think Rimbaud wrote scripts for Sylvester Stallone.'

'How's that?'

'I didn't get it either, sir. A French poet, I hear. She had to spell it out for me.' Harpur wondered if he could keep this going until Iles or Garland arrived for the kidnap meeting, so that no further discussion of Sarah would be possible.

'Colin – this rumour – well, do I deduce from your response just now when you offered Sarah's name – do I deduce that you are aware of this talk?'

'Oh, yes, sir.'

He frowned, approaching the tougher question and breathed a little hard. 'Do I deduce there is something in this rumour about you and her? Colin, I have to think of the Press, the Home Office.'

'She hasn't really been happy at home for quite a time, sir.'

Lane shook his head once more. 'Happiness is— '

Iles came briskly in. 'Ah, sir, happiness is. Is this from the end of *Manhattan*, where Woody Allen's listing all the things that delight him – including that fucking heavywit Groucho Marx, if you can believe it – and gets to the face of the girl he's rejected, Tracey? Then he starts one of those last-reel romantic street runs he likes so much, to find her. Crap, but vintage crap. I'm glad you admire it.'

Lane said: 'No, the happiness of Patsy Leach and Lynette now they're reunited.' The Chief seemed almost as pleased as Harpur for an excuse to shelve the earlier subject. Perhaps he felt his duty had been done in airing it. Harpur wondered whether the Chief had picked up any rumours about Garland and Jane Bish, too. Lane did worry about these things.

'Oh, Patsy and Lynette,' Iles remarked. 'Is that really how it is with those two, sir? Happiness? I get the impression they can't stand the sight of each other.'

Garland joined them and he, Harpur and Iles sat down around Lane's desk. The Chief stood again and drifted back and forth between the desk and the window, working the socks looser as he went so he occasionally trod on the dragging length and stumbled. 'Colin has been outlining the likely defence of those three,' the Chief said.

'They'll plead guilty, of course. What else can they do?' Harpur told them. 'But they're going to say in extenuation that it was all Leopold Easton's doing, and that they went along only because they were terrorised by him. Potter and Maskrey are young, no record, and Mother's a woman, so it might seem half-credible. It could get them a year or two off. The child will say they were decent to her, though Leopold was not. But, then, Leopold we haven't got. They'll argue that as soon as they felt sure Leopold had disappeared they wanted to make arrangements to free the child and went down to bring Ralph Ember up to collect her, knowing he was a trusted friend of the family, as it were. Ember confirms all this.'

'Confirms they were all co-operating with each other?' the Chief asked. 'How can this be? Weren't they attacking Ember when you and Garland arrived in the cellar, Col?'

'Ember is supposed to have fallen into a momentary, uncontrollable rage at seeing the girl in those conditions, that's all. The others had to defend themselves.'

'We accept this?' Lane asked.

Iles, stretching out in his chair, and adjusting the crease of his beige summer-weight suit, said: 'As ever, sir, a question that goes to the very nub, the very nub. Accept? Oh, Ember's got something to hide. Possibly a few things. Some kind of deal has been done between him and the three. They're providing useful stories for one another.'

'But how?' Lane asked. 'This deal?'

'How? Quite, again, sir, if I may say,' Iles replied. 'I wasn't there, sir, at Kew, as you know. This was dear Harpur keeping an important tip to himself, in the usual style, and doing an illicit expedition on to another force's ground, with his inveterate sidekick here, Garland. Oh, they did well enough, one has to concede. Great utilisation of available resources, Garland with the flying video, Harpur the radio. But then they leave all four of them locked together in the cellar for upwards of fifteen minutes as I understand it while they take the girl upstairs and let her phone Patsy Leach – Patsy Leach and me, I might say, since I was doing phone duty. Again. You wanted a senior officer present at all times, sir. In that quarter of an hour those four obviously came to terms and concocted their tales.'

'This was unfortunate, Colin,' the Chief said.

'The girl had become almost hysterical suddenly,' Garland said. 'We had to get her out, fast.'

'Both of you?' Iles said. 'I suppose each had to be present to crow when she made the call, make sure of the kudos.'

Lane held up a hand again. 'Well, it's done. The child is safe. This, as I see it, is a grand achievement, however brought about. The Met can shout as much as they like about carrying out an operation on their ground without their knowledge, but it did work. Colin's information turned out to be first class.'

'Thank you, sir.' Harpur replied.

Iles said: 'Colin straddles so many worlds, has so many dark corners to his life, that one never really knows what he's up to.'

'Oh, I wouldn't say quite that, Desmond,' the Chief replied. 'No.' It sounded as if he meant yes indeed, though. Lane came to a stop and thought for a few moments. 'Ember? What was in it for him, this deal with the three, if it exists? What has he got to hide?'

'There are two people and a lot of bank money missing, sir,' Iles said.

'We can connect him with any of that?'

'Not connect in a court sense, sir – in view of what these three are saying,' Harpur replied. 'We know from Patsy Leach and the child that Ember must have been among the last to see Caring Oliver in this country. And we don't really know whether Caring is alive or dead. But Ember says Caring was leaving to return abroad when they parted. It's just possible. People can disappear overseas. A bit of face surgery, new papers. There's been a search, of course, but no luck, despite all the publicity.'

'Panicking Ralph hasn't got it in him to see off Caring, anyway, surely,' the Chief said. 'Plus dispose of the body.'

'Panicking Ralph's a moveable feast, sir,' Iles replied. 'Always has been. Well, we're all multi-faceted, aren't we, Col?'

'And where's this Leopold?' Lane asked.

'Once again the nub, sir,' Iles replied.

Chapter 33

Ember thought a bit of a holiday was in order and left with Margaret and the children in a hired Acclaim for Italy. Most of Margaret's scars had gone, and he considered she looked really good, a credit. He had sent her out to buy a couple of first-class silk suits and she had one of them on now. Sometimes, he wondered why the hell he ran with other women. But then, sometimes, such as when it was Mother, he had had no choice.

It was a sound idea to put some distance between himself and Patsy and Lynette for a time. These things always blew over nicely if you let them. And then there was Harry Lighterman and the boy called Fritzy who both needed avoiding for a spell, if not a great deal longer. There had been no trouble from either, yet, but he thought that one evening he had glimpsed Lighterman in Shield Place, near the Monty, that long, malevolent body and unhelpful face. He could be wrong. It was possible that all the police activity over the kidnap had frightened Harry far off. And there was nothing to say that Fritzy had ever been in the vicinity at all. Just the same, Ember wanted to be careful. He still held a lot of cash and, what with the holiday and one thing and the other, he needed to go on holding it. By now, it felt as if it belonged to him of right. He had been through a hell of a lot, what with the piping to his head and his place broken up and having to confer satisfaction on Patsy and Mother.

There had been one serious loss, obviously. The Montego had had about £120,000 in the boot, for contingencies, when he left it in Kew. Now, he had to hope above all else that the car had been stolen. It seemed crazy, but was what he needed. Someone somewhere might still be celebrating one of the richest pickings he would ever drive away. What Ember had to pray, and did nine or ten times daily, was that the Montego had not been towed to a yard by the police for prolonged illegal parking. If so, it would be still there, awaiting collection on payment of a fine. The fine would be nothing, but Ember could not risk going to make a check. If he did, there would be a computer transaction and no knowing where that might surface one day. His story, and Mother's, Potter's and Maskrey's story, was that Ember had come to the house for the first time on the day Harpur and Garland arrived, humanely brought by those three to escort the child home, now Leopold no longer dominated them. If that tale became subject to doubt, because the records showed his car was towed away earlier, all sorts of other very serious possibilities would arise. The police could ask where he had been between times, and might go on asking. They might also ask how he knew about the house in Kew and what was his connection not just with Mother, Potter and Maskrey, but the owner, Leopold, and his bank-robber friend in jail, Winston Acre. All these matters were better left.

He had a manager in to run the Monty for a month while they were away. That meant being swindled all round the clock, of course, but it was peanuts, in the circumstances. The month could be extended, in case the Montego did turn out to be with the police and began to send dire signals. He had reported it stolen, naturally – from the Monty car park – but could not be sure this would stop someone like Harpur digging if the car suddenly came to light somehow in a London police pound. If nobody claimed it, would the police open it up after a set waiting time? He thought again of marquee evangelists and one of their favourite texts in his boyhood, 'Be sure your sins will find you out.'

Margaret said as they neared Portsmouth: 'Does this manager know how to get hold of us?'

'We're touring, love. How could he?'

'In case something goes wrong at the club.'

'What could go wrong?'

Venetia said: 'Oh, such as that little maniac who broke up our rooms.'

'I think I vaguely recall someone getting a wee bit rough a while back,' Ember replied. 'Remind me what he was like.'